BLACK FLIES

BY M.W. GORDON

DEADLY DRIFTS
CROSSES TO BEAR
"YOU'RE NEXT!"
GILL NET GAMES
BARRACUDA PENS
DEADLY AIRBOATS
BARBED WIRED
BLACK FLIES

BLACK FLIES

A MACDUFF BROOKS FLY FISHING MYSTERY

by

award winning author

M. W. GORDON

Black Flies
Copyright © 2016
M.W. Gordon
All rights reserved.
Published in the United States by Swift Creeks Press,
  Sarasota, Florida
swiftcreekspress@gmail.com
www.swiftcreekspress.com

SWIFT CREEKS PRESS EDITION, SEPTEMBER 30, 2016

Most of the geographical locations are real places but are used fictionally in this novel. This is a work of fiction, and the characters are either the product of the author's imagination or are used fictionally. Any resemblance to actual persons, living or dead, or to actual events or locales is unintentional and coincidental.

Library of Congress Cataloging-in-Publication Data
Gordon, M.W.
Black Flies/M.W. Gordon

ISBN-13 978-0-9848723-8-1
Printed in the United States of America

DEDICATION

To Project Healing Waters and the many vets who support its activities.

ACKNOWLEDGMENTS

To Iris Rose Hart, my editor, friend, and patient instructor in English grammar.

To Christine Holmes for developing and maintaining my website and designing advertisements.

To the graphic design staff of Renaissance Printing of Gainesville, Florida, and especially Jim O'Sullivan for assistance with the cover, bookmarks, and posters.

To very special people who have provided quiet places for me to write, especially Julie and Jason Fleury of Bozeman, Montana.

To Elsbeth Waskom, Josh Dickinson, Roy Hunt, and Paul Tarantino continued thanks.

To Master Casting Instructors, Dave Johnson and Dave Lambert, who, contrary to this book—in which several MCIs are killed—are alive and well.

And always to my Elsbeths: Buff (wife), Beth (daughter), and Ellie (granddaughter), and to the memory of the first Elsbeth, Betty (mother-in-law).

THOUGHTS ON WRITING

"A novelist must wrestle with all mysteries and strangeness of life itself, and anyone who does not wish to accept that grand, bone-chilling commission should write book reviews, editorials, or health-insurance policies instead."

My Reading Life, Pat Conroy

PROLOGUE

Elsbeth's Diary

So much happened in the year-and-a-half after Lucinda was abducted. Guatemalan President Herzog's search for Dad continued, resulting in the loss of Herzog's two top advisors and a turncoat former CIA agent.

Three innocent fly fishers, including Dad's close friend Grace Justice, were killed by barbed wire strung across the Gallatin River in Montana. Dad struggled with memories of his intimate relationship with Grace, an Assistant Florida State Attorney and a Federation of Fly Fishers Master Casting Instructor.

Palmer Brown, after killing his wife by pushing her off Inspiration Point, proved also to be the killer of Grace Justice. Brown was himself killed by me and my dearest friend Sue, although his target was my dad. Brown first shot and wounded Dad with a rifle and was aiming to finish him off when Sue and I ran toward Brown with our guns blazing.

Dad bears scars of anger from both the shot by Brown on the Gallatin River that entered Dad's back and pierced his bladder and the two shots by Parkington Salisbury a dozen years earlier on Dad's drift boat Osprey *on the Snake River. Both shooters had been Dad's clients fly fishing, and both were determined to kill him months after their floats. Dad had embarrassed Salisbury in front of his wife Kath, and Brown had embarrassed himself in front of Dad.*

Dad vacillated between trying to understand that he had to live his own life and accepting that Lucinda almost certainly had died at the hands of her abductor—former husband Robert Ellsworth-Kent.

1

TO THE FLORIDA COTTAGE

REASONS PERSISTED TO STAY LONGER AT MY cabin at Mill Creek in Paradise Valley in Montana, a half-hour north of Yellowstone National Park. Yellowing cottonwood and aspen leaves dominated the slopes of the mountains around the cabin. The annual color spectacle was difficult to abandon. When the last leaf dropped, I knew I had to rush east to escape the first snowfall, but, usually to my regret, I sometimes lingered for a few more days to fish the Yellowstone.

Last week I ordered a small bronze memorial plaque to honor Grace Justice and only yesterday received permission from the understanding owner of the land to place the memorial on the Gallatin riverbank where Grace was murdered. Brooding over her death, for which I assumed all blame, I ignored increasingly severe urgings by my daughter, Elsbeth, to get on the road and head to Florida. She had already vanished east for classes at the University of Florida in Gainesville. When she last called, I began fibbing that I was en route, supported by the magic of cell phones that did not inform the other person of the caller's location.

One commitment hurried me along on the boring cross country transfer to Florida. Two weeks ago I mailed my check and registered for the late September International Federation of Fly Fishers (IFFF), Florida Council's annual expo at the Plantation in Crystal River on Florida's West Coast. My plans included taking the Certified Casting Instructor (CCI) exam the day before most of the attendees arrived. The CCI is the first—and for many the only—step to the intensely complex Master Casting Instructor (MCI) level.

A second registration I made was for an all morning class in advanced fly casting that would be a special treat because it was to be taught by Rachel Hart, a household name in the national casting community and spoken with the same reverence one used mentioning Lefty Kreh or Joan Wulff.

Hart's fly casting video showed a petite creature with a booming voice she readily used to point out anything wrong with a student's casting. Like "This is supposed to be an intermediate level class; you don't even belong with the beginners. That roll cast attempt didn't roll; it gathered in a snarl you dumped on your right foot. One more cast like that, and I'll personally give you back whatever you paid to take my class so you can try something you might be better at, like quilt making."

Hart wears glasses but never when she's with a man she finds attractive. Friends joke that if you're ever talking to her and she takes off her glasses you're her next target.

Rumors suggested she was again on the hunt because she was ending her fourth marriage, which is remarkable since she's only thirty-four. She doesn't collect husbands; she signs them up as short-term tenants.

Rachel began her first marriage—to Jamad Mutumba, an exchange student from somewhere in West Africa—when she was twenty and a junior at Reed College in Oregon majoring in Classics and minoring in Art History. On the day she received her diploma, she left him stranded with an expired student visa, bought an old Ford pickup, and drove straight to Key West.

She collected a Florida divorce, effective the day she remarried to Carlos Espinosa, a Key West Conch fly fishing guide and Master Casting Instructor. Rachel accomplished what she wanted from that marriage—casting lessons—and celebrated the death of that matrimony by passing the IFFF's CCI exam.

Hart married for the third time—to Anatoly Azarenka, a scary looking multimillionaire businessman from Russia. The union lasted only until she had transferred a little over half of his wealth to a private account in the Cayman Islands. Anatoly was not happy and told her she would "go missing" if she didn't return the money. She responded by reporting him to immigration and seeing him deported. He mysteriously died of food poisoning the week he arrived in Moscow.

She soon married again—to the son of an Irish mother and a Jewish father. Sean Bernstein and Rachel met at her first AA meeting.

Four husbands in fourteen years meant the average length of her marriages was three-and-a-half years. If that continued, she could celebrate her 50th year of marriages with fourteen ex-husbands.

Her present husband had convinced her not to assume his name and to use only her maiden name because Rachel Hart Mutumba Espinoza Azarenka Bernstein was a bit long to explain, although it suggested she hadn't discriminated between races and religions.

Whatever one postulates about Hart's marital philosophy, she's a precise and elegant fly casting instructor. With sufficient separation settlements from her cast-off spouses to stop working, she focused on preparing for the Master Casting Instructor certification. She passed the exam the first time and thus was one of the first U.S. women to become an MCI.

Hart was so busy teaching fly casting in many states and several European countries that when asked at a lecture about being away from her husband so much she responded, "I've consummated that marriage more at fly fishing conferences he didn't attend than at home."

Sean Bernstein moved out of their extravagant Sanibel home on their third anniversary and filed for divorce two weeks before the Crystal River program. Hart was pleased that for the first time she hadn't started and partly paid for the divorce proceedings. This time *she* managed to keep the house. She thought she might try that format more often in the future. As in fly casting, practice makes perfect.

Amused by hearing about Hart's life and anxious to meet her in person, I began my annual fall drive to the Sunshine State. The miles to Florida—which I didn't want to count—rapidly disappeared to the rear, and I arrived at our St. Augustine cottage as the TV late shows were rolling up the carpets, which didn't matter since I hadn't watched such programing since the days of Johnny Carson.

A full night's sleep wasn't to be had. Sleeping in was unacceptable to Wuff—my rescued sheltie—who woke me at 6:00 a.m. *sharp*—4:00 in Montana—impatient for her breakfast. I took her out for a moment, fed her, and went back to bed, trying to explain to her I was too tired to play ball *before* my breakfast.

Wuff was sitting on the corner of my bed watching me for signs of life when I woke a second time at 9:00 a.m. It was time to get up, give her the two tips of my daily banana, and think about beginning a number of telephone calls, first to Dan Wilson at Langley in D.C.

After brewing coffee and warming two frozen sausage links in the microwave, I toasted a stale English muffin and took it all outside to the porch. I sat on a rocker, breathed in the fragrances of the salt marsh flats, and glared at my cell phone.

Half of the calls I've received over the years have led to trouble, and I was in no condition to take on any new requests from Dan Wilson in D.C. for special work in some unstable country. I noticed there were numerous messages for me from Dan, and each was marked IMMEDIATE ATTENTION. That could mean anything from "How you doing?" to "I need you with your gear for a little job" in some country unable to govern itself—Somalia, Sudan, Libya, Gambia, Venezuela, or the one that always caused me to shiver when I heard its name—Guatemala. The mere mention of Guatemala made me worry about its President Juan Pablo Herzog.

Dan has a priority in my life; he has been my link to the "Agency" in D.C. since I entered a protection program a dozen years ago and changed my name from Professor Maxwell Hunt to Macduff Brooks, my occupation from international law professor to fly fishing guide, and my location from Gainesville, Florida, to Paradise Valley, Montana—for the summer—and to St. Augustine, Florida—for the winter. Dan has been more than a link; he has become a friend, which often has proved to be more important.

When I opened his most recent phone message, I read and reread its brief four lines:

Macduff. Call me. Last night the partial remains of the body of Robert Ellsworth-Kent were discovered washed up on a beach at Abaco in the Bahamas. A few parts of a second but unidentified body of a woman were nearby.
Dan

The message made me numb and in no condition to talk. The unidentified body had to be that of my wife, Lucinda.

Eighteen months ago during a ship christening ceremony on the grounds of the Castillo de San Marco in St. Augustine, Ellsworth-Kent forcibly abducted Lucinda, dragged her into his van, and then deliberately ran the van into me as he drove away. My enduring limp was all he left.

Robert Ellsworth-Kent was Lucinda's first husband, the consequence of a brief engagement and a never-should-have-happened marriage in London that lasted only a few weeks during which he abused her badly enough she could never bear a child.

Soon thereafter, he went to prison for attempted murder. Lucinda got a divorce and moved to New York City, where she began working as an investment advisor. She became extraordinarily successful and bought a large ranch that is only a short distance upstream from my cabin alongside Mill Creek.

We met ages ago for Thanksgiving dinner at Lucinda's Montana ranch and years later according to her allegedly married in a small hilltop church in Oyster Bay on Florida's West Coast a few miles north of Cedar Key. I wasn't convinced any marriage ceremony actually took place, but Lucinda insisted it did. It's been more than a decade, and whenever the subject arises, she reminds me that the statute of limitations' time to challenge a marriage has expired.

Ellsworth-Kent never accepted our marriage. He tried to kill us several years ago, failing but causing the death of five fly fishing guides on float trips on different western U.S. rivers in what became known as the "wicker man and mistletoe" murders. U.S. and British police searched for but never found him.

He reappeared eighteen months ago and abducted Lucinda. Until now neither person has ever surfaced. His remains found on a Bahama beach have been identified, but those of the woman—who logically was Lucinda—have not.

Fearing the worst, I declined to return Dan's calls and sat hunched over on my cottage steps for an hour. My excuse was that *he* would call *me* if he learned Lucinda had survived.

Wuff began tapping my knee with a paw, begging for a walk. I agreed, providing me with the excuse to further delay the inevitable call to Dan. We must have been a sight, two friends limping the quarter mile to the mailbox and back. Wuff had been shot a dozen years earlier in a fly fishing incident on my drift boat, *Osprey*.

The time consumed by delaying the call didn't keep me from thinking the worst about Lucinda. . . . Dan's message flashed in front of me, and I had visions of the first scene in *Jaws*. The woman was Lucinda. She was hardly enough to constitute dinner. Her few remains had floated ashore next to Ellsworth-Kent's body. I imagined a leg. A hand with three fingers. An ear.

And not much else.

2

NEWS FROM WYOMING

FINISHED WITH OUR WALK, WUFF IMMEDIATELY trotted into the kitchen and collapsed in her day bed. The bed has her name on the side. A second identical dog bed is at the foot of my king size. Wuff uses her kitchen bed less for sleep than for watching what is going on in the kitchen area, meaning keeping an eye on me. Lucinda's abduction reduced Wuff's flock to one, and she is determined not to become a sheepdog without even one obedient lamb.

Wanting further to avoid calling Dan because I wasn't prepared for disturbing news, I focused on my daily chores—I washed and dried the breakfast dishes, made my bed, watered two plants my housekeeper had left, and then went online but found nothing of interest in the day's *Bozeman News*. Then I turned to the *Jackson Times*.

My laptop had remained shut on the trip across country. I was glad I pulled up the most recent *Jackson Times* because there was an item surprisingly buried—at least to anyone who fly fishes on lonely creeks and rivers in the Western mountains—on one of the back pages:

Arthur Spence, owner of car wash businesses in Jackson and over the Teton Pass in Victor and Driggs, Idaho, remains missing. Spence is one of few certified Master Casting Instructors based in Wyoming. Annually, he has donated considerable time to giving lessons to raise money for charities and last year started a fly fishing casting program for kids.

A week ago Spence left his South Jackson home, telling his wife he'd be gone fly fishing most of the day but would be back in time to take her to her birthday dinner in the Couloir Restaurant at the summit of the Bridger Gondola at the Jackson Hole Mountain Resort, where the view outperforms the kitchen.

Spence's wife didn't know whether he was floating on the Snake with a friend—he had left his own drift boat at home—or was wade fishing on some local creek, which he often did alone.

He didn't return that evening and hasn't been heard from or seen since, despite an extensive search that was called off yesterday.

Arthur Spence was a name familiar to me. He is more than just a fly fisherman. He is one of only a handful of Master Casting Instructors in Wyoming who are certified by the International Federation of Fly Fishers (IFFF), which is headquartered not far from my log cabin. The Federation is devoted to teaching fly casting and offers a rigorous program that certifies casting skills in three programs: the Certified Casting Instructor, the Master Casting Instructor, and a relatively new special group called the Two-Handed (Spey) Casting Instructor. Spence was all three.

My long-time Jackson resident and fly fishing guide friend, John Kirby, probably knew more about Spence's disappearance. They both live in Jackson Hole. I closed out of the paper's website and called John. He didn't answer, which was not unusual because he was likely guiding a client in his drift boat somewhere on the Snake River, which twisted southward alongside the Grand Teton range in Wyoming.

It was evening before I reached John and told him Ellsworth-Kent was dead. I didn't mention the woman's remains. He must have assumed Lucinda was dead and didn't want to disturb me asking about her.

"I wondered when you might turn your phone back on," John said. "I figured you turned it off when you left Montana for the drive east and wouldn't turn it on until you arrived in Florida. I was right. . . . Do I have something to tell *you!*"

"I called *you* and get to speak first. . . . I'm exhausted. There must be a better way getting here than driving," I said, ignoring his "something" he wanted to tell me. "John, the railroads should start some service so I could put my car on the train two dozen miles north at the old charming train station in Livingston, have a private sleeping compartment for two nights that would take me through a deep sleep across the Great Plains states, and I would wake up in Jacksonville facing less than an hour's drive here to my cottage. But truthfully I guess I have little chance of getting across the country without paying the price of being on the Great Plains for two days. About as much chance as your Georgia Bulldog football team has to win the national championship."

"I'll ignore that. You're mean-spirited today," he responded. "You shouldn't be nasty. After all, Ellsworth-Kent was found dead. I assume that's why you called."

"My call is really about a guy from *your* town named Arthur Spence. I was catching up on reading your *Jackson Times* online. Today's edition mentioned he went off fly fishing and has been missing for a week. He never went home and hasn't been seen in Jackson Hole or across the Tetons in Idaho where he has some businesses. . . . Have you ever met him?"

"Spence is the 'something' *I* wanted to tell you about. Every fisherman in Jackson and probably the whole of Wyoming knows about him. I consider Spence a friend. You know him, Macduff, don't you?"

"Yes, maybe too well in view of his death. I had more or less promised to head down to your area and fish with him about a week ago, but I was trying to pack and begin the drive here to Florida and begged off. Spence and I agreed to get together when I returned next spring."

"If you've got a few minutes to listen without interrupting me in the middle of every sentence, I'll tell you what I know about Spence," explained John.

"Try me," I said.

"A month ago I booked Spence to wade-fish in Cascade Canyon in Grand Teton Park. He's a great caster, but he didn't know the Cascade Canyon area, and he wanted me to guide. He never showed up. Not even a phone call canceling. That was about when he went missing."

"Or did he show up and you two argued over using nymphs and you killed him?" I asked.

"*No!* . . . The next day I had a client from Nevada named Scott Bradford who wanted to wade-fish for small brook trout. Cascade Canyon, where I had planned to take Spence, seemed a perfect place. You know I don't care much to guide on wade trips. I prefer to float, but Spence wanted to wade and fish for small brookies. Same as Bradford. I like wading when I'm fishing myself or with a friend but not when guiding. The reality is that we guides can't complain; we don't do many trips of any kind this late in the season. Anyway, I called you about taking Bradford off my hands."

"I was on the road, and my phone was off. Sirius music is the only reason I make it across the Great American Desert. Did you fish with Bradford, or is he missing, too?"

"You're right about your phone. I couldn't reach you. Your phone's usually on airplane mode, even though you're in a car. . . . I was going to make it easy for you to come and guide for a day or two. Sarah and the kids went to Arizona with her family. You could have come down to Jackson; we would have fished a few days together, and then you'd take Bradford to Cascade Canyon. If you would only *answer* your phone! And I *did* fish with Bradford."

"What else do you know about Spence other than that he's a great caster?"

"White male, about forty-five, has lived here for a couple of years. First met him last year at a lecture at the Jackson Public Library by some author whose name escapes me. He writes suspense novels that deal with fly fishing. I dozed during most of his lecture. His main character reminded me of you."

"Get to the point. Don't preach to me about authors."

"OK. But it includes Bradford."

"I think you're digressing. But go ahead"

"Sit down, Mac, if you're not already. There's a lot you should know that hasn't been in the news yet."

"Why not?"

"Most of what I'm going to tell you happened only yesterday."

"I'm sitting. Tell me."

3

CASCADE CREEK IN CASCADE CANYON – WYOMING

"YESTERDAY I MET BRADFORD EARLY AT THE Jenny Lake parking area," John began. "He seemed to be a pleasant guy to spend the day with. He said he lived in Nevada and emphasized that his home wasn't in Las Vegas but in Carson City, the state capital. No mention was made about what he did for a living, or I forgot.

"We took the boat across the lake and hiked up in Cascade Canyon. It was an exquisite spring day, perfect for fishing the creek although we had to be careful fishing in the bright sun not to cast shadows on the water.

"After a half-hour of walking, we stopped where the creek widened, and there was a slope of rocks leading up to Storm Point. Bradford was excited about the hike and the fishing. I felt it was going to be a good day. Much better than you had not long ago with Palmer Brown on the Snake River here in Jackson, Macduff. Remember him?"

"Don't ruin my day talking about Brown," I said. "I'm trying to forget that float, much less the day months later when he shot me on the bank of the Gallatin River. He was worse than Park Salisbury had been a dozen years ago. Salisbury shot me on the Snake River in *your* town. You live in a high crime area.

"The last thing Palmer Brown had said to me, after he shoved my drift boat into the Snake River and it began to float downstream empty, was that he would kill me. He did his best to carry out that threat. . . . Maybe someday I'll learn not to upset clients from hell."

"You were saved by your daughter Beth and her friend?"

"That's what loving daughters do. . . . Tell me more about your day on Cascade Creek."

"I started off with Bradford tying a small #18 Royal Coachman to the nearly invisible end of his tippet. Small fish demand long, finely-tapered tippets. He took a couple of false casts to let line out on his 7' bamboo rod and dropped the fly nicely fifty feet away in an eddy on the downstream side of a solo large boulder, an easy cast unimpeded by any vegetation behind him. He appeared to be a decent caster, and I told him the day would be more actual fishing than giving casting instructions and untying wind knots.

"A brook trout was waiting behind the boulder and rose and engulfed Bradford's fly. He looked around with a grin, but when he looked *behind* me, he lost his concentration *and* the fish. The price of combining inattention with barbless hooks.

"'What's up? You were doing great!' I asked.

"'John, we're being watched.'

"'Maybe she likes your casting. Where is she? Is she good looking?'

"'It's not a female, at least not what you think.'

"'A moose? A grizzly? They're both seen around here often.'

"'Nothing so dramatic. *Much smaller!*'

"I looked behind me, Macduff. A couple of dozen little furry creatures were standing on the rocks that slope up toward Storm Point. They were all staring at us! . . . You know what they were—picas, living among those rocks. I told Bradford they were evaluating and grading his casting.

"'Picas, John? Are they rodents?'

"I told him 'no' and added that they're related to rabbits and hares. They have no tails, I explained, adding the role of park naturalist to fishing guide.

"'I can hear them, John; they're chuckling.'

"'It's thunderous applause only for you, Bradford. Really, they're communicating by *whistling*. Greetings. Or warnings. Whatever picas communicate about.'

"'I guess they're whistling warnings this time, John, not greetings. We look intimidating.'

"'More likely warning their own kind that there was a fox above them on the rocks. Or they spotted an eagle. Or, most likely, a weasel was heading this way on the canyon trail. The weasel is their worst enemy,'" John said he had explained to his client.

"I told Bradford that picas remind me of meerkats in Africa and that I would protect him from picas *and* weasels, all being part of my role as a fully prepared guide. Finally, I thought it was time to get serious about fishing, Macduff, and told him to cast and drop his fly about two feet off some grass along the far edge of the creek. I was sure I saw something rise.

"He tossed his fly—this time a #18 Elk Hair Caddis—sixty feet, four short of where the reeds began on the far side, and let it float slowly with the current. A decent cast but no trout seemed interested.

"I suggested he try again but shift to twenty feet upstream from his first cast. He did, but this time he overshot the water on the edge of the reeds, dropping the fly into the middle of a reed clump.

"'Damn! John, I think I'm losing a fly!'

"I told him to flip it up quickly to each side. He did, but that didn't dislodge the fly. It had been consumed by the two-foot high grass. Next I suggested he pull it straight back, slowly increasing the pressure and hopefully only pulling out a clump of weeds but getting the fly back.

"Bradford tried that, and said he felt some slight movement but that it was heavy. I told him to go slowly. He pulled it four to five feet, to the edge of the grass. It wasn't a fish but there was an occasional flash of reflected sunlight. He was snagged on something that wasn't moving any longer. He was afraid of breaking the tippet, so I said I'd wade out and see.

"'Anything to save a fly, John?'

"'Yes, some of that.'

"The water was well below my hip boots, and the bottom looked firm. Whatever it was, Macduff, it was *not* a fish; there was no movement. From the edge of the grass the 'thing' appeared. It was a large wide-brimmed khaki-colored hat, with the Elk Hair Caddis firmly snagged in the brim. The hat had several small metal pins from outfitters on different rivers from Alaska to Maine. They must have caused the reflection.

"Bradford said it was hardly worth the effort, but I kept wading and picked up the soggy hat, pulled out the fly, and tucked the hat behind my belt, wincing as the cold water ran down into my hippers. I told him it was a price a guide paid for not losing a fly.

"'Apparently the picas enjoyed the show, Bradford.' They were still standing among the rocks, watching and whistling. More likely watching and *jeering*.

"I stood and admired the grass. It was not as high a year ago. . . . There wasn't another place I wanted to be but there—standing alone in a clear, cold mountain stream with the Grand

Tetons rising above while the picas whistled below and fish waited for us in the creek.

"Bradford called and asked if there was any name written on the hat. I looked on the inside of the brim and there was, in faded ink but clear enough to read: 'Arthur Spence!'"

"The guy who was missing?" I asked.

"That's right," John responded. "I waded further into the grass and pulled branches aside.

"Macduff, at first I didn't see anything other than the hat, but as I turned to go back, I saw a booted foot sticking out of some grass ahead."

"A foot? Any more than a foot?" I asked.

"Much more. A leg and then a whole body, all snared by the grasses. Bradford had hooked only the person's hat. The body was stuck, partly submerged and partly supported by the grass. It was a male, confirming the name scribbled on the hat."

"Did you move him?"

"The body wasn't going anywhere. It couldn't float down the creek. The park rangers would want to see it where we found it. . . . I yelled to Bradford to call the rangers."

"Any idea how Spence's death happened," I asked. "Marks on the body? Any sign of blood? Of course, he could have drowned accidentally. It's not the best place to fish alone, and he might have become tangled in the grass after all the day's hikers had left the previous day. It gets cold in the canyon at night."

"I couldn't tell much about the body. There were no marks on his face or hands, and the rest of him was covered by his fishing clothes. There was no visible blood. . . . But there was something small and black hanging around his neck on a string, although I couldn't tell what it was.

"I waded back to the shore. Bradford got through to the park rangers office and contacted a ranger named Jessie Fox who was working only a couple of miles away at Inspiration Point. She apparently left immediately, jogging toward us. At the same time a copter was sent from the search and rescue group at the park entrance at Moose. In this case it was neither a search nor a rescue. But they had to deal with the body. A few minutes later Ranger Fox and the copter arrived at almost the same time.

"Fox told us who she was and then waded directly to the body, carrying a camera. We could see her taking pictures and then struggling to pull the body free of the grass and get it to shore. She was sweating from running, and the sleeves of her stained shirt were rolled up showing forearms covered with tattoos. When she was out of the creek altogether, we could see she was about 5'10" with a pretty face and unkempt ponytail. Her face and neck had no tattoos. She rolled her sleeves down and buttoned them. I think she was embarrassed by the tattoos.

"I told Ranger Fox who I was and introduced her to Bradford. . . . It was strange to be making introductions and see a body lying at the edge of the slowly flowing creek, grass swaying beyond in the slight breeze and snow-capped mountains rising above it all.

"The copter landed a few minutes later, and a rescue officer named Astrid Bjornsen hopped out and joined us. I heard Bjornsen tell Fox that she and the rescue team would fly the body to the morgue.

"Fox acted flustered," John continued. "She was visibly angry about something, but she didn't want to argue with another ranger who was probably a couple of GS levels above her. One of Bjornsen's men later told me Fox had been passed over for promotion a month ago and was trying to show a level of good behavior that her colleagues thought might be beyond her reach. But while Fox didn't want to irritate Bjornsen, she looked at us differently. Not friendly.

"'Stay here, you two,' Fox said to me firmly," related John. "Then she said to me in no uncertain terms that she would tell us when we could leave and only after we answered her questions."

"Was Fox arrogant, stupid, or immature?" I asked John.

"A mix of all three. Bjornsen got me aside and said Jessie Fox was one of the many young rangers who are overwhelmed by their uniform, distressed by poor pay, and in Fox's case disappointed over her rejection for promotion."

"Did the rangers find any bullet holes on the body? Stab wounds? Fight marks?" I asked.

"Nothing," replied John.

"Did Spence drown?"

"Maybe. I couldn't see any sign of a struggle."

"So it might not have been a murder?"

"Good chance, I guess. Maybe he tripped, was caught in the grass, fell, and drowned."

"And no one saw it? He didn't yell for help? What did you and Bradford do next?"

"Answered a few questions and climbed into the helicopter with the body. Bradford asked me when we were on the copter looking out the door if we should offer to stay to answer more questions from Fox?

"'I guess it's up to us,'" John said he'd answered.

"Fox was by the creek looking at us. She seemed angry. I gave her a thumbs-up sign hoping she would take it as a sign of approval."

"Did she?"

"I guess not. She responded by raising her hand, but with a thumb down. . . . Then she came over and *ordered* us to get off the copter. We did, not looking forward to her unpredictability. The two of us walked over and sat on a log by her, looking at her standing and scowling at us like two kids being told what to do by a camp counselor.

"The first thing she asked was why we were in Cascade Canyon.

"'Fishing,' Bradford told her, holding his rod out for her to see.

"'I have to issue you two a citation,' Fox said.

"I asked if she issued many citations for murder and she didn't take it well. She said she knew we were guilty of something and added words she didn't learn in park ranger school.

"Then for the first time she asked me what my name was and demanded identification.

"I said that I was John Kirby and introduced Bradford as a client.

"'What did you say your name was?' she responded, glowering at me.

"'John. John Kirby.'

"'You're a guide?'

"'Yep.'

"She said to me that I should know there was no fishing permitted until mid-July. I told her I knew the rules.

"Then she added that I was really in trouble because I admitted a guide was assumed to know all the rules and I obviously ignored them. She said that meant a big fine.

"My response began to have a sharper tone. I told her that I knew the rules: that Cascade Creek flowed past where we were sitting and ended in Jenny Lake, and then Cottonwood

Creek flowed out of Jenny Lake and after a few miles joined the Snake River.

"'The rules are clear,'" I explained. "'There is *no* fishing in the creeks that flow from the west *directly* into the Snake. Cascade Creek doesn't flow *into* the Snake; it is the Cottonwood that's closed 'til mid-July'. . . . I sat back and grinned at her again.

"'Don't get smart with me,' she replied. 'Why did you two choose to fish where there was a body?'

"Bradford was getting impatient with her and reminded her that the body was well hidden in the grass and that we obviously didn't know it was there. I suspected that Fox was confused and flustered. She asked us if we removed any identification from the body. I told her we hooked his hat—which I handed her—and that it had what we assumed was his name—'Arthur Spence'—written inside. Fox hadn't gone through the man's pockets; she seemed reluctant to touch the body.

"'Who was Arthur Spence?' Fox asked me.

"'A fisherman who's been reported missing. He's apparently from Jackson. The papers reported him missing. I assume you don't read the papers.'

"She scowled and said we were challenging how she did her job. I wasn't sure whether she was going to shoot us both and get it over with or cry. She suggested we three hike back to the boat and she'd think about it on the way. We agreed.

"The trail narrowed passing through woods, and we had to walk single file back to the dock. None of us said anything until we reached the water and stood waiting for the next boat, which was approaching from across the lake.

"'Do either of you think Spence was murdered?' asked a much calmer Fox, sitting on a seat between Bradford and me and looking back and forth at each of us.

"I told her that, even though the creek was shallow, you can drown in very little water, and my guess was that it was an accident, but we all needed to wait for the medical examiner's report because without more we were only guessing. I said it could have been an accidental drowning or a homicide.

"'Or a suicide?' she asked.

"'Maybe,' I added, although my feelings were that while suicide was a possibility, there were more dangerous places in these mountains to end one's life and without suffering the agony of swallowing water.

"Fox then said she knew about the man who may have pushed his wife off Inspiration Point. And that she had been the first park ranger to reach the woman's horribly battered remains. She said she was having nightmares most every night—waking up seeing the remains."

"I'm glad I wasn't with you," I told John. "I don't want to be reminded of Palmer Brown, who gives *me* nightmares. He was a deranged man."

"When we got to the Jenny Lake parking lot, Macduff, and were joined by two other rangers, Fox took me aside and quietly said she thought she could have done better dealing with us and apologized. The two deaths in the park clearly disturbed her. I accepted her apology and said if I were in her position I probably would have acted much worse. She squeezed my elbow, smiled, turned, and left.

"I had told her I could understand how she felt and said we all have our bad days and there were no hard feelings. . . . Then I suggested to Bradford that I take him back to Moose to get his car and that he let me buy him a beer on the porch of the Pizza, Pasta Company restaurant. . . . Thirty minutes later we were sipping cold Snake River Ale and Bradford said, 'At least we caught half-dozen brookies on the walk up along the creek, but I hadn't intended to add a hat and body to my catch.'

"As he began to drive off after we finished, Bradford rolled down his window and said, 'I hope the picas enjoyed the show we put on.'"

"You had an exciting day," I said to John.

"Yeah," he said, "But I think I'd prefer a little less excitement—fewer bodies and more trout."

"Life would be dull without occasional trauma," I answered. "You loved every minute of it."

"Macduff, I don't need one month to fish and find a body caught in barbed wire strung across the river and then the next month find a body at the end of my client's line. Two murders in a *month's* time! You are dangerous to be around. How does anyone hang around you and survive? . . . I shouldn't have said that. You've suffered more than enough with Lucinda's abduction. I'm sorry."

"John, I didn't call you to talk about your guiding trip with Bradford, but I appreciated hearing about it. I've had some news about Lucinda. . . . Perhaps not *really* about Lucinda."

"You don't always make sense," John reminded me.

"The news was that Ellsworth-Kent's body was found washed up on a beach in the Bahamas."

"You've already told me he was dead. Was Lucinda found? . . . You don't have to talk about it."

"We don't know. There were remains of a woman near Ellsworth-Kent. It was probably Lucinda. . . . As soon as I hang up, I'm calling Dan Wilson; he apparently has some news.

I've put off calling him long enough. If I learn anything, I'll call you."

I hung up, walked out to the porch with my cell phone, and realized I couldn't delay the call any further. . . . If Dan tells me Lucinda is dead, I'll have to deal with her death as best I can. But even if he tells me she's alive, she must be so traumatized from the last eighteen months that she'll never be the Lucinda I've known for most of the best years of my life.

Pulling the phone from my pocket, I turned it on to "recently called numbers," looked at it, turned it off, and put it on the armrest of my chair, staring at the blank screen.

4

SAME TIME – THE FLORIDA COTTAGE

PERSPIRATION BEADED MY BROW AS I TAPPED Dan's name on the beleaguered phone and hoped for a message saying he was away and wouldn't return to the office for at least two weeks. Better would be two months. . . . No such luck. He was at his desk and answered.

"It's about time, Macduff," he said. "At least it proves you haven't misplaced your phone—again. . . . What possibly could have caused you not to return *any* of my six calls all marked 'IMMEDIATE ATTENTION'?"

"Forget the small talk. I read your message that Ellsworth-Kent was dead, and I didn't want to face the next question: Were the woman's remains found near him Lucinda's? . . . *Was it her?*" I asked.

There was silence, mostly in my imagination. The hair on my arms stood on its roots. My toes tingled. I wanted to hang up but for a moment couldn't speak.

Then I mumbled, "Well, are you going to tell me who? . . . *Was it Lucinda?*"

"No! We've just learned that the person was a thirty-something waitress who worked at a bar in Abaco."

"Thank God," I said, so weak I set the phone down on the table and hunched over to talk. "I don't really care, but who was she?"

25

"She went by Bambi Meadows. She was three months pregnant. Ellsworth-Kent was the father."

"So much for *High Priest Einar!* How does *High Priestess Bambi* sound?" I added, wanting to divert the conversation.

Ellsworth-Kent alleged that he had been appointed High Priest Einar several years ago in a Pagan ceremony near the town of Kirkwall on the Orkney Islands in Scotland. Not long after abducting Lucinda, he claimed she was appointed High Priestess Onomaris and they married. My daughter Elsbeth and her friend Sue went to Scotland and discovered that the Pagan Federation in Kirkwall had no record of any such appointments or marriage.

"I know what you're going to ask," Dan said.

"*Where* is Lucinda?" I asked hesitatingly, not certain I could handle the answer.

"*She's alive!* We found her."

"Thank God! In the Bahamas?"

"In Hope Town on Abaco."

"Where is she now? Have you seen her? Is she OK? Is she getting good treatment? Have you talked to her? When can I see her? I can leave here immediately. Can she leave soon?"

"Wait a minute. One matter at a time. . . . First, I *have* seen her. But I haven't talked to her, for reasons I'll explain. . . . And, finally, you can't see her; she's not OK. She won't be going to Florida soon."

"Why? What's wrong? Where will she go?"

"You know Mira Cerna, the hypnotherapist from Budapest. She's come here to D.C. She was home in Hungary on a brief break when we recovered Lucinda, who knows and trusts her. Maybe Lucinda shouldn't, but she does, and we don't want to upset her. Mira doesn't know it, but Lucinda's room is bugged, and I watch and listen to every conversation between them. Mira tells me Lucinda isn't close to being ready to be brought back into our world. She's right about that."

"Meaning?"

"I can't explain everything. Mira will talk to you later. Essentially, she doesn't want Lucinda to be de-hypnotized—or withdrawn or whatever it's called—in one quick act. Lucinda might not absorb the shock."

"Was Lucinda hypnotized by Ellsworth-Kent?"

"Extensively. The truth is that Mira claims he was pretty good at it. But *he* finally realized he was in over his head acting as a hypnotherapist and retained Mira to keep Lucinda in that state."

"For eighteen months?"

"Pretty much so."

"Just what was 'that state' Ellsworth-Kent wanted to sustain?"

"Lucinda believing he was the best person in the world to be with and the only one who truly loved her and that she was not loved or wanted by you because you loved someone else and were unfaithful to Lucinda."

"Dan, how did Ellsworth-Kent and Mira Cerna know I was seeing Grace Justice?"

"Who said anything about Grace Justice?"

Grace Justice—a prominent Florida Assistant State Attorney—became my sometime companion several years ago when Lucinda left me to return to live in New York. Lucinda had learned she had cancer and thought I wouldn't want her. Damaged goods or something absurd like that. When the truth came out and we were back together, Grace remained our social friend. Lucinda never asked how close Grace and I had been.

Grace was assigned to investigate Lucinda's abduction, and I began to see Grace again. Dan knows all that. And he knows Grace was killed fly fishing with me a few months ago in Montana.

"You misunderstand, Macduff. Lucinda was hypnotized and *slowly* led to believe you were not in love with her. She was *never* told you were a bad person, but only that there was someone else you loved more, and someone else Lucinda loved more."

"That would be Ellsworth-Kent."

"Of course. Lucinda was convinced, by Ellsworth-Kent and later Mira, that the one who really loved Lucinda was Ellsworth-Kent. She gradually accepted that and began to believe she and Robert were married."

"Married in a Pagan ceremony?"

"Yes. But Elsbeth and her friend Sue discovered there was no record in Scotland of any such ceremony. You've got to understand that Lucinda wasn't able to distinguish reality from the image Ellsworth-Kent projected. She thought her marriage to him was legitimate."

"For eighteen months?"

"Almost, she was forced to take drugs for the first few weeks after the abduction, maybe for months, before Ellsworth-Kent realized he couldn't keep her alive and suppressed under drugs. He had to find some other way. He found it in hypnotherapy. Not long after, he retained Mira Cerna for a very high price; he gave her $500,000 in cash, and she took leave from her hypnotherapy research and teaching position in Budapest. You know Mira has a reputation as one of the most prominent hypnotherapists in the world."

"Where was all of this 'therapy' performed?"

"Mostly in the Bahamas."

"Hope Town?"

"Yes."

"Was Reginald Covington involved?"

"Certainly. He and Ellsworth-Kent knew each other from years ago when they went to public school and university together in England. Ellsworth-Kent was the rich white kid from aristocracy in England. Covington was the black kid from poverty in the islands."

"And Covington, now no longer the poor black kid, provided his fenced-in, guarded mansion on Hope Town for Ellsworth-Kent to confine Lucinda?"

"Yes. It became a kind of private mental hospital with only one patient."

"What did Covington get in exchange for using his home?"

"I'd rather not go into that now."

"Dan, this is going to take time to soak in."

"Take it easy. *Lucinda is alive*. We're going to see that she has the best medical care available. . . . Macduff, I wondered about Mira Cerna at first, but I accept that she slowly became disenchanted with Ellsworth-Kent and Covington. We need Cerna's expertise now. She kept Lucinda in her hypnotic state for months, and she's promised to get her out. But with time."

"Time meaning how long?"

"Mira doesn't know. She's never been involved this deeply for so long. She used the word 'months' several times."

"I think you're saying Mira doesn't want Lucinda exposed all at once to the world she lived in at the time of the abduction. Meaning not seeing me."

"Yes, for good reason."

"Are we talking about two or three months?"

"Yes. Maybe more."

"And I can't see her all that time?"

"It looks that way. More important is that she can't see *you*."

"How does she look?"

"Rail thin. She's lost a lot of weight."

"Complexion?"

"Pale. She was rarely out in the yard at Covington's place. Probably not in the sun more than a moment or two a week in almost two years."

"Vital statistics?"

"She's being checked. Her heart is fine. The doctors are doing all forms of tests that are beyond me."

"Dan, can I listen to the tapes you've recorded of Lucinda's conversations with Mira?"

"No. You wouldn't want to hear what she's said."

"Meaning what?"

"Let's just say her mind has been focused on her past two years."

"Explain that. Are you saying Lucinda doesn't have a very good opinion of me?"

"She doesn't' know you're alive, and she hasn't mentioned you once. If she's aware you exist, she believes you have no interest in her."

"I'm in no shape to act very rationally," I replied. "Any suggestions?"

"Yes. I've talked to a Dr. Maisie Russell at the University of Florida medical center in Gainesville. I know your daughter Elsbeth goes to the university and rents a house there. Dr. Russell is head of a dual program in psychiatry and neurology. She can explain what Lucinda's gone through. And she will understand and treat what you're going through. Dr. Russell told me that as soon as I talked to you to insist you call her. My secretary's emailing you her contact info as we speak. Promise me you'll call her as soon as we finish."

"Well. . . . maybe a little later. . . . "

"No! Now! Dr. Russell is waiting for your call, and you had best pack and head to Gainesville. Anything else to tell me?"

"Does Dr. Russell believe there's something mentally wrong with me?"

"She'll tell you about that. Just go."

When I phoned Dr. Russell, her appointment scheduler was expecting my call and said the earliest the doctor could see me was right after lunch—today!

Thirty minutes later I was packed somewhat and on the road to Gainesville.

I intentionally had omitted discussing with Dan the death and possible murder of Spence at Cascade Canyon.

5

ON THE ROAD TO GAINESVILLE

NO ONE EXCEPT DAN AND MIRA, AND NOW ME, knew about Lucinda being alive. I preferred to tell Elsbeth face to face when I surprised her after talking to Dr. Russell. I assumed she would want to tell her housemate friend, Sue. Telling anyone else might encourage well-intentioned but unanswerable questions about when Lucinda will rejoin me and how she survived the year-and-a-half with Ellsworth-Kent.

That Lucinda was alive and in the hospital and there would be a long and stressful recovery was all I would say. I wasn't prepared for what I worried might be among the questions friends asked, especially how Lucinda might react to learning about my relationship with the late Grace Justice and what Ellsworth-Kent and Covington may have forced on Lucinda.

My housekeeper Jen Jennings would be here at the cottage tomorrow, but friends in Montana and Wyoming had to be called. That included Wanda Groves, my attorney in Bozeman, Montana, who helped me over the past months preserving assets Ellsworth-Kent attempted to extort from me and Lucinda.

Mavis Benton, my housekeeper in Montana, will be thrilled. She had been glum all summer, and I often saw her staring at photos of Lucinda on the log cabin walls, tears running down her face.

The drive to Gainesville was one phone conversation after another. Bluetooth kept my hands on the steering wheel, although my mind remained a world away.

The call to Wanda was completed by the time I went under I-95—content in being under and not on it. As I passed through the vast green vegetable fields of Hastings, I contacted Deputy Erin Giffin at the Park County Sheriff's Office in Montana. Newly appointed head sheriff Ken Rangley joined us for part of the call. In Palatka I reached Mavis at the Mill Creek cabin and in Melrose got through to guide friend John Kirby in Jackson, Wyoming. Entering Gainesville, my last call was to Huntly Byng, the head investigator at the Teton County Sheriff's Office in Wyoming. Truthfully, I didn't remember much of the driving part of the trip, but the time had passed quickly. I went directly to the UF Medical Center, used valet parking, and was in Dr. Russell's office at two minutes before 1:00 p.m.

After sitting for no more than five minutes reading a silly forgettable magazine called something like *Teens* or *Celebrity Divorces*, a *Cosmopolitan* cover-girl look-a-like came out not in scrubs and stethoscope but wearing something spectacular that Yves Saint Laurent or Versace might have created. She was not anorexic like the paper-thin gals who wore those designs at fashion shows, nor was she the least bit heavy. Her complexion made many cosmetic models' skin look like grit sandpaper.

"Mr. Brooks," Dr. Russell said with the soft but strong "r" in the burr of the Scottish highlands, "come with me and tell me how you came to have such friends as Dan Wilson in D.C. He wouldn't tell me who he worked for, only that my seeing you immediately was a matter of national security. Who are you?"

"I'm Macduff Brooks, an ordinary fly fishing guide in Montana. I've taken Dan fishing occasionally. I'm not very important and of no essence to national security."

"I've looked you up online," Russell responded. "Magically, you appear to have been born when you were forty-seven. There is no record of you before that. You are far from ordinary."

For the next forty-five minutes I gave Dr. Russell an honest outline of my life, but limited to *after* arriving in Montana. Some questions I didn't answer if they seemed to be irrelevant to her role with Lucinda and me. Quickly she became aware I wasn't telling all, partly because I suggested she read the *Bozeman Magazine* article because it had everything I might include in my answers to her questions.

"Macduff, if you expect me to help you and Lucinda, you should answer my questions fully and not tell me to read some article."

"I've told you more than I expected I would say when I arrived here. I'm not a threat to national security, but a number of people feel I'm a personal threat to them."

"I'll try to deal with that. Looking at your recent life, I'm not sure before Grace Justice died you truly wanted Lucinda back. You were sleeping with Ms. Justice frequently."

"I won't debate that with you. At least partly because I wasn't sure myself why I kept up a relationship with Ms. Justice when there was some hope Lucinda might return."

Dr. Russell's questions subtly changed from my history to my feelings about Lucinda after I had learned she was alive.

"Macduff, do you feel you're obligated to *renew* your relationship with Lucinda?"

"It's not a matter of renewal. I never spent a moment when I didn't want her back."

"Even when you were in bed with Grace Justice?"

"I guess I imagined that Grace was Lucinda."

"Do you expect me to believe that? If Lucinda had not survived, but Grace had, would you have had the same feelings that you were actually with Lucinda whenever you were with Grace after, say, five years? After ten?"

"I assumed I'd reach a point where Lucinda was only a memory. Grace knew that she would never have a lasting role in my life until we were certain Lucinda had perished."

"Now that Lucinda hasn't perished and Grace is dead, are you totally committed to Lucinda?"

"Yes."

"But you don't know what Lucinda is like now. I can almost assure you she will never be the same person you knew before she was abducted. Will you still be devoted to her when permanent personality changes have become clear?"

"I hope so. Am I right in believing there are different possibilities? One is that she will return to essentially what she was like when she was taken. Another is that she will look the same but be a different person in one or more ways."

"She might *remain* convinced that you do not love her and that Ellsworth-Kent died fully committed to her."

"Dr. Russell, you're talking about something we don't know about: how close to the old Lucinda she will be? You never knew her. I thought your questions to me would have been more along the lines of: how do I think I will react to her and how can I best help her? That's on my mind all the time. I don't know the answer. I want to do my best.

"If the months and maybe years pass and she cannot recover her old character, it will be like caring for a spouse who has Alzheimer's. It would be a question of caring for someone I love no less because she has changed. I knew her before the incident. If she sits in a chair looking at me but not knowing who I am, that doesn't mean I don't know who she is. Give me a chance."

For the next hour Dr. Russell educated me about psychiatry and neurology and how and why I might feel differently than I presumed. She said it might take numerous visits to her office before I was ready to see Lucinda. Most everything she said sounded like canned speech, and I tried to sift through it for glimpses of what she was trying to accomplish.

"Let's talk in another two weeks," she suggested. "By then, I'll have read the article about your years before you moved to Montana. Lucinda will have been in the hands of some very good doctors in D.C., and we may know more about who she has or will become and whether you're capable of helping her."

"I think that's for Lucinda to decide."

Showing up for another session is doubtful, I thought, as I walked to my SUV, wondering why in my lifetime cardiologists, ophthalmologists, and even dermatologists had advanced so extensively in treating patients, while psychiatrists were still considered a fancy way of saying social workers.

If I do return to Russell's office, I may ask her about that.

6

IN GAINESVILLE

AN HOUR AFTER I ESCAPED FROM DR. RUSSELL'S grasp, I parked in front of Elsbeth's rented Golf View, Gainesville, house El and I called home for ten years until her tragic death on the Snake River in Wyoming. For another ten years I remained in the house living alone, inviting only students for seminars and holiday dinners, and never hosting colleagues or old friends.

Sitting in my SUV, I had images of two former students who had been at this house on some of those occasions—Juan Pablo Herzog from Guatemala and Abdul Khaliq Isfahani from the Sudan. They became close friends and two of the students I was most fond of that decade.

What evolved after the two returned to their countries was beyond my possible comprehension and quickly became nightmares. Isfahani had become a terrorist and a principal in an unsuccessful attempt to topple both the Empire State and Chrysler buildings in New York. But he was no longer an issue; I assassinated him in Khartoum several years ago.

Herzog had become a more serious *personal* problem because his target was not against America, but me alone. He nearly killed me in Guatemala more than a decade ago when he discovered I was doing more than teaching law at Francisco Marroquin; surreptitiously I was gathering information for our

State Department. Saved by U.S. Embassy persons, I was flown to D.C. and placed in a protection program, giving up my life as Professor Maxwell Hunt, my occupation as a law teacher, author, and consultant, and evacuating my Gainesville home, the very house I was now sitting before. For my future life, I chose to become Macduff Brooks, a fly fishing guide in the western mountains of Montana and Wyoming.

Herzog frequently has sought me out to kill me, but has not been able to learn who I am, exactly what I do, or where I live. He has come close and lost a niece and a nephew who were sent to find and kill me but lost their own lives. Another niece, seeking me, became disaffected from her Tío Juan and has remained in the United States unwilling to return to Guatemala.

Sitting outside my old house only a few blocks from the law school, thinking "what if?" put me in a trance. Some minutes later, hard knocks on my SUV window caused me to turn. Elsbeth was staring at me not more than a foot away—amazed to see me.

I rolled down the window and said quietly, "Hi, girl!"

"Hi! What are *you* doing here? It's been a week since we talked as you left Montana. You haven't returned a single call. I've been scared silly. Now you show up in front of my house. Should I call 911? . . . Why do you do things like this?"

I got out of the car, and she threw herself at me, breaking into tears. We walked into the house together and went out onto the back porch.

"Don't you dare move one inch. I'll be right back," she said, pushing me down onto a chair.

Five minutes later she joined me again with a glass of Gentleman Jack in one hand and something I didn't recognize in the other.

"It's a piña colada minus the piña but with double rum," she said, sipping.

"What's wrong?" she asked. "How long have you been in Florida? I've called you so many times. I tried Dan's office in D.C., but they said he was out of town until further notice. I called Jen, your housekeeper in St. Augustine, but she's in Virginia visiting family. I haven't said anything to my housemate, Sue, about how worried I am, but she knows. . . . And now you walk in looking like you're in another world. . . . You haven't been in Gainesville in months. And I assume you're not here for a soccer game or you'd be dressed differently. Certainly not wearing a suit and tie. You look a lot like you must have when you were Professor Hunt. Dressing like that when you're in Gainesville is not wise."

I sat for a moment not saying anything, looking out at the yard where so many times I imagined I'd be playing with the child El and I were expecting. The child I thought perished with El but was sitting in front of me staring and waiting for me to say something about the reason for my visit.

"Lucinda is alive," I whispered.

Elsbeth slumped back into her chair, reached for her glass, and knocked it over onto the floor.

"Why isn't she with you? Why aren't you with her?"

"I don't know where to begin. I couldn't face you."

"*Where is she?*"

"By now, in D.C. at a government hospital."

"Was she in Washington all this time?"

"No. She was mostly in the Bahamas."

"Bahamas? Where?"

"At the mansion of a Bahamian friend and former schoolmate of Robert Ellsworth-Kent—her abductor. She had been held in Hope Town for more than a year."

"Kept there by Ellsworth-Kent? Drugged? She couldn't survive being drugged all that time."

"There is much more to it."

"Tell me everything. . . . Why are you here in Gainesville?"

"I had a medical appointment."

"Medical appointment? You have a bunch of good doctors in St. Augustine. Why Gainesville? Dentist for teeth cleaning? Ophthalmologist to check your cataracts? Annual physical?"

"This was a specialist that Dan Wilson arranged for me to see."

"Dan Wilson arranged it? What on earth is going on!?"

"I met with the head of a dual program in psychiatry and neurology."

"A shrink!"

"Yes."

"Why? You've never talked to one before."

"I'd like to think I don't need one now. After two hours with this doctor, I'm certain of that. But I'm here because of Lucinda."

"This is going way beyond me. Let's start with Lucinda. How was she found? Where? What condition was she in?"

I repeated everything I knew to date, including the message from Dan reporting the death of Ellsworth-Kent and the conversations with Mira Cerna about the proposed treatment of Lucinda over the next few months.

"I can't believe you can't see her. Even if she can't see you. That's unfair."

"Maybe not," I replied. "Imagine how Lucinda feels. She may not know that Ellsworth-Kent is dead. She may believe she's married to him and he's away. She might not recognize me.

"Mira Cerna will be working with Lucinda for months, and Dan says her conversations with Cerna are being monitored and recorded. But I trust Cerna; I believe she's sincere in wanting to bring Lucinda out of hypnosis slowly to where she has no positive feelings for Ellsworth-Kent."

"Where will you be? You can stay here with me and Sue. But you should be closer to Lucinda."

"It makes no sense to go to D.C. and sit in some hotel for what could be weeks. Or more. I'll stay in St. Augustine and be ready to fly to D.C. as soon as Dan gives me a green light."

"I'll be over to the cottage *every* weekend. I don't have Friday classes, so I'll come Thursdays after my last class ends at noon. May I bring Sue?"

"Sue's always welcome. She's become family. Remember that together you two saved my life last year after Palmer Brown shot me and was aiming for the final blow."

"If anyone succeeds landing a final blow on you, it will be me—if you don't do as I tell you."

7

THE FOLLOWING DAY – CRYSTAL RIVER, FLORIDA

THE PLANTATION AT CRYSTAL RIVER IS AN OASIS of early Florida elegance set between gridlocked route U.S. 19 and a maze of river and canals. Unless a visitor remains lost in the maze, the water spills west into the Gulf of Mexico which, by its name, identifies Crystal River as located on the "other side of the tracks" of Florida, along a coastal strip with towns named Homosasa, Citrus Springs, Yankeetown, Steinhatchee, and Keaton Beach.

Built barely a half century ago, the Plantation lodging drew upon an imagined classical splendor of a bygone Florida. Current guests are forgiven if they feel they are experiencing Atlantic Coast Henry Flagler era elegance.

Crystal River had never attracted me until the Florida Council of the International Federation of Fly Fishers—home based in charming rural Livingston, Montana, close to my summertime log cabin—began to schedule its annual fall conference at Crystal River. For three days the fly fishers displaced another set of consumptive liars called golfers, whose length of shots off the tee is exceeded only by the length of fish inflated by my group.

Before I left Montana, I reserved a ground floor room at the Plantation with a view of the canals so I could walk out onto an expansive lawn and throw what I thought were perfect practice loops, but they drew suppressed laughter from attending Certified and Master Casting Instructors enjoying evening drinks in front of their rooms.

Two months ago I signed up to take the Certified Casting Instructor test, and, regardless of that outcome, the following day I paid to throw myself at the mercy of Master Casting Instructor Rachel Hart in a class for self-styled advanced casters.

Elsbeth *commanded* that I stay overnight with her and Sue in Gainesville following my summit meeting with Dr. Russell. That meant more hours on the road the following day than I welcomed. After breakfast with the two young coeds, I drove two hours east to St. Augustine from Gainesville, hung up my coat and tie for what I hoped would be many months, collected fly casting gear, and drove another nearly four hours back west to Crystal River. The drive made me understand how one becomes discouraged driving laterally across Florida, in this case east to west. All roads in Florida seem intended to lead to Miami, a destination I dread to even contemplate.

No roads lead from St. Augustine to Crystal River in any manner one would label "direct." I tried by heading west for a while and then south for about an equal time. It meant first retracing the last half-hour of the morning's drive between Palatka and St. Augustine, and then, for my first time ever I passed through Welaka and paid $10 to take the Fort Gates ferry across a narrow neck of the St. Johns River. From the western shore soon I was engaged in involuntary tours of Salt Springs, Bruceville, and its neighbor Grahamsville, and then added even more towns new to me, such as Santos and Shady, only to find myself lost in Top-of-the-World. Finally, I moved on through Stokes Ferry, Timberline Estates, and miraculously entered

Crystal River. I can neither recommend nor remember the route and decided to detour on the way home and visit Elsbeth again in Gainesville.

The Plantation was waiting for me, as were two Master Casting Instructor friends, David Lambert, of Ponte Vedra, Florida, and Dave Johnson, of Batesville, Indiana. They were sitting on the terrace outside our rooms with chilled bottles of Stella Artois and a couple of rigged practice fly rods. If I flunked the CCI exam the next morning, I could claim it was because we all had a second and third beer and the practice rods remained leaning against the wall.

By the time I met Rachel Hart the following morning, I was a know-it-all newly certified CCI. But Rachel quickly took me down an embarrassing notch after she asked me to demonstrate an over-the-shoulder roll cast on the canal in front of us and stood behind me to represent a bush that confirmed a roll cast was the proper choice. Excited, I didn't stop the lift at twelve o'clock but too quickly muscled it back to two o'clock and sent the practice fly rocketing down into her recently coiffured hairdo. The worst was to come. I jerked it back and pulled her with me. The fly was hookless but nevertheless caught in her hair, and we went down together.

She asked me to step aside using a few four-letter words I suspect she reserved for such occasions. She never called on me the rest of the session, but she stared at me a lot. I'm fortunate I hadn't sewn on my new CCI patch after hearing I had passed; she would have ripped it off and tossed it into the canal or stuffed it down my throat.

When the lesson concluded, I was shocked that Ms. Hart asked me to buy her a drink. She said she had heard about the mayhem that allegedly occurred around my guiding and wanted to hear it from me to actually believe it. We walked to the terrace by the pool, sat at a small table in a quiet corner, and ordered drinks.

"I'd prefer you'd call me Rachel. . . . How many clients have you murdered?" she began, taking her glasses off and setting them on the table.

"Not one, and I haven't paid a dollar fine or spent a day in jail. I must be innocent."

"That's what they all say. . . . I read in a paper today about the body they found in Wyoming in a national park. Do you know about that?"

I didn't want to say much. "I was on my way to Florida when it happened. And when I'm in the West, I'm mostly in Montana, not Wyoming. But I did see a brief piece about it."

"What made me take note in the article was that the guy was a Master Casting Instructor. Like me."

"I don't think being an MCI should be related to his death," I said. "It was most likely an accidental drowning. We'll know more when the medical examiner issues his report, if he hasn't already."

"The article I read said the dead man had a black fly hanging from a piece of string around his neck," she noted.

"He did. I know the guide who found Spence's body. He told me about the black fly and said it looked like a Black Marabou pattern. There was no hook; it must have been a practice fly. My guide friend didn't think it meant very much."

"If you'll buy me dinner," Rachel said abruptly, "and another drink, I'll give you some pointers about casting, and you can tell me more fly fishing murder tales."

"When you give me suggestions on casting, remember that I'm a foot taller than you," I said. "We both use nine foot rods. That means my rod tip is much higher than yours, and it's harder for me to pick up line."

"But because your line and loop are all higher," she replied, "your cast should go further. . . . Macduff, if casting is all we're going to talk about, it's time for me to leave." She had removed her sandals and was rubbing her feet up and down my calf. It felt good.

"If you leave, you'll miss my stories about gill nets in Florida and barracudas in Cuba."

"I'll stay! Tell me about the gill nets first," she said, resuming the foot massage. "Dinner can wait. Let's get another drink and take it down by the canal where it's more private."

We did, and I told her about the gill nets, barracudas, and airboats. Two hours later, after dinner by the pool, as we walked back towards our rooms, I knew she was a unique lady, talented and enticing. And thrice divorced, I reminded myself.

I couldn't help thinking about President Jimmy Carter's famous *Playboy* interview when he said "I've looked on a lot of women with lust. I've committed adultery in my heart many times . . . and God forgives me for it."

"God may forgive me for thinking about sleeping with other women, but I don't think Lucinda would," I said out loud as I put the key in my door lock, only to realize two women were unlocking the adjacent room door, looking at me, and laughing.

8

FOLLOWING DAY - GAINESVILLE

RETRACING MY GERRYMANDERED ROUTE FROM St. Augustine the next day would have been possible only by conceding I would make wrong turns and visit a number of towns I missed on the drive to Crystal River. I decided against such an embarrassing retreat across state and instead chose a deviation I knew that about noon would put me back in Gainesville at Elsbeth's house.

It was Sunday, and she and Sue were working in the yard, dressed in old jeans, long sleeved shirts, and wide brimmed hats that tried to defeat the cancer-seducing Florida sun.

"Did they throw you out of the meeting for casting unbecoming to a fly fisherman?" asked Sue.

"Look at this," I said, holding my CCI patch a few inches in front of her face.

"Did you find that on the lawn?"

"Sue, I thought you were on my side for *some* things."

"I am, but not when it deals with your casting, making strange noises with your oboe, or eating unhealthy meals."

"And I was thinking I might adopt you!"

"Not a chance. I have parents at home in Wyoming. *Normal* parents."

"I drove out of the way to receive this welcome?"

"Actually, you're a very good caster—for an old man. But not a good oboist for any age."

"Dad, come in and have lunch," called Elsbeth. "We're having asparagus quiche. It has to bake for thirty minutes after I sprinkle it with Gruyere cheese. I'll leave your cheese off."

"Also, hold the asparagus."

"You need to eat more greens. Asparagus is a good green."

"I had greens for breakfast."

"What? A spinach and egg omelet? Zucchini? Kiwi salad? Green apples? Green bananas?"

"I had green *tea*."

"You're hopeless. Let's go inside. . . . I have some corn flakes that came in a green box."

I was on a second helping of the corn flakes, drenched in maple syrup that came from a tree with green leaves, when my cell phone rang.

Luisa Solares was calling from her rented house in Gainesville. She's a niece of Guatemalan President Juan Pablo Herzog, and the illegitimate daughter of Herzog's Catholic priest cousin beloved as Padre Bueno before Juan Pablo murdered him on the streets of Antigua during an Easter parade.

Herzog sent Luisa to UF to study for a year in a special Master of Laws degree program in Comparative Law created exclusively for law graduates from civil law nations.

Luisa's real reason for being sent was to learn about what happened to Professor Maxwell Hunt, who I was known as until Herzog tried to kill me and I was placed in the protection program by the State Department people who had sent me to Guatemala in the first place to lecture and collect information. Luisa didn't know I was Hunt and has refused to seek that information for Herzog, occasionally igniting his fury.

Increasingly, it hasn't been wise for Luisa to go home, and she has remained in Gainesville to begin the law school's regular JD program, which she might finish in two additional years. I trust Luisa; she has become a close friend of Elsbeth and Sue.

"Mr. Brooks, I have something to tell you," Luisa began.

"I hope it's not that you're withdrawing from the law school and going home to work for your uncle."

"Not a chance. I don't trust Tío Juan. He remains determined to find and kill Professor Hunt, if he can find out who he is."

"He thinks he knows," I said. "A former and now dead CIA agent told Herzog that Hunt changed his name to Walter Windsor and moved to Alaska to work in fishing."

"I hope it takes my uncle years to discover that isn't true," Luisa said. "Alaska is why I called you. You might like to know he sent a top advisor named General Hector Ramirez to Anchorage to search for Professor Hunt."

"You told me about Ramirez not long ago."

"What you probably don't know is that last week Ramirez located a man named Walter Windsor who worked on a halibut fishing boat in Homer, Alaska."

"How did you hear about it?" I asked.

"Family members in Guatemala who prefer not to be mentioned but quietly keep me informed about what my uncle is doing."

"What has Ramirez accomplished in Alaska?"

"He set fire to the boat that Windsor worked on, after he locked Windsor in his cabin."

"Windsor died?"

"Burned to a carbonized brain case. My aunt Victori . . . I mean one of my relatives, told me about it. When the boat burned, it was at a dock in some village harbor on an island in something called the Aleutians."

"What did Ramirez tell Herzog?"

"Herzog wanted Professor Hunt brought to Guatemala alive but that was no longer possible. Ramirez was reluctant to try to transport a charred body to Guatemala City. He told Herzog who, in turn, ordered Ramirez to send a photo of Windsor's head. . . . But his body was *more* than burned.

"When the police arrived hours after the boat burned, they found that Windsor's head was missing. They were more intrigued and occupied by why the head was gone than why the fire occurred.

"Apparently Ramirez flew home and used his diplomatic immunity to get the head into Guatemala without inspection."

"This is becoming like a good mystery story!" I exclaimed. "Do you know what Herzog did with the head when Ramirez showed up in Guatemala and presented it to him?"

"He was elated about Walter Windsor being dead. But my family members sensed he was concerned that he couldn't conclusively link the head to Professor Hunt because it was burned down to the skull? What would he compare it with? Dental records he doesn't have? He would have to find Hunt alive to prove it wasn't his skull."

"Did he keep the head?"

"I don't know. Maybe cremation. He has a lot of enemies in Guatemala who'd love to see him toppled from the presidency. He's egotistical enough to put the skull on display in his presidential office, but that might irritate enough people around him to encourage an investigation."

"Luisa, is Herzog done with intimidating and berating you? He has what he wants. Granted, he didn't accomplish that partly because you couldn't retrieve the information from the law school. But, nevertheless, he got it."

"I'm not going back to Guatemala, Mr. Brooks, at least while Herzog is alive. I feel, as Sue says, 'safe and sound' on my own here in Gainesville. I'm two years away from my JD degree. When I graduate and pass the bar exam, I'll practice law in Miami. I already have an offer from a good firm that focuses on Inter-American issues. . . . Mr. Brooks, I owe you."

"You owe me *nothing*."

"In a way I have *already* partially repaid you."

"How?"

"By shredding a report I drafted for my uncle a year ago. I never gave it to him."

"A report?"

"I'm going to read you part of the report:

Tío Juan, I have what you want. Professor Maxwell Hunt became a fly fishing guide who lives part of the year in Emigrant, Montana, and the other part in St. Augustine, Florida. His new name is Macduff Brooks. He's single, has no wife and no children. Get him and you've settled your vendetta. Your loving niece, Luisa

"I can't believe you'd do this. And you know I'm married and have a daughter."

"I didn't want them brought into my uncle's vengeance that's really directed at you."

"How did you learn about me and Professor Hunt?"

"Partly by what you've just shown about your interest and what *you* know about Windsor. Uncle Herzog told *me* about Walter Windsor. I became convinced you were Hunt from all I've learned about you and Elsbeth over the past year. You don't keep secrets well. I know a lot about you before and after you became Macduff Brooks."

"What now?"

"As we speak, Macduff, I'm shredding the only copy of my draft report. I will never say the names Macduff Brooks and Professor Hunt together other than to you or Elsbeth, or, if she returns, Lucinda."

I was shaking as I turned off my phone. I knew that Luisa was briefed extensively by Herzog about Professor Hunt before she left Guatemala to come to Florida. And she has had considerable contact with Lucinda and Elsbeth. In my frustration and diversion of attention because of Lucinda being gone, I may have said things I shouldn't have.

It made me wonder how many people know more about my having been Professor Hunt than I would like. Dan, of course, and the remaining few CIA agents who took some part in my conversion. Thankfully, that number keeps going down; four of those agents are dead. Grace Justice also knew, but she's dead. I don't think anyone else in Florida knows.

Montana and Wyoming are another matter. John Kirby and Huntly Byng in Jackson know a lot about me, but not about my years prior to moving west. The same is true of Erin Giffin and Ken Rangley in Livingston and attorney Wanda Groves in Bozeman. That's about it. Except for one thing. What did Lucinda, in her condition, say about my past to Ellsworth-Kent and maybe to Reginald Covington?

I don't want to even think about that.

9

FOLLOWING DAY - ST. AUGUSTINE

BACK AT MY ST. AUGUSTINE COTTAGE THE NEXT morning, coffee in hand, I called Elsbeth and told her I was turning off my phone for two days. Mainly, I didn't want to talk to any police investigators, even Huntly Byng. Next, I left a message for Dan Wilson that said if there was any change to Lucinda he wanted to tell me about to call Elsbeth. She would decide whether to drive the two hours from Gainesville to tell me.

After making more coffee, I called a local carpenter who years ago worked on the cottage and gave him a list of needed repairs to the house and dock. Then I scrubbed my flats boat and applied on the transom a name decal—*Office*—finally giving it an identity other than the mandatory revenue producing Florida boat registration numbers. Done working for the time being, I had an urging to take out the boat.

The tide at the dock was dropping close to where it would be too shallow for me to reach the IntraCoastal Waterway—the ICW. I dreaded being stuck on an oyster bank waiting several hours for the tide to change.

With the outboard tipped up to keep the prop barely below the surface and Wuff on the bow searching for sea monsters, we worked our way carefully through the maze of channels and reached the ICW, grounding twice but not enough for me to have to get out and drag. Walking on oyster shells is unpleasant; it destroys shoes and disfigures bare feet and paws.

On this trip my fishing gear was nowhere to be seen. I had planned something other than fishing.

A flats boat is not the most comfortable way to travel; the slightest ruffle to the water's surface causes the boat to pound. Heading north, pound we did. Wuff left her bow perch and came back and lay on the floor next to me, appearing displeased with her choice to follow me to the pier from the cottage and jump into the boat without being asked.

Our destination was Camachee Cove, more or less an hour from when we entered the ICW. That meant passing beneath the historic Bridge of Lions in the center of St. Augustine, in view of the irregular skyline left to the city by Henry Flagler. It was, nonetheless, a most *handsome* irregular skyline.

On the north side of the bridge, the harbor opened up to the Castillo de San Marco to the west and soon the channel to the sea to the east. Gliding beneath the high and gracefully curved Villano Bridge, we immediately turned to port and entered the man-made Camachee Cove Yacht Harbor, home to dozens of cabin cruisers and sports fishermen and nearly a hundred sailboats.

One of the sailboats we had come to check on was the very same I had sailed aboard with its owner, Grace Justice, one night only a few months ago. She had bought the sailboat at an auction of cars, boats, and planes used to traffic in drugs, and she coaxed me to a moonlit sail. And even more.

The boat was a modest 27' Florida-made, twenty-year-old Island Packet. Not designed for serious racing, but good lines and stable. It's perfect for close offshore ocean cruising. I dreamed of using it for that, with thoughts of crossing the unpredictable Gulf Stream to the Bahamas and wandering around the waters of Abaco for a month or two.

Grace Justice had no relatives. Her two significant assets, other than being attractive and unattached, were the boat and a condo within sight of the cove and yachts. I unexpectedly received title to both, a bequest from a fine, professional lawyer lady who died fishing with me on the Gallatin River in Montana. She was sitting in the bow of an inflatable pontoon boat and was first to hit deadly barbed wire intentionally strung across the river to discourage fishing. It caught her by the neck and yanked her out of the boat. She bled out before help could reach her.

A contract had been signed to sell the condo. Although I'd never discussed it with Lucinda—she had been abducted more than a year before Grace died—my plan was to keep the Island Packet, but invest the condo sale proceeds in a small cottage in the Bahamas where our winter fishing would shift from the redfish, sea trout, and flounder found around St. Augustine, to the bonefish, tarpon, and mahi-mahi or dorado dolphin around the Abaco islands.

Abaco had to wait; Lucinda's year-plus Bahama confinement likely hadn't left those islands on her list of desirable destinations for recuperation. The specific place I found most charming was around the harbor at Hope Town in Abaco—a mere half-mile from Covington's mansion where Lucinda was confined. I'll talk to Mira Cerna and get her thoughts on the Bahama idea.

When Wuff and I returned to the cottage as the sun was setting, Elsbeth's SUV was parked next to mine, and she was sitting on the porch. She got up slowly and walked down the stairs and threw her arms around my neck. There were no tears, but something was troubling her.

"Shall I go pour a drink before you tell me why you're here?" I asked.

"No need. There's a glass of Gentleman Jack next to your rocking chair on the porch. Let's go up. When I'm through, you can tell me what you've been doing off in your boat alone without any fishing gear."

We sat. I stared at her. "You look so good to me."

"I hate to add some bad news to what I hope have been a couple of restful days. . . . You told me about meeting Rachel Hart and both having a lesson from her and enjoying a dinner and evening together. You liked her?"

"Yes. She's small like Erin Giffin in Montana and every bit as attractive and bright. Both have arms with visible muscles that were developed more for sport than show. Neither is a weight lifter. Erin is a master at Kendo; Rachel is a master at fly casting. They remind me of each other. I'd like to get them together."

"That won't happen, Dad. Someone named Dave Johnson called me after you left here. He said he's a friend of yours and was at Crystal River with you. He urged me not to let your becoming a Certified Casting Instructor cause you to stop practicing."

"He called just to tell you that?"

"No. To tell you that Rachel Hart is dead. It probably hadn't made the *St. Augustine Chronicle*. But it was on the TV in Gainesville."

"What happened to Rachel? She seemed fine when we had dinner the night before I left the Plantation."

"Dave didn't know the details, other than her body was found in a canal in Crystal River."

"Where? Near the Plantation?"

"Yes. Outside the rooms that face the canal. I think you said you stayed in one."

"That's right. Rachel gave me a private lesson on the grass in front of my room before we went for a drink and dinner. . . . She was bright and happy. Not a trouble in the world, at least what she shared with me. . . . Did she accidentally drown?"

"She might have. That's most likely what happened. Apparently there were no bullet or knife wounds on her. Drowning is what Dave said the police were suggesting."

"I'll go on line and read the Crystal River paper. They may know more today."

"Dad, is there any way this can be linked to you?"

"I don't know why you'd ask. I was gone before she died."

"That may not be true," she said. "The police are going to learn that you had drinks and dinner with her the evening before her body was found early the next morning."

"When I went to my room, I was alone. And several women were entering their room next to mine. They will help me establishing an alibi."

"You could have gone to *her* room after *you* got to your room. If you missed her."

"I don't know what you mean by that. Are you on my side?"

10

REPORT FROM CRYSTAL RIVER

TODAY'S CRYSTAL RIVER PAPER HAD A LONGER and more detailed report, as well as a photo of the covered body of Rachel Hart on the grass next to the canal. Partly blocked by trees, in the background I could see a line of three rooms. One was room 105. That was Rachel's room. I was in 103, next door. The women who saw me enter that night talking to myself were on the other side of me in 101. That's not helpful to my case, nor was remembering that there was an adjoining door between my room and Rachel's.

The article added some information to what Elsbeth had told me:

> *The body of Rachel Hart found in a channel of the winding Crystal River was recovered yesterday and taken to the local Medical Examiner's office. It appears to have been an accidental drowning; Ms. Hart was wearing fishing clothing, including a vest that added considerable weight when wet. Authorities assume she was fishing on the canal bank, lost her balance, and fell in. A fly rod was on the ground near where her body was found. It has not yet been determined if she had been drinking.*

Rachel Hart was a featured instructor at the annual program held by the Florida Council of the Federation of Fly Fishers, the prominent international organization dedicated to teaching fly casting. Ms. Hart was a Master Casting Instructor, the highest level certified by the organization. Her MCI badge was sewn on her vest. Hanging from the vest were forceps, a small device like a nail cutter used on leaders and tippets, three spools of different size tippets, and a hook sharpener. She also carried a net that was attached at the back collar of her vest. Hanging from her neck on a string was a black fishing fly without the hook.

Nothing found on or with the body suggested foul play, although the cause of death remains to be determined by the local coroner and medical examiner.

"Elsbeth! Come and read this and tell me what you think."

She brought her lunch to the small kitchen table, set it down, and looked over my shoulder to read the article.

"There's going to be trouble, Dad."

"I agree. What are your thoughts?"

"*The black fly!* It sounds like the same as the one found on Spence when he was murdered in Grand Teton National Park."

"Who said either Spence or Hart was murdered?"

"Sorry. The Spence *death*. Dad, let the police do their work. Don't bring this up."

"I won't say a word unless they ask. But the black fly doesn't mean Rachel Hart was murdered."

"Dad, *who* wears *black flies* around their neck?" I know only one other—Spence. . . . Don't you think the Crystal River police will want to talk to you?"

"They most likely don't know the details—especially the meaning of the black fly or even about the Spence death in

Wyoming. . . . I'll let the police do their job. If they learn about me and contact me, I'll respond. Otherwise, I'll tend to my own affairs."

"Hold your breath! I'd like a whole fall term here to pass without a murder!"

11

A FEW DAYS LATER - THE FLORIDA COTTAGE

RECENTLY I NAMED MY FLATS BOAT *OFFICE*. When people call me with what they believe needs immediate attention, I can honestly respond that I was stuck at the *Office* and most regretfully wasn't able to consider their request.

I was "working" at the *Office* one October morning, looking back toward the house at three glorious Florida maple trees, each trying to impress me the most with a fall leaf display of summer green mutating first into golden hues of orange and then daily to new variations on a theme of red. The trees have grown rapidly since I planted them a dozen years ago, a substitute for the mesmerizing yellow-gold textures of the cottonwoods and aspens that I have to part with each fall in Montana. When Montana leaves settled on the ground, the snows soon arrived to cover them and when the snows left in April, the leaves had vanished.

Between distracting views of the maples, I struggled at the *Office* with the installation of a Power Pole, a clever device for effortless anchoring so successful it must worry the traditional Danforth anchor folk.

My *Office* cellphone sitting on the console began whistling Vaughn Monroe's 1940s "Ghost Riders in the Sky." My musical beckoning changes daily, which can be confusing. But I get to hear familiar tunes in unfamiliar circumstances. The last call earlier today offered the French singer Charles Aznavour singing the hopeful "Hier Encore," which means "Yesterday When I Was Young."

The French vocalist created visions of the Paris of my service as a newly commissioned U.S. Navy ensign. I was back in my dress white summer uniform walking through the Jardin du Luxembourg. Sitting on a bench, I watched a young boy push off a model sailboat and giggle when it left his hands to flee across the water. A beautiful woman thrice my age wearing black stopped and looked at me and came over, bent down, and kissed my forehead. I felt one or two of her tears run down my face.

"Bonjour, Monsieur. You are the image of my late husband when he served in the French Navy and lost his life at sea. His ship went down and his body was never recovered. Merci, au revoir, Monsieur." She leaned over again and kissed each cheek and then turned and departed, never looking back.

She reminded me of the desperation that comes with separation and quickly brought me to the present on my boat. My phone had stopped ringing, which first brought relief but then confusion about whether the caller might have been Elsbeth, wanting to inform me that a check was going to bounce in her Gainesville bank unless I covered it quickly. Or far more important—it was Mira or Dan with word about Lucinda.

I finally looked at the phone, which identified the caller. It was Huntly Byng, head at the Teton County Sheriff's Office in Jackson. I consider him an exceptional police officer and trusted personal friend.

Byng was the first person who arrived at the Snake River's edge more than a dozen years ago when former and then retired ambassador Ander Eckstrum was killed by a single high-powered rifle shot from the shore minutes before my clients and I were to reach the Deadman's Bar takeout on the river. It was a tragic day. Ander's fifteen year old daughter Kris, soon bound east to begin studies at Yale, was also in the boat. She suffered no physical injury, but the trauma kept her in Jackson for another year.

Within a year, the shooter—Park Salisbury, wearing a disguise and using a fictitious name—arranged for me to guide him. I asked and received his permission to take Lucinda and Wuff along. During the float Salisbury removed his disguise and shot Lucinda, Wuff, and me. Lucinda, in turn, shot Salisbury repeatedly, protecting Wuff who was lying beneath her and bleeding. Wuff took a bullet that left her with a permanent limp. I added another bullet to Lucinda's shots when I finally found my Glock beneath a rag in my guide box and lifted it and fired, but not before I took the last bullet Salisbury ever fired. Lucinda killed him. But I think I deserved an assist.

Foolishly, I had put Lucinda and Wuff at risk, but had she not been there, I would have been taken to the morgue rather than air lifted to a Salt Lake City hospital.

Ander's daughter Kris entered Yale a year later, earned Phi Beta Kappa, and, because of her widowed mom who remained living in Jackson, enrolled at the University of Wyoming for her law degree and three years later settled in Jackson. Kris is now among a handful of highly respected attorneys in Jackson.

I take time to visit with Byng whenever I'm in Jackson, which has proven to be often because of my friendship with Jackson fly fishing guide John Kirby and his wife Sarah.

"Huntly," I asked, "did you forget to tell me something when we talked recently? I'm not in any trouble that I know about."

"You live on the edge of trouble. This has come up only in the last hour and it involves you. Do you know the name Myron Davis?"

"Should I?"

"Not necessarily, but you will from now on."

"Who is Davis?"

"He's the new and ambitious Wyoming Attorney General. I say ambitious because he's determined to become governor and has talked about after serving in the governor's seat for two terms he would run for the Senate, which—joking or not—he has labeled a clever way to retire early and lucratively at taxpayer expense."

"Interesting, but for me hopefully irrelevant."

"Only for the moment," Huntly said. "Davis is pushing us to indict you and John Kirby for the murder of Arthur Spence. Davis is weakest in Wyoming in the Jackson Hole area and wants to make his name known and admired as he prepares for the run to be governor."

"When Spence's body was found by John and his client," I responded, "Bradstone or something like that, I was on my way to Florida from Montana. I was *not* in Cascade Canyon. . . . Your papers may not have covered it, but a couple of days ago a second Master Casting Instructor and fly fisher was found dead in a canal in Crystal River, Florida."

"Why the connection other than they were both MCIs?" he asked.

"There was a black fly—a practice fly with no hook—hanging on a string around her neck."

"Were you involved?" asked Huntly.

"No. Well, sort of. I attended her casting instructions the day before her body was discovered."

"You were with her? Anything more than a lesson?"

"We went off for a drink, which led to dinner and a few more drinks. Then we parted company and went to our rooms."

"You're sure you parted company?"

"Don't go into that. But, yes, to the best of my recollection. . . . I haven't talked to the police here yet. They insisted I drive to Crystal River; I suggested they come to St. Augustine. I don't plan to comment to them about Spence. . . . What about your talking to Bradstone?"

"Kirby's client's name was Scott *Bradford*. He's back home in Michigan, and Myron Davis sees no political value to bringing him into this."

"Have you determined who, if anyone, killed Spence? That would shut Davis up," I asked.

"Regrettably, we haven't. The autopsy concluded that Spence accidentally drowned. I thought that ended the matter, even though I have doubts about his drowning. . . . No one knows the significance of the black fly around his neck—it looked to me like a Black Marabou. It could have been Spence's good luck fly. Or a killer's calling card. You and John must appear to Davis to be two scapegoats who are disposable in exchange for winning the Jackson vote."

"Huntly, tell me more about Davis."

"He's maybe forty-five. Graduate of both undergraduate and law schools of the University of Wyoming at Laramie. He wasn't an honors graduate, not on the law review, and there's no suggestion of his being involved with moot court or serving as a research assistant for any professor. But he was president of the law school political structure. That's not known as a fast track to a job with a good law firm, but it is the way a lot of Wyoming politicians have started."

"What did he do after law school?"

"Worked with the Laramie County District Attorney's office in Cheyenne, the largest city in the state. He's charismatic and was well liked. One of our contacts in Cheyenne said he talked his way onto high profile cases and worked hard to impress his superiors. His record of convictions was exceptional.

"He stayed there for about ten years and then moved to the Wyoming Attorney General's staff as a Senior Assistant. Shortly before his boss—then Wyoming Attorney General Bill Burns—was elected governor, Davis was made Chief Deputy.

"Then he struck gold. The Wyoming governor appoints the Attorney General, and he chose Davis. That was five years ago. Governor Burns is in his second term and has three years to go in what he has promised will be his last term. Davis has his sights on replacing Burns.

"The Spence case made most of the newspapers throughout the state. All noted the fact that your friend John Kirby was guiding when Spence's body was found. Somehow—maybe Bradford talked—*your* name was raised as the originally booked guide."

"Why would anyone pick on me and John?"

"It's *you*. Over the years your name has been associated with murders that have cost counties in Wyoming, Utah, Montana, and, I assume, Florida, far more money than had been budgeted to investigate crimes. You remember the wicker man and mistletoe murders. One was on the North Platte. The city of Saratoga and Carbon County spent a huge amount trying to solve that murder. They still blame you.

"You're a household word, Macduff, and a lot of people think of you as little more than a rich outsider who doesn't work and fly fishes all the time. John's being dragged into this because he's your friend. I predict he'll be dropped from whatever Davis plans as an investigation. *But not you.*"

"Does Davis have any special dislike for fly fishermen?"

"I found out that at one time he fly fished a lot, mostly in Eastern Wyoming. I don't know why he stopped. . . . He's tried to separate himself from the glitz and money in Jackson Hole except for campaign donations. Maybe going after you two will cause him to lose votes from your friends here in Jackson, but Davis may think he'll look better everywhere else in the state. Wyoming's a strange place. There's Jackson Hole, and there's the rest of the state. I imagine more money to buy public office exists in Jackson than the rest of the state altogether."

"What do you suggest I do? Return voluntarily to Wyoming to be interrogated by Davis? I hate to, but I don't want John to be left to deal with this alone."

"It's premature to do anything. I wanted you to know the rumors weren't good even before we were pressured to do anything here in Teton County by the Attorney General's office."

"How do you feel about showing up at my door with an arrest warrant?" I asked.

"If I'm asked to do that, this office will be short of one senior deputy. I've got better sense than becoming a lackey to a Cheyenne politician."

"Huntly, I don't want you to forfeit your job on my account; you're a respected officer."

"Let it play out. I'll cross that road when I come to it."

"I have an ace to deal," I said.

"Meaning?"

"Favors from D.C. I'm owed some. Don't ask."

"I read the *Bozeman Magazine* article about you last year. You worked for the State Department for nearly twenty years, and you wouldn't talk about it in your interview. Are the people who owe you located in a special cooperating Agency located in Langley?"

"Where's Langley? . . . Let's leave it at that."

"When former ambassador Ander Eckstrum was shot on your drift boat, I remember he was wearing your hat. Was the shot meant for you?"

"No. At least I hope not," I said, without wanting to keep the discussion alive.

"But the guy that killed Eckstrum tried to kill you later, when Lucinda saved you and shot and killed him."

"I won't take any credit away from Lucinda, but I did shoot him as well."

"Shooting a corpse doesn't count."

"Let's keep the focus on Davis. Let me know when anything changes."

"Promise. Best to Elsbeth and Wuff."

Huntly didn't know that Lucinda had been found, and I wasn't emotionally prepared to discuss her. When he hung up, I sat in disbelief that I could be dragged into Spence's death. But I realized that politics in Wyoming were no better or worse than politics in Florida. I *never* should have agreed to an interview for the *Bozeman Magazine* in Montana.

Online I found dozens of references to Davis, but nothing surprised me as I read through article after article from Wyoming papers. Then I googled Davis for non-Wyoming comments, including a list of his travel out of state. One item made me stop and read it again:

Wyoming Attorney General Davis gave the after dinner speech to the closing of the annual meeting of the Northeast chapter of PARA held in Delaware. PARA is the acronym for People Against Recreational Angling, an organization with links to some violent protests against nearly any activity that promotes recreational fishing.

I went to sleep that night wondering what benefit Davis saw in speeches that raised the ire of fishermen in Delaware or Wyoming. But perhaps the speech was given before he decided to announce he would run for governor.

12

AT THE FLORIDA COTTAGE

B YNG'S PHONE CALL WAS DISCONCERTING. I knew that Spence's death might result in my being questioned by the Teton County Sheriff's Office—likely by Byng. But I didn't contemplate that some political hack attorney general would play a major role.

Byng is now about fifty-five and is the Lieutenant in charge of all Teton County criminal investigations. That means homicides and other serious crimes. There hasn't been a homicide in years although many remain convinced that last year Palmer Brown murdered his wife by pushing her off Inspiration Point in Grand Teton National Park. Byng has been getting pressure to quickly make a conclusive determination about Spence's death.

The ME ruled that Spence's death was an accident. The case file is on the back burner as far as Byng is concerned. But it may not be for long if Davis leads a movement to blame my friend John Kirby, who found Spence's body while guiding a client in Cascade Canyon. Or to blame me. He prefers blaming me because I'm an outsider, even though I was in Montana at the time and preparing to drive to Florida. I don't want John to take the pressure and blame if I refuse to go to Wyoming to be interviewed by Davis's staff.

Whether I would even be asked to be interviewed was soon answered on my dock as I was gutting one of the few salt water fish I ever keep, a sea trout. I caught it with Dave Fuller's sinking Petti-Coat streamer fishing around a dock on the Matanzas River near the old Spanish Fort. My sloppy fish cleaning job was interrupted by my new ringtone, Ray Charles singing "Georgia on My Mind." Charles went to the Florida School for the Deaf and Blind in St. Augustine. Unhappy with his treatment in both the town and the school, he was expelled, left town, and never returned. He moved to Seattle after asking a friend who was sighted to look at a map and tell him where in the country he could move to and be the furthest away from St. Augustine.

"Hello," I said, giving my left hand a nasty slice from my filleting knife as I manipulated the phone. Dropping the knife, I held my hand over the water and watched blood spatter on the water.

"Brooks?" the caller asked.

"This is Brooks. I see from my phone this is a Wyoming number."

"You're right. This is the Wyoming Attorney General's office."

"Are you the attorney general?"

"No, but wait and I will connect you."

"No thanks. When he wants to talk to me, you have my number. Tell him to call me directly." I hung up, turned the phone off, and headed to the cottage to perform some first aid.

Over the next hour there were seven calls from the same Wyoming number. An hour later I called it.

"This is Miss Nichols, Attorney General Davis's private secretary. Please hold."

"This is Macduff Brooks," I interrupted. "Tell Mr. Davis I returned his call. I'm about to go to lunch and then take some underprivileged kids for an afternoon ride on my boat. I don't want to disappoint them by any cellphone conversation. If Mr. Davis himself will call me direct tomorrow at 8:00 a.m. sharp, I will talk to him. That's Florida time, 6:00 to you."

"I'm not sure he will like that. He's a very busy man. But he doesn't get in *that* early."

"In that case, give him my regrets."

I thought a lot the rest of the day about what Davis was likely to want: a phone conversation and nothing more? Meeting here in St. Augustine to discuss what little I knew about Spence's death? Or, God forbid, flying west to Wyoming to be interrogated by his staff?

In the morning, at precisely 8:00 a.m., my cell phone rang. I was having breakfast. Not the healthy kind I would have if Lucinda or Elsbeth were with me, but two fried eggs, four small sausage links, hash browns, two English muffins, and a delicious cinnamon pastry for dessert. Dessert for breakfast? Why not? Why should the best part of a meal be left only for dinner?

"This is Macduff," I answered. "Am I talking to Mr. Davis?"

"To *Attorney General* Davis. I want to see you here in my office."

"Go ahead. I'm happy to answer your question."

"Not by phone, face to face."

"Let me give you my address here in St. Augustine. We can set up a time and meet at my house or at my office."

"You don't understand, Brooks. I want to talk to you here in Cheyenne. In *my* office."

"I could meet with you at my cabin in Montana. It's a little north of Yellowstone at a place called Mill Creek."

"It has to be here *in Cheyenne!*" he replied, loud enough to wake Wuff on her bed in the corner.

"How about another alternative? I get to Jackson a few times each summer to see a friend and do some fly fishing. We could meet in Jackson. I'll buy you a great Jackson beer made by a local microbrewery."

"You still don't understand, Brooks. This is not a social call. I want you here to answer questions about the murder of Arthur Spence."

"Spence? Murder? The Jackson ME autopsy report concluded it was an accidental drowning and that closed the case."

"We have reason to believe that it was a murder and that you were involved."

"Do you know where I was when it happened?"

"Jackson. More specifically, in Grand Teton National Park."

"Mr. Davis. Your information is incorrect. I was in my Montana cabin packing for my annual fall five-day drive to Florida."

"We have evidence about you and Spence to the contrary."

"And what evidence is that?"

"We'll discuss that when you get here. We're the state with jurisdiction to prosecute a crime committed here."

"We can talk about that when you get *here*," I replied.

"I can ask the Florida authorities to send you out here if you don't come voluntarily."

"Have I been arrested in Wyoming?"

"Not yet."

"The 'Florida authorities' you mention will have to have good reason to agree to my extradition. I'll need to be arrested.

73

I don't think they'll take your word over the results reached by both the sheriff's office and the ME in Jackson. It was an accidental death. . . . Mr. Davis, the newspaper articles in various Wyoming cities suggest you are unlikely to be elected governor unless you broaden your base to include places like Jackson."

"I don't know what you're talking about. Let's keep any talk about the next gubernatorial race for another time. I'm talking about a homicide involving *you*."

"Let's not waste each other's time, Mr. Davis. You do what you have to do."

"I was hoping you'd cooperate. I didn't want to bring in your friend, John Kirby. He's even more of a suspect than you. But he's also a respected Jackson resident."

"Meaning, don't upset a local voter and his many friends. Instead, place blame on an outsider, even though he's not been arrested and the death was ruled accidental. Not a very sound way to be attorney general. . . . I might have mentioned that all my phone calls are recorded. You know—'to help us better serve our clients.' Maybe the Jackson newspaper would like to hear our conversation when you start campaigning for governor."

"You basta . . . " Davis started, then realized it wouldn't sound good on a transcript.

"One other thing. When I went online, an article in the *Rehoboth Daily* in Delaware discussed your speech in Rehoboth not long ago. Remember?"

"I think you're mistaken."

"You spoke to the annual meeting of People Against Recreational Angling at Rehoboth Beach. Your speech was protested by a dozen local fishing clubs. I wonder if you'd send me a copy of that speech; if not I'm sure it's available somewhere online. When you start campaigning in Wyoming, the fishing community there will welcome hearing it."

There was silence. Apparently we were disconnected.

13

A CALL FROM D.C.

THE TELEPHONE WAS AN INVENTION MARVEL. But sometimes I think it has brought me more grief than pleasure. One call I hoped would bring good news was yet to come—from Mira Cerna in Washington.

Mira Cerna is one of the world's most highly respected hypnotherapists. She's on the faculty at Hungary's leading university in Budapest. Ellsworth-Kent retained her to help him keep Lucinda hypnotized. She didn't know Lucinda had been forcibly abducted. Ellsworth-Kent told Cerna that Lucinda was terminally ill and hypnotherapy could divert her terror of dying to something more helpful, such as her love for Ellsworth-Kent. Cerna also was told I was an abusive ex-husband who Lucinda needed to forget.

After the first month of her abduction, Ellsworth-Kent sought Cerna for help. He was beginning to worry that, even though he had done a remarkable job sustaining her hypnosis for weeks, Lucinda might come out of it on her own. Mira was paid a significant fee—purportedly $500,000 and all expenses—to fly to the Bahamas, where Ellsworth-Kent, with the help of a prominent local friend, Reginald Covington, had Lucinda confined. Hypnotherapy soon convinced Lucinda that, although I was not an *evil* person, I never loved her the way Ellsworth-Kent, her former husband of two months, did.

Only days after Ellsworth-Kent's body was discovered washed up on an Abaco beach in the Bahamas, Dan Wilson, my CIA contact in D.C., located Lucinda and took her from Covington. Mira Cerna came from her break Budapest to join Dan in Hope Town, and they flew from there to D.C. in a private government jet where Cerna began to slowly convince Lucinda that the truth was very different from her understanding, which had been induced slowly by Ellsworth-Kent's deft use of hypnotherapy and then by Cerna's assistance to assure that such status would endure.

Lucinda's beliefs were slowly altered to convince her that only Ellsworth-Kent loved her and was worthy of her. Cerna has warned us that reversing those beliefs must be done over time. How much time was troubling me. I wanted Lucinda back.

"Macduff?" Cerna asked when I answered her call with a quiet: "Hello."

"Yes, Mira," I said. "I think I'm pleased to hear from you. How long has it been since you said I couldn't see or talk to Lucinda for a while?"

"It seems like years, but it's only been weeks."

"Is she progressing?"

"Yes, faster than I thought she would."

"Meaning?"

"She's regained weight, and her coloring is better. We have her in the sun for brief spells. She was low in Vitamin D."

"Does she walk?"

"Yes. She never lost that ability. Ellsworth-Kent kept her weak and not interested in walking anywhere except around the house and yard in Hope Town. We've retained a physical therapist who comes in every day to work with her. In addition to losing weight, she lost muscle tone. She's beginning to show arm and leg strengthening."

"Does she stay at the hospital?"

"She sleeps there so she can be monitored. We're pushing her and want her watched. But during the day she's up and away from her room. She's no longer napping."

"Has she been walking on the hospital grounds?"

"Macduff, yesterday we drove . . . or rather I drove, to Georgetown. She loved walking and seeing the old homes. We walked for two hours without stopping a minute to rest on a bench or wall."

"Do you talk to her?"

"She doesn't talk much. That's an issue we haven't worked out."

"Does she say *anything?*"

"Yes. She asks where Ellsworth-Kent is."

"Does she refer to him as Robert?"

"No."

"As Ellsworth-Kent?"

"No. She refers to him as High Priest Einar."

"As a friend?"

"As her lover. Now that her health is so much improved, we are about to begin to work on her feelings about you and Ellsworth-Kent. It may change fast, but we have to begin slowly."

"Why didn't you start correcting her as soon as she referred to Ellsworth-Kent as a high priest?"

"We wanted first to make her strong physically and not induce a stroke or heart attack."

"Was that a real risk?"

"We don't know. This is a very unusual case. The doctors are taking it step-by-step."

"Has my name been mentioned by you or by her?"

"No. We're uncertain how she'll react when we first say your name."

"When do you think that will occur?"

"Next week, we hope."

"Can I be there?"

"No. Mentioning your name is one step; seeing you is another."

"Mira, based on what you've done so far, will she return to her mental state before the abduction happened?"

"I'd like to say 'absolutely.' But the answer is 'maybe.' Be patient."

"Is it possible she'll never be brought out of her current mental state?"

"Yes."

"Would she die?"

"Quite possibly. She might live but never recognize you. If we talk her out of her devotion to Ellsworth-Kent, but can't get her to remember or want you, it will be a sad case. She probably would have to be institutionalized for the remainder of her life."

"I've wanted to call you every day since we last talked, Mira. Every time I pick up the phone and think of calling you, I lose my composure. I can't function for hours."

"I understand, and I'm sorry I don't have much to tell you. I'll call as soon as I have anything more. Good or bad. Keep yourself occupied."

Dropping the phone on the floor, I realized how much I was trembling. I made it to the bedroom, sprawled across the bed and thankfully was soon asleep.

I didn't wake until mid-afternoon the next day.

14

A CALL TO BOZEMAN, MONTANA

ATTORNEY GENERAL DAVIS FROM WYOMING troubles me. Anyone in a position of power in state government, in order to achieve personal goals, can create problems for others. Myron Davis is a prime example. He is the quintessential politician who spends years moving from one office to another, elected or appointed, within the state system. If he can't move up, he'll move laterally or even take a step down to qualify for and preserve a costly, undeserved pension.

Wyoming has a pension plan that is more than generous. Davis could receive a pension of seventy percent of the average of the highest three years of salary. He could hardly do much better if he were in the Greek or Brazilian government.

He has all of the three state employee benefits—pension, prestige, and power. Having talked to him yesterday, it seems the last—power—is what he cherishes most. Power is available for doing good deeds or drastically bad deeds. I place what he wants to do with me and John Kirby in the latter group. He wants us brought down so he can go further up.

Davis will take time to consider our conversation and decide how to respond to my less than supportive comments. If I stay away from Wyoming and if he decides to try to have me brought to him by using his power, I should be considering my choices.

There is one person, from neither Florida nor Wyoming, with whom I need to talk. She is Wanda Groves, my attorney in Bozeman. My phone call with Cerna yesterday was scary and left me exhausted. After my long sleep, a shower and a good lunch encouraged me to try Wanda.

"Macduff, you can't be calling again about Ellsworth-Kent trying to steal your assets. That was substantially solved when he apparently became *hors d'oeuvres* for some sharks. You seem to attract issues with hungry fish—sharks or barracudas."

"Don't go there, Wanda," I replied, wondering about how she learned of Ellsworth-Kent's death. "I called you about something very different."

"I can't imagine what. Tell me," she said.

"Do you know the name Arthur Spence?"

"Not that I can remember. Did he die on your boat?"

"You would say something like that. The answer is 'no,' but he did die fly fishing, although I wasn't with him. It occurred in Grand Teton National Park in a place called Cascade Canyon. And it was ruled an accidental drowning by the ME in Jackson Hole. That was also the conclusion of Huntly Byng, the chief homicide investigator for Teton County."

"Macduff, you know I don't practice criminal law."

"I know, but I wanted to run some facts by you and see what you think generally as a lawyer and a friend. If I need a criminal law specialist, I have one here in St. Augustine, and John Kirby should know one in Jackson."

"Tell me about Arthur Spence."

I spent the next hour telling Wanda about Spence and answering occasional questions. I also told her about my conversation with Davis. She agreed with most of my assumptions, but urged me to talk to a criminal lawyer in St. Augustine if Davis sent someone to Florida after me and to retain one in Jackson or Cheyenne if he enticed me to Wyoming. She also told me to tell John Kirby to get a lawyer.

"I have a good criminal lawyer here named Muirhead," I told her. "I used him when one of the local investigating police got a bit too testy when my flats boats was incinerated a few years ago and killed a man. If I need a lawyer in Jackson, John said he will help."

"Macduff, you haven't mentioned Lucinda. Should I ask?"

"I'd be concerned if you didn't, but her progress has been slow. I don't know. Please don't press me."

"Keep me posted."

"I promise."

15

A CALL TO JACKSON, WYOMING

DEPUTY HUNTLY BYNG ONE DAY, GOVERNOR Myron Davis the next, then Professor Mira Cerna, and today Attorney Wanda Groves. When will it end?

But I'm an impulsive person, and before I can sleep comfortably, which for the last few weeks has been a challenge, I need to talk to John Kirby.

I tapped out his numbers on my cell phone and sat back hoping he might not answer. I was tired. But it wasn't my day.

"Hello, Macduff. I just got in from a day on the Snake. My client and I floated your favorite stretch from Deadman's Bar to Moose. *Great* fishing, especially around where Cottonwood Creek flows into the river. Hope you've had a relaxing week on your flats boat on the salt water marsh creeks. You've told me you were going to name it *Office*. Did you spend a lot of time at the *Office* this week?"

"I spent two hours two days ago at the *Office* replacing a bilge pump. It was clogged and short circuited because of raccoon poop! Any ideas on how to keep raccoons off the boat?"

"Keep watch from midnight to four every night and carry a shotgun."

"I had the mid-watch so often on my destroyer when I was in the navy in Newport that I vowed to never again stay awake at those hours."

"Poison the raccoons!" John suggested.

"That might kill Wuff. You're no help."

"How is Wuff?" he asked, ignoring me.

"I've been back here in Florida for less than a month, and I haven't spent even fifteen minutes letting her run on the Summer Haven beach. I'm glad she can't talk. She'd sound like Lucinda or Elsbeth. They're three of a kind. . . . I should move to some secluded home in the Keys and not tell anybody. Including *you*. . . . *Especially you!*"

"You can't move until you have Lucinda back. You don't think straight when she's at risk. Any news?"

"I'm confused, John. She's progressed physically by recovering weight, spending time in the sun, and walking with Myra Cerna. But I'm concerned that she may never be the person you and I knew."

"And loved. Anything Sarah and I can do?"

"Not yet, but if I ever get Lucinda back to Montana, I'm going to beg that we spend a few days with you. She'll need to be with good friends. . . . Have you talked to Huntly Byng lately about the Spence death?"

"No, and I don't intend to unless Byng calls me. As far as I'm concerned, Spence's death is for the National Park and Teton County to deal with, and since it's officially been determined to have been an accidental drowning by both, I'm not involved. End of story!"

"You soon may become involved."

"Why do you say that?" John asked.

"Do you know the name Myron Davis?"

"A political hack in Cheyenne. He's our appointed attorney general and is determined to be governor. He's not popular here in Jackson."

"If he convinced people that you and I were responsible for murdering Spence, would he pick up votes in Jackson?"

"He'd win the gubernatorial election."

"That significant? Has Davis called you?"

"No. Why would he?"

"He called me and made some accusations."

"Did he say you killed Spence?"

"He said you and I were involved, and he's obligated to investigate."

"Investigate! Huntly Byng here accepts the accidental drowning decision by the ME."

"Davis wants his office to do the investigation and has demanded I fly to Cheyenne for questioning. He actually said 'interrogation.'"

"Are you going?"

"In any other similar case, I'd tell him to go . . . well, you get the idea."

"What's different about Spence's death?"

"You."

"I didn't kill Spence!"

"I'm not suggesting that. I may avoid Davis by refusing his demand. In fact, for the most part, I already have. But I don't want to leave you hanging as the only *available* suspect."

"I know the criminal lawyers here in Jackson. Several would be thrilled to take on Davis. Don't give me a second thought. Davis has no evidence that suggests Spence was murdered."

"There is one thing you should consider, although Davis apparently doesn't know about it. Have you read anything about a fly fishing instructor named Rachel Hart? Maybe you know her?"

"Do I?" John responded. "I took some lessons from her in a program in West Yellowstone last year. She's as beautiful as her casts. She asked me to join her for drinks and dinner."

"I won't ask what you did. She was found dead in a canal on the west side of Florida, a place called Crystal River."

"Murdered?" John asked.

"The local coroner said there was no evidence of foul play and ruled it an accidental drowning, just like Spence."

"Case closed!"

"It should be," I added. "But there is one link between the two deaths."

"Each person has tried without success to teach you how to fly cast?"

"That's unkind. What's common is that each of them had a black practice fly hanging from a string around their neck. It looked like a Black Marabou."

"You don't think Davis knows about Rachel Hart?" John asked.

"Possibly not, and he won't learn it from me."

"Or me. . . . I'm happy to talk with anyone he sends here. By here I mean Jackson, not that black hole of politicians—Cheyenne. Besides, there's nothing in Cheyenne that's worth seven hours driving four-hundred-plus miles to get there. Plus fifty bucks each way for fuel and more for overnight costs."

"Regardless, Davis is determined to get us both to Cheyenne," I responded.

"Then how's he going to score points with Jackson voters unless he shows up here?"

"I think he's a slow learner. He doesn't realize he has to face Jackson area voters sooner or later. . . . John, your comments are exactly why Davis hates Jackson. I suggest you tell him you would be delighted to fill him in on what he obviously doesn't know and welcome him to Jackson. Tell him he should come and maybe visit the site of Spence's death up in Cascade Canyon."

"Will he buy that?" asked John. "He'd never make it up Cascade Canyon. From photos he's too fat and out of shape. He might have a stroke. . . . Come to think of it, I should invite him!"

"Are you agreed we will both demand he come to us? I'll insist he come to Florida unless he wants to wait until late next spring and see me in Montana. You're easy. He uses a state plane and flies to Jackson. In reality, he doesn't give a damn about you, John. And even less about me. He wants *votes*. And that makes him dangerous. But also vulnerable.

"John, I called my attorney Wanda Groves in Bozeman. She only does civil work. She told me to urge you to retain a criminal defense attorney in Jackson. Know any?"

"I do," he answered. "There are some *very* good criminal law practitioners here. Sometimes I think too good. No one seems to go to jail. Not even Palmer Brown."

"Don't say that name. I won't sleep tonight. My scars still hurt where he shot me."

16

A WEEK LATER – ST. AUGUSTINE

AN EMPTY HOUSE FILLED WITH THE MEMORIES of two happy people is a lonely place when one of the two is absent. Even when one is away only for a few hours at a meeting or shopping. Our sheltie Wuff has always stretched out by the front door when Lucinda or I was gone. No longer. Wuff must have some instinct that tells her Lucinda is not coming back. Wuff stays pretty close to me now. She's confused and unhappy. It isn't easy for a sheep dog to have her flock reduced to one.

If Lucinda had died at the hands of Ellsworth-Kent, Wuff and I would have grieved, helped by Elsbeth and Sue and many friends. Time would have healed some of the wounds, and at some point in the grieving process, weeks or maybe years after, the visible signs of the departed one would vanish, assisted by the need to eliminate reminders of a terrible loss.

Most photos would come off dressers, tables, and walls. Her clothing that might have lain unworn in drawers or hanging in closets would be given to friends or charity or discarded. A rarely driven second car would be gone and favorite fly fishing rods and gear passed on to something like Project Healing Waters. It would have been difficult enough to remove her belongings that could be seen: soap she was using in the shower, clothes that carried her scent, or perfumes that mixed with her fragrance.

I hadn't reached those stages. Not yet. Not when there was even the faintest hope that she would someday walk through the door and share a rocker on the porch or a day with me on our flats and drift boats. My expectations were always that Lucinda would return as the same person I saw abducted.

But what if she returned as little more than a shell of how she left. She suffered eighteen months of mental abuse, of her mind being twisted and distorted to eliminate me and accept one she feared for decades with good reason—Ellsworth-Kent.

It's doubtful she'll walk in, grab my hand, and head us to the couch or bedroom, whether to simply sit or lie together. She may need her own space for a time.

What if Cerna or other medical experts can't free Lucinda of her feeling that I don't exist or if I do exist that I have no love for her? Little good would come from living out our lives together. She might prefer to live alone for the rest of her days, feeling abused by and distrustful of all men.

One matter kept entering my thoughts. Would I feel any differently had Grace Justice not been killed fly fishing with me in Montana, when she was caught by her neck in barbed wire strung across the Gallatin River? If Lucinda did not recover, would Grace have become even more important to me than she had been at the time of her death?

The more each day closed without hearing from Dan Wilson or Mira Cerna, the more I assumed the worst. They have asked me not to call. They promised to let me know of *any* changes to Lucinda. But as the weeks went by, no calls came.

Was I wrong thinking that was an ominous sign?

17

THREE WEEKS LATER – THANKSGIVING IN GAINESVILLE

DAYS PASSED WITH NO WORD ABOUT LUCINDA. The eve of Thanksgiving arrived with the promise of a meal with Elsbeth and Sue the next day at their house in Gainesville. In the morning I drove there thinking that if Guatemalan President Juan Pablo Herzog learned that the skull on his mantel were not mine, the place where he would renew his search might be this same house. A few years before Elsbeth and Sue rented it for their years at UF, it was the residence of Herzog's nephew Martín Paz, sent to Gainesville to study and to discover what had happened to Professor Hunt.

Martín died. Lucinda and I were following him after he left a UF soccer game where he failed to locate us in the stands—disguised as we were. Coming around opposite sides of a building, we confronted each other. Before he could shoot us, a gun was fired from behind us that killed Martín. Lucinda and I were certain that Dan Wilson was behind our being saved, but to this day he denies any involvement.

I never pass the signs that we are entering Gainesville without thinking *any* visit to that city is unwise. But my thinking is blurred by my desire to visit Elsbeth.

Elsbeth and Sue had decorated the house and dinner table with some red maple leaves gathered from the cottage yard. On holidays both gals—Elsbeth raised in Maine until she was seventeen and Sue raised in Jackson during the same years—succumb to the traditions of their family history. They know that Thanksgiving remains special to me because it was the day I met Lucinda at her ranch on Mill Creek not far from my cabin. Others had been invited to the dinner, but declined at the last minute announcing by email—affirming their rudeness—that they had received and accepted a last-minute offer to be flown by private jet to Peter Island in the Caribbean for the holiday.

Lucinda's guest list thus was diminished to one unknown fly fishing guide. She decided to host the dinner anyway, and after I fell on ice as she opened the front door, she let me in laughing, gave me two drinks, and fed me at the long dinner table with the places for the missing guests set but with their plates turned upside down.

After dinner our conversation continued before a fire in her great room and thus began a romance between a moderately comfortable fly fishing guide and a relatively wealthy investment advisor. From that romance an engagement and wedding blossomed, and a decade of memorable years passed before Lucinda was abducted and taken from me.

This year's Thanksgiving dinner table was set for five. Elsbeth, Sue, and me, and I assumed two young men from the university they hadn't mentioned but wanted me to meet. At the time the gals had planned to carry the turkey to the table, the other two had not arrived. Memories of my first Thanksgiving dinner with Lucinda!

When we sat and I was about to dissect the turkey, the doorbell rang. It had to be the two tardy guests. Elsbeth said she would greet them and hurried to the front hall. I hoped she wasn't angry. If the two late arrivals were talking as they entered and walked to the dining room, I couldn't hear them. I was concentrating on slicing turkey for five.

It wasn't two university boys, but apparently only one addition—Dan Wilson.

"What brings you to Florida, Dan?"

"A free meal. And you doing the serving?" Dan pulled up a chair between Sue and me.

"Well, four made it. That's pretty good," I commented.

"*Five* made it. I brought a guest," Dan corrected.

"Great," I said, as two arms behind me slowly wrapped around my head. The fragrance of a perfume that had to be sage overwhelmed me. Only one person I've ever known wears that iconic perfume.

Whoever it was, she brought her lips across the back of my neck to kiss my right ear as she whispered, "Want to see the tattoo on my butt?"

Before I could respond, she had turned my chair, sat on my lap, and shifted the target of her kisses from my ear to my lips.

I was so shocked that I gagged on a piece of turkey I had snuck into my mouth as she came in behind me and I began convulsions that landed me on the floor choking and struggling for breath.

Twenty minutes passed before I regained enough composure to sit up and realize it really was Lucinda sitting on the floor next to me.

"Remember the first Thanksgiving we met?" she whispered, "You slipped on the ice in front of the door at my ranch on Mill Creek. Now you choke. You have trouble with Thanksgiving dinners."

"I met you on Thanksgiving those fifteen years ago, and I get you back on the same day. I have a lot of thanks to share. But . . . but what's happened? You're acting normal, as if we've just come home from that boat christening where I lost you."

"I remember little about that day. Robert took me off on a private plane that landed in the Orkney Islands in Scotland. I was confined in a house on the outskirts of Kirkwall. He began immediately to put me under hypnosis. I don't remember another day of it until Mira Cerna reversed that hypnosis last week, as though nothing happened for some eighteen months. That time remains a black hole. . . . For the best."

"You two, may I interrupt a minute?" Dan asked. "Mira Cerna didn't want to bring Lucinda out of those years burdened by remembrances of them. Mira was a miracle worker; she struggled since we found Lucinda in Hope Town, but accomplished what she says is the apogee of her stellar career.

"When Lucinda came out of the hypnosis a few days ago with no recollection of those past months, she asked, 'Where's Macduff?' Mira was exhausted and overwhelmed and said she was through teaching. She went home to Hungary to retire immediately from the university in Budapest and write a book on what happened, of course using a fictitious name for Lucinda."

"You remember *nothing* about those months?" I asked, incredulous at what happened.

"*Nothing*," Lucinda replied, "except for a little about the flight to Scotland. I don't remember being taken to the Bahamas, as Dan told me, or anything about Hope Town where he found me at Covington's house. I didn't know Robert died until Dan filled me in today. I'll bet the poor sharks choked on Robert."

"Do you feel OK? You're not as thin as Dan described. I guess he and Mira fed you well the past few weeks. You look spectacular!"

"I've been exhausted since the hypnosis ended. Other than that, I'm OK."

"Where do you want to go?" I asked.

"First, a bedroom here for a long sleep next to you. Then, when we get to our St. Augustine cottage, I want to walk down to the dock and go out on the tide on what Dan said you've named the *Office*. I want to feel my hair blow and the salt spray on my skin. You know I haven't been outside much over the past months."

"How do you feel about going to the cottage?"

"Fine, I think. Does it look the same?"

"Pretty much, except all the photos we had hanging I removed and burned. And all your belongings. The same at the log cabin in Montana. There isn't a sign of you at either place. We have to start from the beginning."

"You don't mean that?"

"Of course I don't mean that. They kept me hoping all that time."

"Are you two going to pay *any* attention to me and Sue?" asked a smiling Elsbeth, getting up from her chair and again tightly hugging Lucinda. "You can't imagine how we've missed you," she added, Sue nodding and joining in the hug.

"It's going to take a little time for me to catch up with what you two have been doing," Lucinda said to the two gals.

"We have a lot to tell you," said Sue. "Beth and I even went to Kirkwall in the Orkney's searching for information about you. We'll tell you about how you became High Priestess Onomaris in the Pagan religion."

"Do I want to know that? Should you be calling me that?"

"No," replied Sue. "We discovered you hadn't been made a high priestess. It was make-believe by Ellsworth-Kent."

"Wow! I do have a lot to hear about."

"And you'll also want to hear about Macduff's involvement in murders. Several on the Gallatin, one in Grand Teton National Park, one or two in Italy, and a few weeks ago one in Cascade Canyon in Wyoming and another not far from here at Crystal River."

"Macduff!" Lucinda said, turning toward me looking shocked, "You need me here to keep you out of trouble. Have you been in jail? Or been shot?"

"Some trouble is brewing right now with the Wyoming Attorney General."

"And how is your longtime nemesis, Juan Pablo Herzog?"

"For the moment he thinks my charred skull is decorating his mantle."

"I don't want to hear about that. Can't you behave when I leave you alone for a year or two?"

"Wait a minute. I was only present when two of those deaths took place, both on the Gallatin. I was *not* responsible. I was never charged and won't be. . . . The more recent deaths in Cascade Canyon and at Crystal River are another matter."

"I'm tired. Let's have dinner, and then I think I'll retire upstairs."

"Not before I've seen the tattoo."

18

THE NEXT DAY TO ST. AUGUSTINE

SEVERAL TIMES DURING THE NIGHT, I AWOKE from a deep sleep, sitting up abruptly and sweating. Each time I looked next to me to be certain it was Lucinda. I lay back and gently put my arm around her. At 4:30 a.m. it happened again and this time I carefully got up and sat in a chair facing the bed.

At 9:00 a.m. I was still in the chair, and Lucinda began to move. Her arm reached over to my side, and when it touched nothing, she sat up and loudly called out "Macduff!"

"I'm here."

"Come closer," she added. "How long have you been sitting there?"

"Only a few minutes. You slept well."

"As I hoped you did. Can you blame me for being so happy to be back with you?"

"I'm happy for you," I said, exhausted from a night with little sleep.

"Oh, Macduff! I'm awful. I have memories of only a half-dozen days without you. You've had to endure eighteen months not knowing where or how I was. That's long enough for you to assume I was dead and find someone else."

I waited for her to add "Did you find someone?" but she didn't ask.

I knew it would be hard for me to address my relationship with Grace Justice. If Lucinda learned the depth of that time with Grace, would she forgive me? I would never hear about *her* relations with Ellsworth-Kent because she doesn't have any memories of those months and whatever Ellsworth-Kent and Covington did to her. Perhaps more accurately: "did with her consent."

Dan says Mira Cerna believes Lucinda might someday regain memories of those months. I preferred she wouldn't. That would only cause her unneeded anxiety about succumbing to Ellsworth-Kent—and maybe Covington—and feeling disloyal to me. How long could she endure?

Should I volunteer information about the nights on Grace's boat, in the Montana cabin, and at her condo? Would Lucinda feel I was justified because we all thought she had died? But how could that be after her letter came affirming she was alive and content with her life?

Should I tell her what Mira inferred happened between her and Ellsworth-Kent, both by his force and later her alleged consent? Whatever evolves in the weeks and months to come, right now I want to enjoy looking at her, smelling her fragrance, and hearing her voice.

I wonder what she's thinking.

19

A WEEK LATER – ST. AUGUSTINE

NO WEEK IN MY LIFE HAS EVER PASSED MORE swiftly or with the ecstasy expressed by us both during Lucinda's first week home at the cottage.

Wuff went berserk when she saw Lucinda. She coerced enough treats from us both to last a year. Her flock of two was back.

I hadn't tried to draw from Lucinda details of our life before her abduction, and I planned never to ask about her months with Ellsworth-Kent. Maybe the phone call she answered while we on the porch having breakfast was good for her and helped her rejoin and play a leading role in the tumultuous world we had known together.

The call was from Cheyenne. I had programmed the ringtone within hours of Lucinda's return, choosing Handel's "Hallelujah Chorus," and turned the volume on high so it filled my day with joy and expressed how I felt about her return. Lucinda answered the call.

"Good morning," she said.

"This is Wyoming Attorney General Myron Davis's secretary calling for Macduff Brooks. Who am I speaking to?"

"His mistress," Lucinda said, grinning. I had filled her in on my issues with Davis and my expectation that he would try to get me to Cheyenne.

"Is Brooks there?" the caller asked.

"He's still in bed. I exhausted him."

"*Wake him*," she ordered.

"He'll be up in a few minutes. When Mr. Davis is ready to speak to him, have Mr. Davis call direct, not using a secretary who should have better things to do." Lucinda tapped the off button on the phone.

I was thrilled by her response. How did I get along without her? I guess I didn't, as Elsbeth has repeated to me weekly.

Twenty minutes later the "Hallelujah Chorus" began again. This time I picked up the phone.

"This is Attorney General Davis. I don't appreciate you're rejecting my secretary's calls. And I don't like you're having a mistress. You're married and committing adultery."

"Then call me direct," I responded. "My time is valuable. We talked no more than a week ago. If you have something new to add, please go ahead. If you don't, I have other things to do than chat with you."

"A fly fishing guide's time is valuable?"

"That's what I said. Shall I speak louder?"

"I want you here, Brooks, on Monday at 9:00 a.m. sharp."

"I've told you that Cheyenne's not on my map. Come here to St. Augustine and we'll talk. It will be recorded. And my attorney will be with us. By the way, YouTube finds you amusing. Your advocating curtailing recreational fishing has been seen by nearly everyone in Jackson. Plus, I've been telling all my fishing friends about it."

"When I get you, you're dead meat, Brooks. You'll rot in one of our jails while I'm governor."

"Davis, you're wasting my time. Take this name down. If you want me, call him. He's an attorney in Jackson." I gave him the name. I don't know if he wrote it down. I hung up.

"Macduff," Lucinda exclaimed, "you're a sketch! He's going to throw you in jail."

"Only in Wyoming and this Macduff Brooks is not going there until Davis is out of office. Hopefully, he'll get whipped in the election in three years."

"Are you serious that we can stay away from Jackson for three years? What about our trips there to see John and Sarah Kirby and fish the Snake?"

"We'll go. I won't let Davis know when we're in Montana. If he calls, I'll tell him we're in Florida. My cell phone won't inform him otherwise. We'll take your car and you drive. And I can use a disguise. Don't you worry; we'll go and I'll fish with John."

"What does that pompous fool think he's doing?" she asked.

"Be kind. He's a politician struggling to obtain needed votes. He must take Jackson to win the election for governor."

"Why do the voters in Jackson dislike him?"

"He hates people with money. His father was enormously wealthy and, for reasons I don't know, disinherited him. The father has a big house in Jackson and a private jet, and I suspect his son is jealous. Davis lives on what he earns, and in Wyoming that's not enough to live as comfortably as he did growing up. He is said to get money in other ways, most of them questionable."

"What's next with Davis?"

"He will never agree to come to St. Augustine, and I suspect his staff lawyers have told him he needs far more evidence for the Florida courts to grant an extradition request that I be sent to Cheyenne."

"So it's over?"

"Probably, a lot can happen before the next election for governor in three years. But he has to gain the support of the Jackson voters. That means he may keep after me."

"If Spence's case is re-opened and his death proves to have been a murder, Davis could be a problem if the Jackson police don't solve it quickly."

"Do you think it was not an accidental drowning?" she asked.

"Spence was an exceptional fly fisherman. He was methodical and paid attention to details. The water depth where his body was found was shallow, about eight inches."

"Can someone slip and fall in that depth, land in some dense grasses in only eight inches of water, become entangled, and drown? I have doubts, Macduff. On the other hand, do you know anyone with a motive to murder Spence?"

"Not a soul. I've never heard anyone say a bad word about him."

"So we wait and continue to read the Jackson newspaper," she commented.

"And tell John to do the same and keep us informed about any rumors in Jackson about Spence's death."

"What would you like to do today?" I asked.

"Take naps with you."

"All day?"

"I have a lot of time to make up."

"Any chance you'll want to leave the cottage?"

"Not 'til next year. . . . It's after Thanksgiving. Let's start Christmas decorations."

"A tree?" I asked.

"Of course. A huge one."

"Wreath on the door?"

"Of course. With a big red bow."

"Little white lights strung along the porch rails?"

"Of course."

"Anything else?"

"Of course. Lots of presents for me and lots of eggnog for both of us."

"With rum?"

"Lots."

"Let's get started."

20

THE FOLLOWING DAY

"THE COTTAGE LOOKS BEAUTIFUL. LET'S TEST the eggnog," Lucinda suggested as the sun began its early afternoon winter descent through the pines to fade from view in the west.

"Porch or dock for the eggnog?" she asked turning to Dan Wilson and me. Dan had gone to Miami for a few days after our Thanksgiving dinner in Gainesville, and on his way back to D.C., he stopped at the cottage for his first visit ever.

"Porch," Dan suggested. "Tomorrow I'll help put lights on the dock and have some more eggnog there with the setting sun. I have to leave the next morning."

Wuff followed Lucinda, and I followed Wuff into the kitchen. Wuff had not let Lucinda out of her sight since we arrived at the cottage. Hopping around and whining at the living room window, she had watched Lucinda walk up the cottage steps. Wuff has not acknowledged my return.

We all took the eggnog to the porch, ladled some into small cups, sprinkled it with cinnamon, and relaxed in our well used rocking chairs.

I downed three cups of eggnog before I asked what I had wanted to ask for hours.

"Lucinda, since Dan is here, I'd like him to tell about his rescuing you and what you said when Mira brought you out of your hypnosis."

"I'd also like to hear about the rescue," Lucinda pleaded. "It remains a blank to me."

"Dan, tell us and also how you fed Robert to the sharks."

"Wait a minute! I had nothing to do with Ellsworth-Kent's death.

"When I arrived in the Bahamas with two agents from our Miami office, we parked our plane at Marsh Harbour, rode the ferry to Hope Town, and went directly to Covington's house. It was about 8:00 p.m.

"An unshaven guy who looked mean and serious answered the door. He was a foot taller and a hundred pounds heavier than me. I thought we were in for some trouble, but then he stumbled and went down. He was tanked. I stuck my pistol in his pockmarked and stubble-covered face. He quickly looked much less mean and serious.

"Three other men were sprawled on chairs in the large living room facing the water and singing a pub song: 'Now this is number four; she's begging me for more. Roll me over in the clover, lay me down, and do it again.'

"All four were bulky and mean looking. They had been doing some serious drinking. There must have been a hundred empty beer bottles scattered on the floor. Not one of the four was able to function enough to challenge us. We were lucky; they outnumbered us. Had they not been drunk, we wouldn't have fared well. One struggled and got up from his chair, reached out to hand me a beer bottle, and fell over and smashed the glass top of a coffee table.

"Within minutes all of them were gagged and their wrists tied. We escorted them to a basement storeroom, pushed them onto the floor, and taped their ankles. For good measure we separated them and tied them to different support posts."

"All this time you never saw Covington or Ellsworth-Kent?"

"No. Neither was in the house. I thought that seemed unusual. We learned later that Ellsworth-Kent went fishing with the young woman he met at a bar in Hope Town. Covington had been home when Ellsworth-Kent went off to fish, but an unexpected phone call caused him to leave and take the ferry across to Marsh Harbour to meet someone coming in on a flight from West Palm Beach. Apparently, his 'staff' started their binge as soon as he left the house.

"We went from room to room looking for Lucinda—how we learned she was at Covington's house is another story and involved Mira Cerna, the Hungarian hypnotherapist. On the second floor we broke open a very thick and secure door to what was a bedroom. Despite our noise, Lucinda—looking beautiful but very thin—remained seated twenty feet away on a cushion on a window seat. Staring out the window, she wasn't tied or restrained."

"Did she recognize you, Dan?"

"No. She didn't move or acknowledge us, but soon turned her head, smiled and said very softly, 'Hello, come and look at the water. It's a beautiful iridescent green fluttering in the slight breeze.' Then she turned her head back to look out. She was mostly oblivious to us."

"What did you say to her?"

"I said, 'Lucinda, Robert sent us and asked us to take you to meet him in Marsh Harbour.'

"She got up immediately and walked off with us, smiling the whole time but saying nothing. She seemed to be in a trance. Lucinda knew me well enough from years of friendship, but she never gave a hint she had ever met me before.

"We checked on the four in the storeroom, left the house, went to the city dock, took the ferry back to Marsh Harbour, and a cab to our plane. The pilot was ready. We took off, banked north, and headed directly to our next stop—Washington, D.C.

"Lucinda was taken to a private hospital the Agency uses in embarrassing situations. The same hospital you were in years ago, Macduff, when we brought you back from your beating in Guatemala. . . . I went home and began to call you, over and over. You didn't answer for days. Apparently, you were driving back from Montana with your cell phone off."

Lucinda was absorbed in what Dan was saying. She watched him without turning her head or blinking, but she squeezed my hand tightly.

"I was in my SUV on the last day of crossing the country from Montana," I explained. "When I got to the cottage, I did everything to avoid hearing that the remains of the body found near Ellsworth-Kent were Lucinda. I should have called you, Dan. I was scared of what I might learn. . . . I even did some repairs to the cottage to keep me diverted. Then I got the courage to call you and learned the dismembered gal wasn't Lucinda. She was one of Ellsworth-Kent's many playmates in Hope Town. He wasn't a faithful companion to you, Lucinda. The girl was pregnant."

"I guess I didn't know about that," Lucinda commented quietly. "Or I didn't care. Its part of the past I don't recall at all. Maybe I will someday."

"Let's hope not," Dan said. "You don't need to relive those terrible months."

"I don't remember them being terrible. Why do you say that?" she asked.

Ignoring her question, Dan asked, "Do you remember what you said the day Mira brought you out of your hypnosis?"

"I remember everything from that moment to this. But not before. I think I looked at you and Mira and the doctor and asked, 'Where am I?'"

"I said that you were in D.C."

"Then I asked Mira, 'Who am I?'"

"That told us a lot," added Dan. "In your time under hypnosis, you came to know Mira very well. Regardless of what she did to you using her hypnotherapy skills over several months, she made up for it by bringing you out slowly."

"Then I asked, 'Where is . . . I forget his name . . . Mac something?'" She looked at me with her trademark Cheshire cat grin.

"You *know* who I am! . . . After my conversation with that guy Davis in Cheyenne," I said, looking at Dan, "I wasn't sure being blotto in Hope Town wasn't a good way to spend my future."

"We'll give you a few days to decide," he said. "I can have the Agency plane take you two to Hope Town and turn you both over to Covington. I'll bet he misses you. Say the word."

"She's not going, and I'm not going," I said loudly.

"Are you talking about abducting me?" Lucinda asked us.

"You bet," I said.

"I'll stay here. I'm not leaving this cottage."

"For how long?"

"*Long.* I'll tell you."

"Dan," I asked, again changing the subject, "how did Lucinda get to Gainesville to surprise us on Thanksgiving?"

"When we thought Lucinda was ready, I called Elsbeth," explained Dan. "She's a very competent young lady. But she didn't believe Lucinda was OK, and she couldn't talk. I told her to hang up and call me back. A little more composed, she called a half-hour later and asked if Lucinda could be brought to Gainesville on Thanksgiving. I told her 'yes' and you know the rest."

"Lucinda hasn't been out of my sight since," I added. "Or Wuff's. When we go out, Lucinda won't even excuse herself to go off to a restroom. She grabs my hand and pulls me with her.

"Even into the stall?"

"Absolutely."

"Oh, boy! True love."

"I want a favor," Lucinda asked, turning to look at me.

"Anything," I answered, "except I don't have to eat all your exotic meals, and I won't give up playing my oboe."

"Denied and denied," she replied. "My former rules were merely suspended, not terminated."

"Now you're back to sounding like a lawyer," I replied. "What are we having for dinner? Leftover turkey I hope. It should last another month."

"Discuss food and oboes later, you two," Dan said. "What's the favor you want, Lucinda?"

"I want to remember my life *after* the abduction as starting not when Mira got me out of hypnosis, but a bit later. At our Thanksgiving dinner."

"That works for me," I said.

"And me," added Dan, refilling his eggnog.

21

EARLY JANUARY - ST. AUGUSTINE

CHRISTMAS AND NEW YEAR'S FLASHED BY. NO calls came from Attorney General Davis in Wyoming or from Dan Wilson. Elsbeth spent the holidays with us—university classes resumed four days into the new year.

Her roommate and closest friend, Sue, had flown to Jackson Hole the week before Christmas to be with her aging parents. Her dad's memory had been fading, and he'll have some tests in mid-January to detect signs of Alzheimer's. Sue may go back to live with her parents when she receives her degree from UF. I don't know what she'll do as a career; she has long talked about law school, and we both hoped that would be at UF.

The holiday was a confusing time for me; dreams reflected my elation with Lucinda being home but with an infusion of momentary doubt that her presence was real. I have never thought much about the rhythms of hypnotherapy. I had placed it alongside fortune telling and holism as variations of fraud. But how many times have I daydreamed and drifted off into another world, come out abruptly, and wondered what happened? Was it so very different?

It was not me but Lucinda who had lived in that other world she cannot remember. Nor do I wish her to. I will live with my imaginings of how she survived those months. That she lived contentedly all those months has to be considered; she came away with no signs of physical abuse from Ellsworth-Kent or others who assisted him.

Not once in the nearly two months she has been back with me—more exactly fifty-one days and a few hours—has she shown any sign of even a momentary return to her hypnotic state with Ellsworth-Kent.

I don't know if she often thinks of that time and tries to re-create what happened. Would returning to Hope Town and seeing Covington's house and other places they may have visited create images of her time in Hope Town, tragic or pleasant, and cause them to surge into her life?

How do I feel about going to Hope Town? I shouldn't go if I haven't purged myself of a desire to see Covington dead at my hands. Considering life in Bahama's Fox Hill prison—a graduate school for criminality housing scores of Americans—should be enough to bring me back from visions of leaving the body of Covington hanging on his front door like a Christmas wreath, wrapped in palm fronds and tinsel.

My dreams sometimes have focused on the more subtle treatments Dan's Agency people were trained to provide. Ricin? I had memories of the death of Bulgarian Georgi Markov in London who was jabbed with an umbrella tip containing toxic ricin. He died a painful death. One wonders if the Bahamian authorities would be able to do a sufficient medical exam of a body to even identity ricin as the killer.

Does wishing make dreams come true?

22

A WEEK LATER - ST. AUGUSTINE

LUISA SOLARES CALLED ME THE DAY BEFORE classes began at the University of Florida law college. She called to wish us a belated Merry Christmas and joyous New Year. Christmas had been a big event in Catholic Guatemala, where people weren't embarrassed to have a nativity scene on their front lawn and send each other cards that said "Merry Christmas" rather than something like an innocuous "Season's Greetings" or "Happy Holidays."

I was surprised Luisa had planned to go home for the holidays. She told us several months ago that her relations with her uncle, Guatemalan President Juan Pablo Herzog, had not improved, and she was scared to go to Guatemala for any reason.

"Luisa," I said. "Guatemala for Christmas! Had you missed your family enough to chance running into your Uncle Tío?"

"I not only ran into him, Mr. Brooks; he insisted I go to a dinner for fifty people at his official residence, the Casa Presidencial."

"All fifty were family?"

"Mostly, you know how big Latino families can be. Even including illegitimate kids like me. I don't know how many others present were the same. It's not polite to talk about that."

"Did you talk to Uncle Tío?"

"He asked me to join him in his office. More like an order. I followed him worried about what he might do. His office is the room where he shot and killed his most trusted advisor, Coronel Alarcon. You must remember that."

"Vividly! Alarcon had learned who I was and where I lived and was about to tell your uncle. That is, until Alarcon saw his own wife—without a stitch on—come running out of your uncle's bedroom.

"Luisa, what did he want you to do in his office? Did he apologize for being so mean to you? Run *you* around his desk?"

"Dios mío! He pointed to a skull on the mantel behind his desk and said, 'Luisa, that is former Professor Maxwell Hunt of the University of Florida. I have finally won!'"

"I was shocked and felt sick. It looked like a head from the Amazon, eyes and mouth stitched closed. Most of the hair and skin had burned leaving mostly bare skull. I didn't say a word and went to the ladies room and lost my meal and quickly returned to the dinner table to have safety in numbers. I didn't want to go to Guatemala, but I acted impulsively because it was Christmas. I caught a flight back here the next day. It's so hard, Mr. Brooks. I want to be able to visit some of my family but not be scared and have to avoid 'Señor Presidente.' What has Guatemala come to?"

"How did you feel seeing the skull on the mantle of his office?"

"It wasn't recognizable. I knew it had come from Alaska. But I felt better knowing it was not *your* head. I have to find a way to keep him happy. I don't know how. I talked to Elsbeth on the phone yesterday, Mr. Brooks, for the first time since mid-way through the fall term that just ended. She told me about Lucinda. That's why I really called; it's such wonderful news. Please invite me over to see her sometime this term."

"I will. And I'm glad you're back safely. . . . I keep hearing good news about you at the law school, including that you've been invited to be on the law review. That's prestigious. Congratulations."

"Thank you, Mr. Brooks. It's a dream to be at the law college. You may not know that my grandmother, María Luisa, once received an important international law award there. . . . Give Lucinda a hug and tell her I can't wait to see her in person. You two deserve each other."

"Is that a compliment?"

"Of course. I love you both. And Elsbeth. And give Wuff a pat for me. . . . Ciao."

23

THE SAME DAY

IT WASN'T MORE THAN TEN SECONDS BEFORE MY phone rang again. I assumed Luisa was calling back to tell me something she forgot to mention. But it wasn't Luisa. It was a strong voiced woman named Rosalie Abbott, who introduced herself as an investigator for the sheriff's office of Florida's Citrus County. She spoke rapidly with a trace of Boston "Hahvuhd yahd" accent, reminding me of President Kennedy. "You must know what I'm calling about, Mr. Brooks."

"I don't even know where Citrus County is," I replied.

"It's on the West Coast, south of Cedar Key and Oyster Bay where we were married," Lucinda whispered to me.

"Don't scare me," I whispered back at her.

"My office is in Inverness," Abbott said. "It's the county seat."

"I'm still at a loss."

"Does Crystal River and the Plantation mean anything?"

"Of course. Is Crystal River in Citrus County?"

"It is. Have you ever stayed at the Plantation?"

"A couple of times. For a fly fishing group that meets there in September or October." I knew where she was headed, and I wasn't going to offer anything beyond a polite and brief answer to her questions.

"Were you at the IFFF program last September?"

"I was."

"When did you arrive and where did you come from?"

"I arrived on Thursday afternoon and left early Sunday morning to drive to my daughter's house in Gainesville."

"Was she at the Plantation with you?"

"No."

"Was anyone with you?"

"Not a soul."

"Does the name Rachel Hart mean anything to you?"

"Yes."

"Who was she?"

"An instructor at the program. I had a group lesson with her on Saturday morning. She was as skilled a fly caster as I've ever known."

"Did you see her after your casting class?"

"Yes, a couple of times during that afternoon at some of the booths that were selling fly fishing equipment. . . .You're going to ask me if I knew she was dead. The answer is, not until later. It was on the IFFF's website about a month after she died."

"For another *month* you didn't know she was *murdered?*"

"Murdered? A friend, Master Casting Instructor Dave Johnson, called me a few days after I read the IFFF website and told me that Rachel had died. He said it had been ruled by the ME to have been an accidental drowning."

"That's correct. But I've re-opened the investigation."

"Why?"

"Did you have drinks and dinner with her?" she asked, ignoring my question.

"Yes."

"Are you married, Mr. Brooks?"

"Yes. My wife was in Washington."

"Why didn't you mention the drinks and dinner when I asked if you saw her after the casting class?"

"I thought you were interested in how well I knew her as a casting instructor."

"I didn't limit my question to that. . . . The time of death of Mrs. Hart was about 4:00 a.m. Where were you at that time?"

"Sleeping in my room."

"Can anyone affirm that?"

"I'm not in the habit of sleeping with someone as thanks for giving me a casting lesson. When I left Rachel Hart at about 10:15 the evening before, she went to her room, and I went to mine. I stopped at the men's room near the entrance to my building. So I was at my room about 10:30."

"Why go to a men's room in the hallway? I assume your room had a bathroom?"

"I had several beers before and after dinner. I was in a rush to use the nearest bathroom."

"Did anyone see you go into *your* room?"

"Yes, I was talking to myself and having trouble with my door key. Two women came down the hall, saw and heard me and started laughing, and went into their room next to mine."

"So you might have decided not to go into your room and gone somewhere else? Say to Mrs. Hart's room?"

I paused for a few moments, and said, "Your interrogation is over, Ms. Abbott."

"Why is that? I can have you brought here."

"Perhaps. If so, I'll have an attorney with me."

"You don't need one. This is just an investigation."

"Meaning if this investigation results in my confessing to a murder, the conversation won't be used?"

"I didn't say that."

"I know that and I know the purpose of an investigation. I'm not your assistant in conducting that investigation. You're on your own."

"Do you think you're a lawyer?"

"Sometimes I think I should go to law school."

"You're nothing more than a fishing guide. You're joking if you think you could be a lawyer."

"You may be right. . . . You don't need to waste your valuable time with someone who is 'nothing more than a fishing guide.' Call me when you want to come here to St. Augustine and continue our conversation. Bill Muirhead is my attorney. You might want to check him out." I pushed the button to turn off my phone.

"Macduff," Lucinda said, having heard our conversation, "you didn't tell me about your involvement in the death of that casting instructor."

"I wasn't *involved*. I met Rachel Hart on Saturday morning. She's married, for the fourth time, although I understand it's on the rocks. I was one of twenty-some participants in her casting class. Because I had passed the Certified Casting Instructor test that morning, she gave me a one-on-one lesson after the class in how to do a couple of fairly sophisticated casts. . . . We agreed to meet for a drink at the outside pool terrace late that afternoon, and we remained and ordered some food. There were several others having dinner.

"After dinner, Hart and I walked toward the wing where the rooms were and said goodnight. I thanked her for the casting lessons; she thanked me for the meal. That was the last I saw of her. She headed to her room, and I went to the men's room. Then I went to my room where I had trouble opening my door. I went directly to bed and slept soundly until my alarm went off at 6:00 a.m. when I dressed, had breakfast, and drove to join Elsbeth and Sue at their house in Gainesville. End of story."

"If you're asking if I believe you, it's not necessary. I don't know what happened to you while I was hypnotized. And I don't *need* to know what you did during that time. You had good reason to believe I was dead and begin a new life."

"How did I ever find you those years ago?" I asked.

"You didn't. I've never told you but that first Thanksgiving when we met I had schemed to get you to dinner. I had seen you earlier that week fishing in your part of Mill Creek and wondered 'Why can't I find a guy that looks like that?' You belonged on the cover of *Fly Fishing*."

"I don't believe you. You were stalking me!"

"Believe it! I asked you to Thanksgiving dinner and the 'other' guests were all fictitious. In fact, they were colleagues who said they would help me trap you."

"No! . . . But you did trap me later."

"I was aghast when you fell on ice at my front door. That wasn't planned. I probably should have taken you to an emergency clinic, but I helped you up and into my ranch house. The rest is history."

"Deception is grounds for annulment."

"If you even think of that, Dan Wilson will help me dispose of you."

"Dan Wilson! What does he have to do with this?"

"He was frustrated in dealing with you," Lucinda exclaimed. "He was relieved when I took over. Dan has been my dear friend ever since. . . . So what do you have to say?"

"I'm so confused. My first wife El tricked me into taking her to a prom. She convinced me at the prom that no other girl would ever want me. I soon agreed to become engaged, and later when I was graduating and about to go off to Navy Officer Candidate School, she convinced me to marry her. . . . I have to admit that it turned out to be wonderful. But it ended when she died in Wyoming. . . . I might have saved her."

"Macduff, I'll give you a little lesson. El and I both pursued you. That's what girls do. You gave in to El, and you gave in to me."

"I hope I won't be a three-time loser," I mourned.

"Not a chance. You're mine! Forever!"

That night I had a dream that I never married, but narrowly managed to escape two very determined and clever women. I moved to an island in Penobscot Bay in Maine and lived out my life in secluded splendor. . . . In the morning I woke up, thought about all that, and murmured to myself, "Shut up. You don't know when you're well off."

I vowed never to question Lucinda again, except when it came to nutrition.

24

A MONTH LATER - ST. AUGUSTINE

I DIDN'T HEAR FROM ATTORNEY GENERAL DAVIS in Cheyenne or Deputy Abbott in Citrus County for four to five weeks. The time was well spent. Lucinda and I were never apart. Her ever present Cheshire cat grin was back. I was being fed "nutritious" meals, and I didn't dare go near my oboe. I worried every moment that our life was too good to be true. And too good to last.

Daily, I ran online searches seeking whatever might be said about either Arthur Spence's or Rachel Hart's death. They both had been pleasant to talk with the one time I was with each of them. Not another word about either person was spoken by Lucinda. I found nothing in my daily online searches. Expectedly, if readers weren't viewed as being interested, the newspapers took that to mean "forget it."

Lucinda worked at convincing me I had nothing to worry about. I had good attorneys I previously used in Montana and St. Augustine. John Kirby promised to give me contact info about one or two in Jackson, and Dan assured he would "correct" any action that went against our interests. To make it easier, I promised to avoid Wyoming.

No article in Wyoming newspapers ever mentioned Hart's death in Florida; no article in Florida newspapers ever mentioned Spence's death in Wyoming. But two factors were common to the Spence and Hart deaths in what little was written about either. One was that each body was found with a black fly—a hookless practice fly—hung on a cord or string around the neck. I've never known anyone to wear a fly around the neck, black or any other color.

The second common element was that both were FFF Master Casting Instructors. There aren't so many MCIs that make that fact irrelevant. What was strange to me was the newspapers and the criminal investigators—including autopsy reports—in both Wyoming and Florida seemed to quickly treat the cases as closed.

Accepting the coroner's and ME's conclusion that the deaths were accidents convinced the newspapers to change their attention to more important issues, such as reporting various abuses by politicians, attracting more tourists, and adding more sheriff's vehicles to provide deputies with places to nap at road construction sites.

Only two people—for separate reasons—were persisting to concentrate on the two deaths. Wyoming Attorney General Davis was using the Spence death to help him become governor, and the Florida Citrus County investigator Rosalie Abbott was using the Hart death for advancement to who knows what—being appointed as a state attorney or judge or offered a job at a prestigious law firm that was beyond her reach coming out of law school.

Sooner or later someone will link the two deaths, and both investigators will turn the heat on again, *if* it served their own interests. When they do, I don't plan to be the source of either investigation into the meaning of the black fly and MCI links.

25

FEBRUARY - PLANNING FOR HOPE TOWN

THREE MONTHS SOON BECAME HISTORY AFTER Lucinda rejoined me. Most of the time, it was as though she never left. Occasionally and unintentionally, however, I mentioned offhandedly that such and such happened to me during the time she was under Ellsworth-Kent's control, a comment which until spoken wrongfully assumed she would be able to reply. She never pursued these diversions, but quickly changed the focus to avoid opening that long void to any discussion.

On the other hand, Lucinda herself made no references to that long time about which she said she had no memories, good or bad. For my part, I *never* asked her to revisit those days.

One exceptionally warm winter day in late February, after the groundhog hadn't seen its shadow a few days earlier, Lucinda turned to me at breakfast—chin resting on her joined hands and her coffee cup idle on the table waiting to be refilled.

"What's up today, Macduff?" she asked. "You've had me painting the living room—that's done; doing the spring plant trimming—that's done; and dusting off and recharging my photo equipment—that's done. I'm tired of working. I want to play. We were on your flats boat, the *Office*, briefly last evening for a welcome cruise down to Fort Matanzas. I need more. *Entertain me!*"

"We could go search for and catch rattlesnakes near this property," I answered, remembering the huge one coiled on the cottage steps more than a decade ago, exhibiting its signature buzzing of the tail, and anxious to strike.

"No? OK, we could drive to Gainesville and join football fanatics panting over spring Gator football practice. Or we could stay here and visit the t-shirt and junk stores that are unneeded and clash with the elegance and history of St. Augustine.

"We could even step up a notch and go tour Palatka. Or even stay right here and redo our Christmas card list, or maybe open Turbo Tax and start our income tax. The world is waiting for us!"

"Why don't *you* do any of those while I walk around the Castillo de San Marcos in St. Augustine and hope someone will abduct me and take me to the Bahamas."

"You miss the Bahamas? How can you miss it? You didn't see much of it, spending your entire time in a trance inside Covington's home?" I immediately regretted saying that.

"I want to go to Hope Town with *you* and stay where you described you vacationed with El for a week before she died. You talked about a small pink house that teetered on the edge of the harbor. But I don't want to stay in that house and have you relive memories of your times with El. You added that there were a lot of small, picturesque rental cottages around the harbor."

"What if we ran into Covington?"

"Invite him to our place and shoot him," she exclaimed, grinning.

"That's what worried me when you mentioned Hope Town."

"Spoil sport! OK, I promise not to shoot him. After all, he was my caregiver for eighteen months. Instead, we could poison him."

"No."

"Oh, fuss! I'll wear sunglasses and try to behave."

For the fun of it, I went online and printed out information on flights from the U.S. to Marsh Harbour, the description and address of a perfect cottage overlooking the harbor in Hope Town, and a place where we could rent a boat.

Dan Wilson will be upset to know we're planning to spend a week in the Bahamas. Especially because he might have disturbing information on the current activities of Reginald Covington. The only thing I knew was that his house was not on the harbor's rim, but somewhere along Kemp Road on the northernmost peninsula.

Dan was at his desk at Langley when I called and explained our plans.

"Should we be worried about Covington?" I asked.

"Yes, *if* you knock on his door and introduce yourselves and say you'd like a tour of the house where Lucinda spent so many months. But if you stay away from the peninsula where his house is and have Lucinda *always* wear sunglasses, you should be OK."

"What about being seen at the Marsh Harbour airport?"

"That could be a problem. It's a funnel for people heading for the various Abaco islands. . . . No. Never mind. I think I can help with your trip if you'll do something for me while you're there. Give me your trip details."

I told him about where we planned to fly in from, the cottage on the harbor, and our intended boat rental.

"When do you intend to go?"

"Next Saturday, four days from now."

"Don't make any flight or lodging reservations. I'll get back to you today."

In late afternoon Lucinda and I headed to the grocery store, the liquor store, and a cheese shop—which I refused to go into because of the rancid smell. When we returned to the cottage, I wrapped the cheese she bought over my objections in three layers of foil, dropped it into a Ziploc bag, and hid it in the refrigerator behind some lettuce, hoping Lucinda would forget it. It could remain there for years and smell no worse.

We finished putting away groceries and were talking about what to take to Hope Town when the phone began its ring. After the earlier call to Dan, I had changed the ringtone to the Barefoot Man singing "Layin' Low in Abaco."

Lucinda answered.

"It's good to hear *your* voice," said Dan. "Macduff usually sounds like he's chewing gravel."

"I'll tell him your kind words," she said, turning on the speaker.

"Got a pencil?"

"I do."

"Write this down."

"OK, go."

"A jet from our Agency will pick you up at the St. Augustine airport Saturday morning at 9:30. It will have some things for you, including diplomatic passports and photo identity cards, all under the names Roland and Sylvia Casey. Sign them.

Leave your real passports home. You'll fly directly to Marsh Harbour where you'll be met by one of our agents named John Smith. He's based in Nassau and will walk you through customs and give you keys for a small, outboard powered boat which he will take you to. Can you find your way to Hope Town by boat? If not, Smith probably knows it. He'll have a house near yours. Once you've met him, you'll be happy to have him around."

"We'll get to Hope Town easily," said Lucinda. "Macduff's done it before. He knows the islands pretty well. He's nodding."

"When you get to the harbor at Hope Town," Dan said, "you have to slow the boat to near idle. And stay on the port or left side. About a third of the way around the harbor, not far past a restaurant with a bar that juts out over the harbor, you'll see a white house with bright green shutters and a wooden walkway to the pier and dock. There are two green plastic Adirondack chairs on the dock. The dock's *your* exclusive place to tie up. The keys to the house are—guess where?—under the mat. The place is yours for a week. There are bicycles on the porch. You can ride or walk anywhere in the village. Have fun."

"Wait a minute," I called out, listening from across the room. "What's the price of all this? Remember that I'm just a poor fly fishing guide."

"The flight is on us. It's a 'training' flight. John Smith will talk to you when he arrives on Sunday. He'll tell you the cost for what we don't provide."

"Will it be in dollars? I don't have any Bahamian money."

"Don't worry. Smith will give you an envelope with some Bahamian dollars when he meets you. But you really don't need them. The Bahamian dollar is pegged to the U.S. dollar at one to one. Everyone accepts either currency. You're not going to repay us in money. You'll owe me. Follow Smith's instructions."

"Dan, you have never spent this much on us without it costing us some blood."

"If things go right, the expense will be worth it to us and to the two of you. Remember, if anyone asks, you are Roland and Sylvia. Start practicing calling each other those names. . . . I think you're going to enjoy *this* time at Hope Town, Lucinda. I thought you'd appreciate a chance to see your old friend, Covington."

"Old friend!" exclaimed Lucinda.

"John Smith will keep an eye on Covington's house."

"What does Dan want from us?" Lucinda called out when Dan hung up, her expression showing a mix of wonder and concern.

"I have an idea what it is."

"Share it with me? Does it involve Covington?"

"Yes. He's the star of the show."

26

FOUR DAYS LATER - HOPE TOWN

F RIDAY MORNING LUCINDA AND I PUT THE LAST few items in our bags. She had packed light, one small carry-on with an assortment of bikinis, sun block, sandals, a broad brimmed floppy hat, and two pairs of sunglasses with oversize lens. She also had her hair done, changing its color, style, and length. It didn't fool me, but I hope it will fool Covington.

"Covington may recognize your tattoo," I said.

"I'll cover up. I'm taking a beach kimono. I'll save the bikinis for when I'm alone with you."

"You won't need the bikinis when you're alone with me."

"I'm going to be alone with you every minute from when we walk out this door to when we walk back in again a week later. So, I guess I need nothing."

"OK. You can fill your bag with some of my fishing gear."

"I knew you had a real motive. I may prance around wearing only my tattoo."

"I'm beginning to realize what I missed these last months."

"I'll make it up to you," she said.

"Too much of anything is not good for you."

"Try me."

Twenty-four hours later I looked down as our small government jet lifted out of St. Augustine, and saw my first aerial view of the old fort where Lucinda had been abducted. I didn't ask her if she wanted to lean over me and see it.

A few minutes later we both watched cars driving helter-skelter on the Daytona beaches, and soon after that the space center at Cape Canaveral came in view. Twenty minutes later we banked east, passed over a rough Gulf Stream flowing north against a strong wind blowing south, and soon saw the first of the Bahama Islands.

"The turquoise water can't be described," Lucinda exclaimed, looking down. "It's gorgeous."

Fifteen minutes more and we banked and dropped to land softly on the black tarmac that had to be Marsh Harbour.

By the time our pilot touched down, taxied, parked at a small building near the main terminal, shut down the twin jets, and opened the door, a man was standing at the foot of the steps, smiling.

"I'm John Smith. You must be Lucinda and Macduff," he said in a whisper.

"No. You have the wrong plane," Lucinda said as she stopped on the last step before she set foot back on Abaco. "I'm Sylvia, and this is my husband Roland. We're the Caseys."

"Of course! My mistake," he said louder and then returned to a soft voice to say, "It's probably a good idea to start using those names as soon as you set foot on Bahamian soil."

Smith was pushing six feet. He wore wrinkled lightweight tropical khakis with a cloth belt that bore silhouettes of bonefish. His shirt was an old long sleeve Columbia with frayed cuffs and collar. Dirty white canvas Keds sneaks showed wear and laces that had broken and been retied.

His face and hands were so tanned it had to have been the handiwork of an Agency makeup expert. A tan cap that said

"Island Marine" on the front finished an outfit that didn't give a hint of CIA.

"I thought you'd be wearing black shoes, a dark blue suit, white dress shirt, and red, white, and blue tie?" I said, shaking Smith's hand.

"My official uniform's at home. I don't know how anyone wears a suit and tie in this heat. This outfit is far more comfortable. I'd like to live here and always dress like this. It beats Miami or D.C. . . . Let's get off the tarmac; it's partly why it's so hot. It's throwing heat up at us."

"I don't want us to take a taxi to Albury's Ferry Service landing," Smith turned and said. "That's the usual next step to Hope Town. There's a Marsh Harbour to Hope Town ferry, and the ferry dock is generally crowded with people. I've reserved a 21' Boston Whaler with a T-top that's waiting for us at a private dock in town. The guy I rented it from said there was an Igloo on board filled with water and local beer."

Lucinda and I were dressed the part as much as John. We both wore long white pants and long sleeved white shirts. They all showed wear. I had a blue cap; she wore a bright orange one.

The boat was perfect for our needs. Lucinda loved it and took over the helm steering us east toward Elbow Key and Hope Town Harbour.

"Who's ready to try the local beer?" asked John, who had sat down at the stern, lighted a cigar, and put his feet up on a cooler.

"I think the beer is under your feet," I said. "It must be Kalik. Try it. It's good stuff."

Within ten seconds, John and I had taken our first sips and smiled at each other.

An hour later Lucinda and I were sitting in lounge chairs on the porch of our rented cottage in Hope Town looking at the harbor activities, including a ferryboat loaded with kids all dressed alike. They wore white shorts or a dress, scarlet shirts or blouses, and carried books sticking out of knapsacks. Smith was unpacking at his nearby lodging. The sun had dropped in the west and was behind the century-and-a-half old iconic candy-stripped lighthouse.

Lucinda had a glass of Montana Roughstock Whiskey I had brought to St. Augustine from Bozeman last fall to use at a time like this. For me—as usual—a glass of Gentleman Jack.

"I like the way we came here," Lucinda said. "An hour and a half on a private jet from St. Augustine. An easy boat ride from Marsh Harbour across what is truly a jeweled inland sea, ending at our pier not thirty feet from where we're sitting. . . . I approve of the idea of having a weekend place here. You buy us a home, Macduff, and I'll buy us a small plane."

"Gulf Stream jet? Oh, boy!" I said.

"No," she said. "A single prop Cessna, like the one we used to fly to Key West from Cuba a few years ago."

"Will we have a full-time pilot?"

"Yes. You."

"You trust me?"

"I'll wear a parachute," she answered.

"I could sit here the entire week and never leave the porch," I commented, moving my chair to be out of the sun and closer to Lucinda.

"Even at night?" she asked, frowning.

"Nights are exceptions so I can renew my energy."

"Not with my plans for you."

"Dan and John wouldn't approve of our not leaving this porch," Lucinda noted. "Come to think of it, what are we supposed to do for Dan? John gave me a package, small but heavy. Shouldn't we open it?"

"I don't want to start work yet. I'm enjoying sitting here with a drink and looking at you," I said.

"In that order?" she asked.

"You're a *close second*. Let's have another drink and then we'll open the package. Deal?"

"OK. Reluctantly."

When we opened the package, there was this letter:

Roland & Sylvia:

We have been trying to convince the Bahamian government to extradite Reginald Covington to the U.S. to stand trial on multiple charges, including conspiracy in helping Ellsworth-Kent commit the five murders on different rivers in the West, but also for the murder of the owner of an airboat in Florida, on various drug charges, and now for the abduction of an American citizen. That's you, Sylvia.

The government in Nassau has absolutely refused extradition, partly because we have the death penalty, but also because Covington is one of a few citizens who are too important to fail, like big banks in the U.S.

We want Covington. It would be easy to kill him. Security on the island is a laugh. But the DEA insists on your bringing him here for trial on the drug issues. Other parts of the DOJ want him for the other reasons.

We have decided to kidnap Covington. There is precedent. Two decades ago our DOJ kidnapped a Mexican doctor named Alvarez-Machain, who had helped a Mexican drug cartel keep a DEA agent alive so he repeatedly could be tortured. The agent died. Justice sent a plane into Mexico below the radar. Alvarez-Machain was kidnapped from his medical office and flown to El Paso and then on to L.A. to be tried. He challenged the way he was brought—being kidnapped—as opposed to coming voluntarily—which he refused, or by extradition—which Mexico refused. The U.S. Supreme Court did not find the kidnapping relevant to the jurisdiction issue and let the trial proceed.

You are going to help us kidnap Covington. I expect Sylvia will be pleased to see Covington tried in the U.S.

By now you have met John Smith. He will have more details for you, including the details for the kidnapping.

The letter was not signed.

"What else is in the package?" Lucinda asked.

"Let's see," I said, opening the remainder of the wrappings. "There are two small Smith & Wesson 638 Airweight revolvers with silencers and two boxes of cartridges. Also an ankle holster for me. Lucinda, you have a pair of Khaki pants with a holster added in the rear. Your shirt can hang over the pistol. There are also two small stun guns."

"The Agency must want him alive, if possible," commented Lucinda. "Or they wouldn't have given us stun guns, which I intend to forget and leave here. John hopefully will tell us more."

Smith finished unpacking, called Dan in D.C. to tell him we were here, joined us, had another Kalik, and told us details about getting Covington.

After the sunlight had mostly vanished, we walked fifty yards to the most popular place on the island—The Conch Shell Restaurant & Bar.

"What should I order to eat?" John asked.

"Having been in Hope Town less than a day and not in this restaurant for twenty years, you're on your own," I responded.

"There must be a lot of conchs around waiting to be picked up off the bottom," John observed, looking at the menu. "For appetizers they serve Conch Cakes, Conch Fritters, Conch Fingers, and Conch Soup."

"And a main course of Cracked Conch," I said, which John settled on. Lucinda had Crawfish Pad Thai, a noodle dish, and I tried pasta called Rock Lobster Linguine.

Lucinda said she was too full when John ordered Bahama Key Lime pie, and the waiter asked me what I'd like. I followed John—I've never met a Key Lime pie I passed up. I didn't get to eat much of it because when it arrived, Lucinda decided she was still hungry and she saved me the last bite.

I begged off on another beer and wondered why I hadn't had a Kalik for twenty years, especially since it's now available in the U.S. I guess it goes best with turquoise seas, and we don't have those off St. Augustine.

"We working tonight?" Lucinda asked. "I've had enough Kalik to dull my senses."

"Me, too," added John.

"That leaves me alone," I said. "I guess I'll sit on the cottage porch and watch the sun drop and the lights come on."

"Me, too," added John.

"I want to take another piece of the pie home," I said. "I didn't get much of my first piece."

"Me, too," added John. "Like you, Macduff, I had only one bite."

Lucinda didn't say a word. She sat looking at the two boxes of take home pies and grinned, with further expectations. If she were Wuff, she'd be drooling.

Sitting on our porch, we were all quiet, complementing the clarity of the night. Our eyes were focused on a rising nearly full moon that was entrancing. A few late arriving boats silently moved across the harbor, their navigation lights suspended above the water. Voices could be heard, skippers calling quietly to a person on the bow who was told to drop an anchor or pick up a mooring.

"Macduff," Lucinda said to me after John went off to bed, "Dan hasn't called us to talk about his letter. Or does he consider it a directive?"

"We'll call him first thing in the morning."

Sunday breakfast we cooked in the cottage kitchen. When we opened our windows, we could hear "Amazing Grace" drifting from a nearby church.

As we finished eating, Lucinda prodded me again to get on the phone and call Dan at his home. I obeyed, and Dan's wife answered and called him. I turned up the phone's speaker.

"Get settled in your Hope Town cottage?" Dan asked.

"We are. Dan, we have your package and your letter. And now we have some questions."

"Shoot!"

"Did he say 'shoot,' Macduff?" asked Lucinda, who was loading her Smith & Wesson. "I'm ready."

"He didn't mean to shoot your pistol," I said. "He was asking for our questions. For a moment I thought you were under hypnosis again and you thought it was Robert on the line. And you were ready to obey him and shoot me."

"Will you two stop that and get to your questions?" said Dan.

"This is more than a slight favor you're asking from us," I said. "Why us? You have lots of agents, and more than a few are in Miami near here. Aren't they better to use?"

"Covington is known to be in Miami frequently. We think he can identify most of our people based there."

"Then send someone he doesn't know—from D.C. or Ontario or anywhere."

"There's no one better to identify Covington than Lucinda. There's something strange about him. He hasn't been photographed often. We have *nothing* in our files, but Lucinda knows him."

"Dan," she interrupted, "I was hypnotized. I may not recognize him. I'll try."

"There's another reason to send you, Lucinda. Payback time for you. I thought you might like some revenge. . . . Forget that. I never said that. . . . I assume John Smith is there."

"He is. But he's out taking a morning walk. You should see him. He looks like he's lived here all his life. . . . Is he an experienced kidnapper?"

"That's not a joke. He was a principal part of the Department of Justice's kidnapping of Alvarez-Machain in Mexico. It went very smoothly. Not a shot was fired. He'll be helpful to you."

"You gave us pistols and stun guns. Are we supposed to shoot Covington or stun and kidnap him?" I asked.

"Use the stun gun. We want him here in D.C. The pistols are only for defense in case you face weapons."

"Like a half-dozen of Covington's henchmen with AK-47s! Our two little Smith & Wesson revolvers don't seem an adequate response. I'd prefer a can of bear mace," Lucinda responding, fretting.

"You won't be alone," said Dan. "John Smith will be with you, along with six agents disguised as vacationing fishermen who will be well armed.

"Covington should not have more than two or three guards. He downsized his staff after Ellsworth-Kent died and we got Lucinda back. . . . That's why we're rushing; we think one or two new bodyguards may be away training. We're trying to draw two others off to Nassau on errands for Covington. You may face *only* Covington and one or two other guards."

"We just knock on his door and when he opens it invite him to come with us. If he objects, we stun him?"

"Something like that. We're playing with an idea of knocking him out and having him taken on a stretcher to the jet in Marsh Harbour and telling the airport security people he's heading for the hospital in Nassau for emergency aid."

"So it really hasn't been planned down to crossing 't's'?"

"I think we're close enough."

"If he pulls a gun, do we shoot him?" Lucinda asked.

"If you're endangered, of course. But don't let that happen outside his home, such as in a restaurant."

"And we do what if we're left with a bloody corpse?"

"If he's dead, leave him and get out. If he has any life left, bring him home with you. . . . How would you like his skull bleached and mounted for your Mill Creek mantle? Something to sit and look at on an cold winter night before the fireplace?" Dan asked.

"I'll forget you said that," Lucinda responded.

27

THE FOLLOWING DAY

// "TIME TO GET SERIOUS, YOU TWO," JOHN SAID, taking the last bite of a fried egg, bacon, and sausage Lucinda cooked specially for him, after giving me a plate of fruit!

The Monday morning sun ignited the lighthouse across the harbor. A boat glided up to the town dock to pick up a dozen waiting school children and take them to Great Abaco.

"What schedule are we going to follow today?" Lucinda asked. "I'm anxious to go after Covington."

"We haven't decided yet. That's why we have several days," answered John. "And, I worry what you mean by 'go after.'"

"I hope he resists so I can kill him," Lucinda said enthusiastically.

"*Stun*, but not kill," insisted John. "Lucinda, you don't even remember how Covington treated you. The person who abducted you was Ellsworth-Kent, not Covington."

"I'm convinced Covington and Ellsworth-Kent acting together were responsible for my abduction and confinement, not Ellsworth-Kent alone. And I remember *some* things about Covington." She turned her head away not wanting to say what she remembered.

"We have three bicycles," I commented. "We need to be familiar with Covington's house. I suggest we ride by the house heading to the end of the road. When we come back, don't stare at the house. Use side glances. And *always* wear sunglasses.

"On our way back, when we're passing his property, I'll fake a bike breakdown. I'll squeeze my brake hard and create a skid that ends in the bike falling. Lucinda, who we want to identify the house—and nothing more—will continue back to the cottage as though she were going for help.

"Then I'll fiddle with my bike. Maybe someone will come out, likely more to see what's going on than to help. If no one comes, I'll knock on the door, tell them I've had a breakdown and need to call a friend to bring some tools and help us. I'll say I've left my phone at our rented house at Tahiti Beach, several miles from where we're truthfully staying. What I want is to get into the house and see if other people are there."

"It might not work," said John.

"They might shut the door in my face. But they *might* let me in," I said. "Or at least *see* in."

"And recognize you and shoot you," said Lucinda.

"Covington doesn't know me. . . . Lucinda, do you remember anything about the layout of the house? I know it's been months since you were in the house and not yet hypnotized."

"There are a few things I remember. Like the general layout downstairs. Where the kitchen is. And the great room that leads outside to the pool. Upstairs, I only remember the room I was kept in. I prefer not to go into that room. It's where Covington first rap . . . let's forget that."

It was the first time Lucinda made any reference to abuse by Covington. It made me inclined to forget the stun gun and go with the Smith & Wesson.

"If I had a better opinion of our justice system," I said to Lucinda after Dan hung up, "I'd follow Dan's orders and get Covington back to D.C. alive for trial. But the truth is he's likely to go free or end up with some kind of compromise, agree to a suspended sentence, and return to his old tricks livingly lavishly at his house here in Hope Town.

"If that happened, Lucinda, you and I would be on his list to find and deal with, likely meaning to terminate us. We agree we don't want to kill Covington unless *he* starts something. Dan insists we take Covington to D.C. alive, if possible. Let's interpret that loosely.

"How can we assure taking him alive is *not* possible?" Lucinda asked.

28

A DAY LATER – HOPE TOWN

LUCINDA WASN'T ATTRACTED TO THE IDEA OF bicycling past Covington's house, and she begged off going. She drew sketches depicting what the interior looked like, but didn't offer to explain why the sudden change. I didn't want to push her. Since her return, she hasn't been consistent about her emotions.

Given a chance, Lucinda might have gone in gun blazing. Or, more problematic, she might have knocked on the door, and when Covington opened it, her hypnosis instantly returned, and she asked where Ellsworth-Kent was so she could return to live with him contented to be his high priestess.

John and I decided to go together. He would pretend to help me work on the bike and hope someone would come out. It didn't have to be Covington. Anyone might be a source of information.

It was Tuesday, our fourth day in Hope Town, and all we'd done was talk. With some hesitation, in the afternoon we tried our bicycle ploy. It was my first view of Covington's house, a gaudy, fake stone, poor mix of Palladian and gothic style more common to Miami or Palm Beach.

A fifty-ish lady in a maid's uniform came to Covington's door, but she didn't offer any help, even though my knee was bleeding. She listened to my plea for help but appeared to be scared and said "no." Although the door remained open enough so I could partly see in, all I noticed was a small vestibule leading to a large room with windows beyond. Importantly, there was no trace of anyone else being present.

The bicycle plan half failed. What little we achieved was at the cost of an unintended broken bicycle chain and for me a bloody knee from miscalculating my rapid braking, which caused my fake accident to become a real one. We walked our bicycles home.

After lunch at the cottage, John went off to the small grocery for a few items for our breakfasts and lunches. He came back excited. I was in the kitchen; Lucinda was relaxing on the porch. We could hear John as he hurried in.

"Listen up, folks! I was at the counter paying for the groceries when a *treasure* walked in the door," he exclaimed, panting. "It was a middle-aged man with a scantily clad young woman wearing sun glasses.

"The grocery counter clerk stopped ringing up my things and said, 'Mr. Covington, sir, it's very good to see you.'

"Covington looked fit, and I could understand how he attracts women, besides laying out a lot of money."

"Who was the woman?" Lucinda asked.

"He called her Candi. Didn't mention her last name. They both walked up to the counter and were standing next to me. Covington was rubbing her butt with his hand. She snuggled against him and returned the rub. Then she rubbed me!"

"And you abducted her, and she's in the golf cart waiting to be untied and brought in?"

"Don't I wish! She was a knockout. But I behaved and ignored her rubbing. Well, I *tried* to ignore her. Covington pushed my stuff aside and paid for two bottles of rum he'd pulled off the shelf. Then he nudged Candi toward the door, and they left. I was stunned."

"Would you recognize her again, without her sunglasses?"

"Maybe not her face, but as to the rest of her, you bet. Especially, I'd recognize her butt."

"If that's all you two can talk about," interrupted Lucinda, "I'm going out on the town looking for someone who'll rub mine."

I raised both hands and pointed at myself. "Me! Me!"

29

NEXT EVENING – HOPE TOWN

WEDNESDAY AFTERNOON, JOHN SAID HE'D treat us all to dinner and entertainment at the Conch Shell, where we had consumed multiple variations of conch the first night. The entertainment was to be the Bahamas' most popular island singer—The Barefoot Man. Based in the Caymans, he often appears in the Bahamas at Nipper's on Guana Key and was to do a special performance at Hope Town. One doesn't go to Abaco without listening to The Barefoot Man singing favorites songs such as "Hopetown Ferry," "Layin' Low in Abaco," "Man Smart-Woman Smarter," "Victoria's Got a Secret," and "Save the Lap Dance for Me."

We arrived early so we could enjoy dinner before the songs began. John suggested a booth at the opposite end from where The Barefoot Man would sing and where we could hear one another talking quietly. The booth before ours was empty; the one beyond ours held a couple sitting across from each other. They were speaking quietly, his an English Oxford accent, hers bedded somewhere in our Deep South.

I slid in next to Lucinda, with our backs against a head-high partition separating us from the next booth.

"Leave your sunglasses on," John said to us both. He was wearing the pair the Agency issued him, apparently for use in clandestine activities. I guess this evening qualified as clandestine.

"No one's going to recognize me," Lucinda said. "My hair is a far cry from the shoulder length light brown hair that Macduff hadn't wanted me to alter since the evening I met him. Plus, I'm wearing light weight black slacks and a black long sleeved blouse. Jeeze, guys, I don't look a thing like Lucinda did . . . . And my makeup is horrible. You two dressed me. I look like a whore."

"We'll protect you, unless you don't want us to," John added, smiling.

Three Kaliks were placed on our table, and orders for dinner were taken. Lucinda looked at John and asked, "Are we set for Saturday?"

"I hope so," he answered.

"And we're going to Covington's house and break down the door and barge in?"

"I wouldn't put it that way," John replied. "We are going to *knock* on the door, wait for someone to open it, and then barge in."

"Using for persuasion our toy pistols?" asked Lucinda.

"In one hand and in the other the stun guns," John said.

"We have an idea how many are in the house," John responded, looking at me and ignoring Lucinda. "Covington should be there, plus his housekeeper, who will likely answer the door as she did when we knocked after your bicycle crashed. Also, at most two armed bodyguards. Dan has been using a satellite to watch the house. It's of no help inside, but it tells us how many are outside, especially around the pool. Over the past week every morning between 7:00 and 7:30 a.m., a person comes out of the house in a robe and sits by the pool for breakfast. It must be Covington. Two men also are present, standing in different locations. Recently, there has been another person at the table. We believe it's Covington's newest playmate, Candi."

"Are the men armed?"

"Probably. But it's unlikely the girl has a gun."

"What kind of weapons?"

"Strangely, they don't appear to have automatic weapons like AK-47s. They certainly have pistols. From what we understand about Covington, he likes these morning times to be quiet. The two men stand well away from him and try not to stare at him. We assume he doesn't like being reminded he's living in an armed camp. It may be a carry-over from when Lucinda and Ellsworth-Kent were there. They may not have wanted to scare Lucinda by standing around with guns."

"Ellsworth-Kent and Lucinda are gone. Covington might have re-armed."

"Yes, but he may be reluctant to go back to having several guards standing around. What does he have to worry about?"

"I suspect he always has reason to worry. . . . What are the odds we can succeed?" I asked.

"I wouldn't try this unless I was certain there was a very high chance of it going smoothly and without a shot fired," responded John.

"If shots are fired and Covington isn't killed, we have to get him to the plane in Marsh Harbour," Lucinda added, looking doubtful. "We could be stopped before we leave Hope Town or when we get to the dock at Marsh Harbour or at the airport before the plane leaves. And even when we're in the air, the plane could be ordered to land, at least until it's out of Bahamian territory."

"All true," replied John. "I'm not going to discuss it now, but we have most of those issues covered."

We were nearly finished with our dinner when there was a commotion at the Conch Shell's front entry.

"Do you have your guns with you?" John asked, putting his pistol in his lap.

"Yes," said Lucinda, also setting her S&W in her lap."

"Mac, what about you?"

"I was going to bring it, but I left it on the dresser," I said.

Lucinda rolled her eyes. John looked down to avoid eye contact with me.

The commotion was little more than very loud talking by four people entering.

"That's Covington," said Lucinda quietly, staring at the man with the girl and reaching up and touching the center nose rim of her sunglasses to assure she was wearing them.

"It *is* Covington," assured John. "He's been drinking and is supported by Candi who's wearing a very thin dress that shows she forgot her underwear. Probably left it on her dresser like you did your gun, Mac. She also had left her footwear somewhere."

The other two were large men who wore tropical clothing—Bermuda length shorts and short sleeved knit shirts. The portions of their arms and legs that showed were chalk white from lack of exposure to the sun. . . . The two men had not yet been drinking enough to show it.

John and I looked at the group; our expressions suggested not one of the four was carrying a gun.

"I don't think they're armed," I whispered to John so Lucinda could hear me.

"I'm amazed, but I agree with you," John whispered, nodding.

The four were shown to seats by an obsequious and nervous waiter who apparently knew Covington and was afraid how he might act, especially if the service was too slow or the entertainment too loud.

Covington was so preoccupied with his girl Candi that he never looked our way. To our good fortune they were seated in the booth immediately before ours and behind Lucinda and me. John was sitting looking between us, directly across their table and into the faces of Covington and Candi. Covington pushed in so he was against her. His left arm appeared to be somewhere on her lap.

We could hear Covington and Candi talking. They had quieted somewhat, but were so close to us we heard nearly everything they said, without leaving any impression that we were listening. Much of the communication between the two was taking place under the table.

They ordered drinks. Candi asked for a Goombay Smash, Covington a Margarita, and the other two Kaliks.

We dared not talk loudly among ourselves except for not always truthfully expressed holiday topics. John started it.

"Roland, you missed the best fish we hooked today," John said, looking at me and loud enough for the four to hear.

Our conversation stayed on fishing, turned to golf, and then the beaches of Abaco and our getting some welcome tan. Lucinda mostly nodded or shook her head, not wanting to have to disguise her voice. When she did talk, it was barely a whisper affirming she was participating, but suggesting she had a soft voice.

It was *what* they talked about that kept our attention. We quickly learned the girl's full name was Candi Treat.

"I want you to take me the next time you go to Miami," Candi pleaded to Covington.

"Next week. I'm staying here until Tuesday. We'll fly to Miami first thing Wednesday. That's less than a week away. We'll stay in Miami for two or three days. You can shop. Keep it under $10,000. I know how you like to spend money."

"What's so important to keep you here for almost a week?" she whined.

"I have a couple of guys flying here in two days. They'll replace Al and Freddie who left last week. You know I'm down to two guards, and they're sitting across from us. They can't be on duty all the time." Covington looked at them and added, "Why don't you both go home and get some rest."

"Thanks, boss. We started this morning at 6:00 a.m. sharp," said the heavier of the two. "We've had some long days this past week."

"And you'll be paid handsomely for it. You both look like hell. Go back to the house and go to bed. That's an order. Candi and I are fine alone."

"I'd like that," Candi said, looking at Covington. "I have some private talk I want to do with you."

"You sure we can go, Mr. Covington?" said the other thinner man with a scar that ran from below his right ear to under his chin.

"Yes! Go! Take your beer bottles with you."

Not counting whatever alcohol Covington and Candi had consumed at the house before they left for the restaurant, they finished their first Conch Shell drinks since they sat down not more than fifteen minutes earlier. This time they both ordered double shots as The Barefoot Man began singing "Let's Do It Again."

"Macduff and John," Lucinda whispered, her face expressing the biggest grin since she returned to me, "I have an idea!"

"You're going to Covington and tell him you have the hots for him and to get rid of Candi?"

"Not quite that. But I do have some hots for him. I want him to roast in hell."

"Tell us your idea."

"Why wait until Saturday to take him and risk dealing with those two thugs? Let's take him *now!*"

"Are you serious? Walk over and invite him to take a little plane ride to D.C. Tell him he'll be arrested, indicted, tried, convicted, and hopefully executed. At least placed in jail for the rest of his life?"

"Trust me," Lucinda said whispering, sliding out of the booth and standing. "Are you two with me, or do I do this alone?"

By the time we could answer, she had turned around, taken two steps, and slid in the side of Covington's booth only minutes before vacated by the two bodyguards."

"What the hell do you want? Get your ass out of this booth," Covington said forcefully but quietly to Lucinda. "What's your name?"

Lucinda took her sunglasses off and stared at Covington.

"Remember me?" she asked.

Covington had taken a last sip of his second Margarita and choked. "You! . . . I told Ellsworth-Kent we should have killed you."

"Yes, it's me." Lucinda said. "If you feel something against your crotch it's not Candi's fingers. It's a Smith & Wesson waiting to screw up your prostate. One move. One bad word, and your sex life is over, followed shortly by the rest as you bleed out."

"What do you want?" he mumbled. Candi was sitting back in the corner looking as though Lucinda might take out a knife and deflate her exaggerated breasts.

By this time John and I had stood up and were next to their table, trying to block the view of anyone in the room.

"Candi," said Lucinda, "you're going to get up and help your man exit the restaurant as gracefully as possible. As soon as you start, the two men with me will step in alongside to help you. Let them. I'll be behind you."

Candi was drunk and too scared not to obey. John and I took Covington from Candi and helped him through the restaurant. He mumbled a lot but offered no resistance. People had seen drunks before in bars, and no one paid much attention.

"How did you get here from Covington's house?" John asked Candi.

"Golf cart. It's half-a-block away. Cars aren't permitted in the town."

We all squeezed into the golf cart and headed to our cottage. The cart hit so many bumps Candi threw up all over Covington. We were at the cottage in a few minutes and pulled off between some bushes that blocked any view of the cottage from the road.

Abandoning our false names in our rush, I said, "Lucinda, pack for both of us. John will get his own bag. I'll stay with these two. Be back quickly."

"Candi's cute, Macduff. But she stinks. Behave while I'm packing."

Covington remained sozzled. Candi, who was now appearing merely tipsy, sat looking at me wondering what we were going to do."

"Are you going to kill me?" she asked.

"No. You've done us a service getting him drunk."

"Is that good?"

"Much better for you. You're safe. Pull out his wallet and hand it to me."

She did. I opened it, took out all the money, and threw the wallet into the trash.

"Candi, here's over a thousand dollars from his wallet. You keep it. He won't need the money. We're going to have our government feed and house him."

"You mean you're taking him and leaving me?"

"That's right. But stay with us until we tell you to leave."

"When I leave, I'm going back to his house," Candi exclaimed with a smile. "I know where he hides nearly a million dollars in cash in his bedroom and where under his desk he taped the number of a Caymans bank account that has millions more. I'm going to live in luxury without him. Even if you let him go, he'll never find me. Will you please keep him for a few days?"

"Promise. . . . Enjoy the rest of your life."

She leaned over and kissed me.

John and Lucinda arrived with all our bags.

"Where are we going?" asked Lucinda. "I've done my part."

"I've got it from here," responded John. "You two help me get Covington into the boat."

"You take the golf cart, Candi, and go get Covington's money and offshore account number. Watch out for his two bodyguards, but I expect they're sleeping it off. I'm sure Covington owes you a lot for your favors. I urge you to get away from the Bahamas. Good luck. Enjoy being rich," I told her.

John started the outboard and moved us slowly out of Hope Town Harbour.

"Macduff, I love this town," said Lucinda. "I guess we'll never have a place here."

"Wait 'til we see what happens to Covington. He may spend the rest of his life in a Wyoming, Idaho, Montana, or Florida prison. . . . Don't give up your dream of spending weeks on Abaco every winter."

"We're out west of Elbow Key," I said ten minutes later, the hull slapping against a slight chop. "You can look back and see the lighthouse flashing at Hope Town."

"You're right. We're heading north," John said.

"Are we taking this little Boston Whaler all the way to St. Augustine?" I asked John.

"No. We'll be off it in twenty minutes," he replied.

"In the water or on land?"

"Neither," John answered to surprised looks from Lucinda and me.

"I hope you know what you're doing. Does Dan Wilson know about this?"

"Yes, he does," a familiar voice answered from the cellphone John was holding up facing us.

"Dan Wilson?" exclaimed Lucinda. "Where *are* you?"

"At Langley. I'm watching you on satellite."

"Was whatever we're doing your idea?"

"Working with John, more or less, yes. With some help by Lucinda's improvisation. How's it going?"

"The next hour will tell," said John. "Listen, everyone. Including you, Dan. I've got to get this boat through a narrow harbor ahead."

"What's this place we're entering?" I asked. "Not very big but a nice harbor."

"It's Man-O-War Key," said John. "Ever been here?"

"Years ago," I said. "Don't we turn left inside the channel and work our way north to the town."

"That's right."

"John, as I recall there's no airfield on Man-O-War."

"There is now," he said as we slowly passed the tiny town.

"Do I see ahead what I think I see?"

"If you mean a float plane, yes. In a minute you'll see a guy on one of the pontoons waving. He's going to fly us out."

As we neared the plane, I read something on the side.

"John, that says 'Bahamas Air-Sea Rescue!'"

"So it's does."

"Are we stealing a Bahamas government plane?"

"No," John answered as the pilot pulled off a magnetic sign bearing the name and tossed it in the cockpit.

"I'm Jimmy," said the pilot.

"Can I have the sign?" Lucinda asked. "I want to put it on our cottage wall. You guys are *our* Bahamas Air-Sea Rescue team."

"It's yours," Jimmy said, rolling up the sign and handing it to Lucinda.

With effort we got Covington into the plane onto the floor behind the seats, but only after a thorough dunking in the water to get rid of the worst of his smell.

"Any chance of our being tracked by Bahamian radar?" I asked Jimmy as he taxied to take off.

"Not much. We're going to stay low under any radar until we're over the Gulf Stream, then climb and head north to St. Augustine."

"How do you land on a runway with pontoons?" I asked, thinking about the runway at St. Augustine.

"We've got both. We're an amphibious aircraft. There are tires in the pontoon that drop down. We're going to land and drop you and Lucinda off. Then I'll go on with John and your guest to D.C."

An hour-and-a-half later it was reassuring to see the St. Augustine runway lights getting closer and closer, until they surrounded us as we touched down. We had been gone less than a week. Covington was ours, tied up and comatose on the floor. I wondered if he comprehended what was happening to him. He may have been dreaming of Candi. Little does he know about her now.

Lucinda and I jumped down with our bags and said goodbyes over the noise of the prop.

John replaced me in the right front seat, and we watched as the plane rolled away to the far end of the runway and came racing back by us to lift off and begin a bank north toward D.C.

Exhausted, we walked to our car and began the forty-minute drive south to our cottage.

When we walked in, there was a note on the table from Elsbeth:

Where have you two been? I came by to say hello. I couldn't get a call through to you. Someone scrambled my phone. I finally reached Dan's number in D.C. and was told he was unavailable for another week. What's up? Call me when you get in.

"I don't think she wants to be called at this hour," I said to Lucinda, who was already headed for the bed, scattering her clothes on the way. "Dawn light will soon begin to filter through the trees. And I'm too tired to talk."

"Me, too. I'm going to have good dreams thinking about Covington confined somewhere in Langley."

"But when he's sobered up, he'll be thinking how to get out of this and come after us," I responded.

"I do wish we'd had to kill him," she said.

"Another time."

30

FOUR DAYS LATER – ST. AUGUSTINE

FOR THE NEXT FEW DAYS WE SMILED A LOT AT each other but never even once did either of us start a conversation about our brief few days in Hope Town. Dan left a message the evening after we arrived in Florida that everything had gone smoothly in escorting Covington into a cell and turning him over to the "authorities." I'd never asked Dan who those authorities were and what they would do with him.

But then problems arose. The papers called the act kidnapping—which was true—and the debate began about its legitimacy as a way of getting personal jurisdiction before a U.S. court. I thought the issue was settled with the *Alvarez-Machain* case dealing with the Mexican physician.

The Bahamian government was outraged at what had been done to Covington, blamed the CIA, and harassed U.S. tourists. Some U.S. tourism companies retaliated, pointing out that U.S. visitors brought in much of the $5-6 million spent annually on tourism and that roughly half the Bahamian population worked in tourist-related activities. Seven scheduled Florida-based cruise ship visits to Nassau were canceled, the number of air passengers from the U.S. dropped drastically, and few private boats from the U.S. entered Bahamian territorial waters. The Bahamian harassment diminished.

That didn't moderate the actions of the Bahamian government that were specific to Covington. He had many people on the islands indebted to him for favors. His supporters began a campaign for his extradition back to the Bahamas arguing comity and reminding the U.S. that the Bahamas had received and agreed to an extradition request a decade ago by sending back to the U.S. the "Barefoot Bandit," a U.S. teenage fugitive who stole a plane in the U.S. and crashed in the Bahamas.

Covington's lawyers immediately pointed out that each of the states—Florida, Idaho, Montana, and Wyoming—that might have a claim to Covington had the death penalty, and for that reason insisted that Covington could not be sent to the U.S. The Bahamas said it was the same as the U.S. experience with Mexico. His lawyers overlooked or ignored the fact that the Bahamas, unlike Mexico, *has* the death penalty.

Newspapers throughout the U.S. argued against extradition of Covington, especially those in the four states that were believed to want him.

Dan Wilson sent us another message that there was much confusion within the Justice Department: Send Covington back, send him to one of the four states, or try him in federal court on yet to be determined charges.

Lucinda and I paid attention only because we were concerned that if Covington were extradited, he would be freed of charges, but not his hatred of us.

The thought of Covington going free frightened Lucinda.

"Macduff, what can we do?"

"Nothing. It's out of our hands. . . . I know how that disturbs you. It will be months before it's played out. Let's agree that I will keep track of Covington's case and only bring you in if I believe there's a rational reason to worry. Right now, four states and the Justice Department all want to try Covington. Any court doing so and convicting and sentencing him to jail would mean we wouldn't have to worry, at least for the duration of his sentence. When I think we should worry, I'll tell you. Agreed?"

"Reluctantly," she whispered. "I want to go west with you and sequester ourselves in our log cabin. I hate to place the whole weight on your shoulders. When do we leave for Montana?"

"In ten minutes," I suggested.

"I'll be ready! Since you're not giving me any time to think about what I'll need in Montana, I'll wait and buy it *all* there. We can go by way of the stores in Jackson Hole."

"I can't be seen in Wyoming," I noted.

"I don't need you with me to shop. I'll drive to Jackson as soon as we reach our Montana cabin."

"I was kidding about the ten minutes. Today's April 1st. We can leave in a week. Take your time and take *everything* you need for the summer."

"Jackson still sounds good. I'll take my time packing and still head for Jackson and buy out all the stores on the square. I'll bet Erin Giffin and Wanda Groves will go with me."

"How would you like to go to Hope Town and delay driving west? You can get ready to welcome Covington home if the U.S. grants extradition."

"I thought we weren't going to mention him."

"Sorry, I panicked when you said shopping."

31

FIVE DAYS LATER – MONTANA

WE DIDN'T RUSH ACROSS THE COUNTRY. AND we didn't pass through even a corner of Wyoming. We suffered interstates and drove north to Indiana to place flowers on Lucinda's mother's grave. Then further north to Minneapolis and into Canada to Winnipeg in Manitoba province where we joined Canada's major east-west Trans-Canada Highway, which runs between St. John's, Newfoundland, in the east and Nanaimo, British Columbia, in the west. Those quaint bookend cities both require a ferry crossing.

The trip west from Winnipeg went through Canada's equivalent of our Great Plains, no less boring until we reached Calgary in Alberta where the Canadian Rockies begin. We passed through towns with colorful names like Moose Jaw and Swift Current in Saskatchewan and Medicine Hat in Alberta.

"Macduff," said Lucinda with a wince of curiosity. "I'm looking at the U.S. and Canada atlas. We're in Calgary. It's *west* of Bozeman. Shouldn't we have turned south sooner?"

"No and no. Two reasons," I replied, exhibiting my earlier decades as a professor giving a class. "We are a little west of Bozeman from a line drawn due south from Calgary. We'll go south from here along the edge of the mountains, cross into the U.S., see Glacier National Park, keep a bit east of due south and stop in Missoula and Butte, and an hour later be in Bozeman. You remember Bozeman?"

"Of course I remember Bozeman."

"We visited Glacier and Missoula a few years ago."

"For a whole day. They deserve more."

"What's the second reason for being so far west and not turning south sooner?" she asked a few minutes later.

"To fish. Tomorrow we're going to get our licenses, rent a canoe, and float the Bow River right through the middle of downtown Calgary. The water is so clean and clear we'll catch trout."

We did exactly that. Lucinda caught several trout while I paddled. My immediate reward was seeing her fish for the first time in two years. My long-term reward would be to watch her do the same for many more years.

The following morning we drove south on a provincial road along the foothills of the Rockies and encountered few vehicles. Halfway to the U.S. border, we stopped at Willow Creek Park and took Wuff for a walk along a beautiful stretch of the creek. No one was in sight. But we could see trout!

"I don't know about you, Macduff, but I can't pass this up," Lucinda said, staring at the creek.

We left the SUV in a deserted parking area by the creek that varied from ten to thirty feet wide and looked like the trout must have designed it.

"How do you want to do this, Macduff?" Lucinda asked as I rigged two 7' rods. "I use the rod, and you carry the net?"

I ignored her.

"Why don't *you* walk downstream fifty yards or so to where the creek disappears into woods," I said. "*I'll* go upstream seventy yards so and fish downstream."

"If you're upstream wading, you're going to stir up the creek and send dirty water down to me. That's not fair!"

"I won't get in the water. We don't need to here. Meadows line both sides of the creek. Easy casting. The banks look walkable even though there appears to be no paths. I can't believe no one else is here.

"Remember to look before you fish. You want fish that are feeding. Watch for riffles that have areas that are unruffled. That may mean some deeper water under the smooth spot. If the water is moving faster through a run, fish immediately in front of and right behind boulders. You're going to see all kinds of water. When you see a pool, watch for where the water enters it and then spreads out. Pools are good places to find pods."

"Pods? I thought groups of fish were called schools?"

"They're called lots of things—shoals, clusters, packs, and more esoteric names like gleans, hovers, and what I like—fleets or flotillas."

"If they're fleets or flotillas, are they on the surface?"

"We refer to a flotilla or hover of trout when they are rising to the surface to feed, but call them something else, like a swarm, when they stay on the bottom. We use nymphs to fish for swarms but dry flies for flotillas."

"You're so erudite. Since *we're* chasing fish this morning, are we a posse of fly fishers?"

"If we *pray* to catch a big fish, we're a congregation?"

"I know why you're sending me downstream and you're staying upstream. What do you call us if we fish together?"

"If Elsbeth were with us, you two would be a gaggle."

"You're not giving me much advice on how to fish. Like what fly to start with."

"OK. I'm going to try an old standard to start. A little #18 Yellow Humpy that has caught more than a few fish for me over the years. I suggest you. . . ."

"Don't suggest. Let *me* choose. You've been a good teacher. Now be quiet and watch your student at work."

"What will you start with?"

"Elk Hair Caddis. Also #18."

"OK. Wave if you catch one," I said and turned north following the creek but away from its edge enough not to throw a morning shadow on the water.

I watched Lucinda go south, rod in one hand and waving over her shoulder with the other. A year ago at this time I was living a lonely life. Occasionally, Grace Justice helped me, but she was not Lucinda. . . . I stood and watched Lucinda walk the fifty yards and then step carefully into the edge of the creek.

When I reached my starting point, I looked and saw her rod bend.

"She could be hooked on the bottom," I thought aloud. But then the bottom moved. I watched as she lifted her net, held up a nice trout, looked at me, and waved.

I grudgingly returned the wave. What luck! I tied on my Yellow Humpy, took a couple of false casts, and dropped the fly at the bottom of a run. A trout came to the surface and took the fly and swam toward an eddy behind a large rock. I looked downstream to see if Lucinda saw my rod bend. But she was busy; she had another on her fly. In a few moments she turned and looked at me and waved again. This time I saw only two fingers.

For a moment, I thought I'd caught one, but turned to see my rod was straight. I didn't wave at Lucinda.

I shifted to the same fly Lucinda has chosen, a #18 Elk Hair Caddis. When I finished and looked toward her, her rod was bent again. It's the right choice of fly, I thought, but for the next half hour I didn't see any sign of a single trout, while Lucinda's rod bent and she waved every few minutes.

I checked my line. No problems with my leader or tippet. I must have snagged something and lost the fly. What fly to use, I wondered, a slight panic settling in.

"I know!" I thought. "When the fish aren't rising to my fly, I drop a nymph down in their midst for instant action.

"Bead head or not?" I pondered. A bead head would send it to the bottom quickly. I reached for my bead head nymph box, but it was missing. I knew who took it. Oh! Maybe a Prince Nymph without a bead head would work. I found one and tied it on.

Looking downstream without turning my head, all I got was a side view of another wave. Damn! I've been fly fishing since I was nine. Lucinda didn't hold a rod until we met. She's catching most of the fish. Life is not fair.

I looked toward Lucinda and saw another wave. This time she raised both hands. I couldn't tell how many fingers were raised, but it was more than five. I sat down and set my rod down on the creek's bank.

"I've waited months to see this sight," I thought out loud. "Whatever fly fishing has brought to my life is embedded indelibly here on a small Canadian creek at the foot of snow-capped mountains."

We both were half-way back to our car, often glancing at each other. Lucinda would cast a few times as she walked slowly to join me; she hooked something about every fourth cast. I would cast a few times and, frustrated at no action, pull my fly out and try sometimes else. I spent most of my time changing flies.

"Macduff, this was a hoot!" she said, joining and hugging me while I stood there with my rod in my hand. It had not been bent not more than twice during the past two hours.

"Life *is* unfair. Can there be a God?" I asked. "I put one fish in my net! One! And it was about nine inches long. I don't have to ask if you did better."

"I lost count. I've never caught so many fish. How did you ever find this place?"

"A friend told me about it. Most people who come to Calgary float the Bow, the river we canoed on yesterday."

"We *must* come back here. After I give you some lessons," she said laughing.

"I took off my Yellow Humpy when I saw you catch one. I put on a #18 Elk Hair caddis, just like you used. It didn't work for me."

"I didn't use it. I decided on my walk downstream to go with an Adams Trude. . . . Maybe I should call you on my cell phone every half-hour and give you some advice."

"And to think I missed you all these months and dreamed about being with you on a creek like this!"

"Let's go home," she said, suddenly looking lost. "I can't wait to see the cabin. We can drive through Glacier Park and stay tonight, then have lunch in Missoula, and stop for a couple of hours at Butte to see the old copper mines and great Victorian mansions. And then go around Bozeman without stopping until we get to Mill Creek."

"I want to sit next to you on our porch tonight and give you some advice about selecting the proper fly," she added.

32

THE FOLLOWING EVENING – MONTANA

OUR HOUSEKEEPER AT BOTH THE CABIN AND the ranch, Mavis Benton, was waiting on our cabin porch when we arrived, taking a brief break from getting both places ready. She had not seen Lucinda for three years, reflected by the long hug they exchanged. Wuff ran circles around them and then looked at me and barked. It was 5:00 p.m., her dinner time. She had adjusted her time frame for the two-hour difference. She was entitled to prompt meals at 6:00 a.m. and 5:00 p.m. *local time*, regardless of where we were in the world.

After emptying our car with help from Mavis, she left. Lucinda grabbed my hand, and we walked down our road to where the Absaroka Mountains open onto Paradise Valley. When we returned, she headed us a short way upstream alongside Mill Creek. It was high and frothing from the melting snow in the mountains.

Back inside the cabin, Lucinda again took my hand and walked me through each room. Her eyes were moist and occasionally I felt some trembling. She had said nothing since we began our walk. But sitting on our bed, Wuff next to us, she turned to me and spoke quietly.

"I missed all this. Paradise cabin in Paradise Valley."

"We have time to enjoy it," I said. "It's mid-April. We'll stay until the day after Thanksgiving. That's seven months. . . . What would you like to do tomorrow?"

"Go visit friends. Have lunch at Ted's Montana Grill in Bozeman. And end the day further up Mill Creek with a picnic and a little fishing."

That was how we spent the day, except we didn't fish up along Mill Creek. I delayed us enough in Bozeman that we didn't return to the cabin until a half-hour before sunset, escaping a repeat embarrassment of fishing on Willow Creek in Alberta. We went directly to our bedroom to put on sweaters and grab a blanket, then poured a Montana Roughstock Whiskey and a Gentleman Jack, and watched the sun go down from our porch.

The last top sliver of the sun burst like fireworks, and the day fell dark. We didn't move. I studied the outline of Lucinda's face in the sparse light from an emerging moon. I was about to touch her cheek when our peace was shattered by my cellphone.

"Should I answer it?" I asked, looking at the cellphone threateningly.

"What might we miss if you don't?"

"Notice that we won the Florida lottery. Attorney General Davis calling from Cheyenne to apologize for wanting to arrest and try me. John Kirby asking me to fish the One-Fly Contest in Jackson with him in September—and promising to pay all the fees."

"Answer it," she ordered, and I touched the on button.

"Macduff Brooks?" asked the caller.

"Who is this," I answered, turning on the speaker so Lucinda could listen.

"Rosalie Abbott, Chief Investigator for the Citrus County Sheriff's Office. I know it's very late. I'm working at the office. I assume you're in either St. Augustine or Gainesville?"

"Neither one," I said. "But it's two hours earlier here."

"Where are you?"

"Outside Florida. At home."

"At home? You live in Florida."

"And outside Florida, where we have our *principal* home. We're here for seven months and in St. Augustine for the five coldest months, usually December to April."

"Don't play games with me, Brooks. What state are you in?"

"Montana."

"Why did you leave Florida? I told you we wanted you here as part of our investigation of Rachel Hart's death."

"Rachel Hart died *seven* months ago," I reminded her. "Your medical examiner ruled her death an accidental drowning. What have you learned recently that suggests otherwise?"

"I believe Ms. Hart was murdered."

"Why do you believe that?"

"She was a good swimmer and careful when she fished."

"How do you know that?" I asked.

"My assumption from reading several pieces about her. We have no record of her ever having an accident."

"Like falling into the water?"

"Yes."

"I'll bet that she fell into the water a number of times. That's what happens when you fish. You wade into fast moving water. Sometimes you lose your balance and fall. And maybe drown."

"That's not what happened at the Plantation. The water was calm."

"But there is a tidal flow and a bank that is easy to fall off. Ms. Abbott, you're wasting my time. I have work to do here as a guide. I'll be back in Florida in early December."

"I want you next week."

"Have you arrested me?"

"No."

"Why not?"

"I need more evidence."

"And you want me to provide that evidence?"

"I want to talk to you."

"You're doing so now. What questions do you have?"

"Were you having an affair with Rachel Hart?"

"I met her the day before she died. I thought an affair took at least a few hours longer. . . . Anyway, the answer is 'no' but I can understand why men would like to have an affair with her. At least four turned affairs with her into marriages, however brief."

"I'm getting nowhere with you. I don't need a lesson about affairs. Please just answer my questions. . . . You were with her much of the day before she died," she said, preferring a statement to a question.

"In the morning, I was in a group having a lesson that lasted about two hours. In the afternoon, I saw her once or twice at one of the booths in the large convention space. There were at least a hundred people in the room."

"What about that evening?"

"The last time I saw her that afternoon she asked me to have a drink with her at the pool terrace. I met her there at about 6:30. There were a couple of dozen people present. It was getting to be dinner time, and she asked me if I wanted anything to eat. I said 'yes,' and we sat by the pool for dinner. I guess we talked about fly fishing until perhaps 9:30 or 10:00.

We walked to the wing that contained our separate rooms. I saw the restrooms when we entered the building and I needed to use the toilet. I didn't want to wait until we reached our rooms, and stand in the hall talking while I kept my legs crossed. Rachel walked on, I assume to her room. I said goodbye, and I didn't see her again. About 7:00 a.m., I had the breakfast buffet and left for Gainesville by 8:00. . . . I had a good time with Hart but hardly an affair."

"Did you ever go into her room?"

"No. Did you check her room for fingerprints? Mine should be on some of her fishing equipment I carried back from our lesson."

"I can't discuss the fingerprints."

"I take that as either a no or you did check but found no prints of mine."

"When you were having drinks or dinner, did you ask her to go to bed with you?"

I didn't like Abbott's unorganized and increasingly intrusive questions. It was time to challenge her.

"If you must know, I asked repeatedly to go to bed with her, in either her room or mine. Or in my car. Or on a chaise lounge at the darkened pool after dinner."

"Hart said no?"

I couldn't believe Abbott was serious.

"Hart slapped me hard. Harder each time I asked again."

"That made you mad?"

"I loved every minute of it. I like rough sex."

"Did you follow her to her room?"

"Are you kidding? She would have killed me. I knew when finally she said 'enough' not to pursue it anymore. I went to the restroom."

"And to get even, you went to her room about 2:00 a.m. and killed her."

"Before I answer, would you like to give me the Miranda warning? Do you know it?"

She stumbled through the warning, not suggesting she didn't know it but that she just forgot to warn me.

"I gave you the warning when we last talked."

"And you recorded it so you could later prove it in court?"

"Of course. . . . Maybe."

"Ms. Abbott, I hate to be mean, but you aren't prepared to ask questions about Ms. Hart and me," I added condescendingly.

"Then come here where I will be prepared."

"From Montana?"

"If that's where you are, of course. This is important."

"Let me suggest something. We schedule a telephone conference call after you've prepared a little better. . . . Sorry, I should never have commented on your preparation. I'm busy getting ready for fishing. You must know I'm a guide. Besides, it's too hot to be in Florida, at least until October."

"You're making me mad. I don't recommend that. Where will you be in the next month if I want to reach you?"

"Right where I am this moment. In my log cabin in Paradise Valley, Montana."

"You'll swear to tell the truth?"

"Yes. Will you send me a bible? Gideons never made it this far west."

"You're playing games again."

"When you want to do the conference, call me first about a proposed time. I will check with my Florida attorney, Bill Muirhead, to be certain he can be on the line."

"You don't need an attorney. This is merely an investigation."

"Then it won't be used by you as evidence to arrest me?"

"I can't agree to do that."

"Be prepared for Mr. Muirhead to object to most of your questions if they are anything like what you've been asking me."

The phone went dead.

"I'm glad I'm on your side," Lucinda said.

"And I'm glad Muirhead's on my side."

"Macduff, can prosecutors be this poorly prepared?"

"You just heard one support that idea. . . . Now, are you ready for bed?"

"Are you kidding. After that call?"

"It exhausted you to listen?"

"Not really. But you asked me to go to bed with you, and I get to slap you around first.

"I can hit as hard as Rachel Hart," she added.

33

A WEEK LATER – MONTANA

THE WEEK PASSED WITHOUT A WORD FROM MS. Abbott.

"Macduff," commented Lucinda the next morning after we walked to get our mail, "I think the Rachel Hart death investigation is at a standstill. Listening to you and Abbott, her county doesn't have close to enough reasons to get a judge to issue a warrant for your arrest."

"That's true in a perfect world. Nobody ever accused Crystal River or Citrus County of being part of a perfect world."

"What's Abbott's motive for accusing you?"

"She hasn't shown her cards yet. I've never met her. She can't have anything against me personally. At least nothing I can think of."

"What about against me?"

"I don't think she knows any more about you other than we're married. Certainly not about your abduction. And Dan Wilson mostly kept our kidnapping of Covington out of the papers. He does not talk to investigative reporters."

"Abbott has to have a reason."

"She does. County investigators are overworked. She doesn't need just another case. . . . I wouldn't even try to guess her reason. Something I did she doesn't like. Something she's trying to hide. Something she's being pressured to do. Or something she feels she has to achieve, like be appointed the Florida State Attorney.

"She hadn't contacted you in *seven* months. Has anything happened in the last month that would renew her interest in the case?"

"Only one thing I can think of. She's learned about the Spence case in Wyoming and about my alleged link to that death. But remember *that* death was also ruled accidental. The two deaths are not connected. The fact that both Spence and Hart were Master Casting Instructors isn't enough. And the IFFF that does the certification is highly esteemed. It's a significant achievement to be a MCI."

"I agree, with one reservation. The black flies found tied around each body's neck. Have you ever seen a guide or fly fisherman with a black fly string necklace?"

"No, and I don't know why either Abbott or Davis hasn't learned about both black flies. If they investigated carefully don't you think they would learn that Spence and Hart were both MCIs and were both wearing black flies?"

"That would lead them to looking for something that linked only the two. There are dozens if not hundreds of MCIs. But you and I know of only two people found dead with black flies around their neck. And not hanging from fancy necklaces. They were hanging from common string. So where are we?" she asked.

"Safe in Montana for the time being. Far from Cheyenne and much farther from Crystal River. Unless they arrest me formally, I won't be sent to either state by a Montana court."

"What happens in another seven months if Abbott learns we're back in Florida and she can reach you?"

"Maybe we *won't* be back in Florida. You raise a good point. Are you ready to spend the winter here?" I asked her, thinking her answer would be a quick "No way!"

"And snuggle with you under a big quilt? You bet! . . .This cabin is not well heated. But our ranch is. . . . Does mentioning the Thanksgiving day we met there scare you?"

"Only because a year later you told me we were engaged and another year proclaimed we were married."

"Has it been so awful?"

"Maybe not. A few oddities for any married couple to face. This cabin was rigged with enough explosives to start a landslide through the Absaroka Mountains. Three of us were shot on *Osprey*, Wuff included. Ellsworth-Kent chased us on five rivers around here and years later abducted you. My flats boat was incinerated with a body on board wrapped in a gill net. We had to flee Cuba in a tiny old Cessna. A good friend and two others were strung up on barbed wire on the Gallatin. . . Otherwise, it's been a pretty normal marriage."

"You don't know what normal means. . . . If there is a 'black fly' killer, are we in danger again?" she asked.

"I could say 'no' and later regret it."

"We could retire, sell all our houses and the boats, move to southern Spain, and buy a comfortable house on a hillside facing the Mediterranean."

"And then?"

"I could knit. You could tie flies."

"Black flies?" I asked.

"Anything but. . . . We'd miss Mavis and Jen, our housekeepers."

"And John Kirby in Jackson, as well as Huntly Byng."

"Plus Erin and Ken here in Montana. And Wanda," she added.

175

"I could name a dozen more. But one name keeps us here," I noted.

"Yes, Elsbeth."

Lucinda knew it would be impossible for me to be so far from Elsbeth. At least until her education is finished.

"So much for Spain," Lucinda agreed. "But that doesn't mean we can't be in either Florida or Montana more. Whichever is safer. Florida because Elsbeth is there? But after graduation she could go anywhere."

"You know where she wants to go? Stay in Gainesville and go to UF's law school?"

"Does her roommate and friend Sue want to do the same?"

"I don't know. Sue hasn't said much. Her dad is ill. My read is that if Elsbeth stays at UF, Sue will stay also. If Elsbeth goes elsewhere, Sue may go back to Wyoming."

"Macduff, it hasn't been so bad. You have a devoted daughter, a devoted dog, and a devoted wife. We spend summers in one of the most beautiful mountain settings in the country. And in the winter, while our friends here in Montana are shoveling snow, we live on the edge of salt water marsh flats in sunny Florida. How many people can say that?"

"All that's good. But Wuff was shot a decade ago and limps. You and I have bullet scars. A lot of people no longer will fish from one of our boats. We do scare people."

"You don't scare me, Macduff. Do I scare you?"

"I won't answer that without my attorney present."

34

THE NEXT DAY

WHEN I WOKE, LUCINDA'S SIDE OF THE BED was empty. That was not surprising; she often was drawn to the kitchen by imagined aromas of Antigua coffee or whining by Wuff waiting for breakfast.

I slept soundly until I heard three rapid blasts from a car horn not far from the cabin. The driver must have opened the outer gate and come in.

Throwing on a robe, I walked to the window next to our front door. There was a Park County Sheriff's Office SUV in our drive. The driver stepped out and immediately was embraced by Lucinda. I couldn't see the figure, but when they parted I recognized Erin Giffin.

Recently promoted to Undersheriff of the County she is now second in rank of the fifteen-member department which is led by another friend, Ken Rangley, who for the last year has been *the* Sheriff.

Erin is a diminutive forty-something-year-old and a tireless phenomenon. She's a Kendo sword fighting expert who I have known since my first year in Montana, well beyond a decade ago. She's barely over five feet tall and barely over 100 pounds, much of which has to be her extraordinary brain. She has a Ph.D. in Forensic Sciences. Erin has never married, and I view her as Park County's most eligible bachelorette, which I remind Lucinda every time she nags me.

Lucinda and I usually don't ask Erin about whether she is seeing someone. I think it's an example of a gal exceptionally proficient doing something she loves and not feeling any need for a spouse. But Lucinda says someday she'll trick some unsuspecting male into an engagement and marriage before he knows what hit him. I commented to Lucinda that Erin's not that devious and that I know of only one woman who is.

Early in our friendship, I worked with Erin on two cases. First was when Julie Conyers was raped and brutally murdered. Julie was one of the owners of the Shuttle Gals. Whenever I had a float with a client, one of the Shuttle Gals drove my vehicle and empty trailer from where I had launched my drift boat in the river and left them where I planned to take out the boat. One day, when my client and I arrived at the Loch Leven take-out on the Yellowstone River, I saw that my trailer had been backed into the shallow water at the edge of the river. Julie's nude body—except for her breasts that had been horribly cut out—was nailed to a large wooden cross that, in turn, had been strapped to the trailer. It was not the only such mutilation of members of the Shuttle Gals; more would soon follow.

Not long after Julie's murder, Erin and I met to discuss Julie's case and enjoy dinner at Ted's Montana Grill on the attractive main street in Bozeman. It wasn't our first meeting. Years ago, she found me on the floor of my cabin near death, emaciated and in rapidly declining health. I was suffering from severe depression over feeling I was losing Lucinda, who was in a coma in the Salt Lake City hospital.

Lucinda and Wuff and I had each been shot on *Osprey* a year before Julie's death, as we three drifted on the Snake River in Wyoming with a crazed former client who was wearing a clever disguise. Lucinda survived the coma, but came out of it with amnesia. She slowly recovered at her mother's home in Indiana.

Erin again entered our lives when anti-fishing activist Hannah Markel and Lucinda's former husband, Robert Ellsworth-Kent, decided to kill Erin and then Lucinda and me on the Yellowstone. They failed, and since that turmoil Erin has enjoyed a pleasant few years without a homicide in Park County.

This time, Erin had sought us out. As she walked toward the house and I rushed to the bedroom to dress, I wondered whether the call was social or professional.

"Hi, Macduffy," Erin said, hugging me when I entered the kitchen. "How long has it been?"

"With you, always too long. Congratulations on becoming the undersheriff. Is that something like an undertaker or an underdog or being underfoot?"

"No, it's related to being underpaid. . . . The county needs to increase your taxes and my pay."

"Next you're going to tell me either that I'm under arrest or you're married. Or both."

"Not yet, but I'm working on that . . . I mean the arrest part but not marriage. . . . Macduff, does the name Carter Davis mean anything?"

"Our Montana governor?" I answered.

"I'm surprised you knew that. You don't like politics. Or most politicians."

"I know his term's up in a year or so. Are you going to run to succeed him? Your Kendo sword might be useful when you're in office."

"What do you know about Davis?" she asked.

"Nothing. . . . I've never thought much about him. I guess he's OK. Besides, I'm having enough trouble with a different Davis, the attorney general in Wyoming. Do you know anything about *him*?"

"Yes, I talked to *him* this morning. He called from Cheyenne. He's a cousin of our governor, and I understand he wants to be the next Wyoming governor."

"Did you talk about politics?"

"We talked about *you*."

"Did he mention a man named Arthur Spence?"

"He did. He believes you murdered Spence."

"The short story is that he needs votes from Teton County to be elected governor. He wants to make a big splash in Jackson, so he's using the Spence death, calling it a homicide and pinning it on me."

"What have you done to Davis to make him so mad?" Erin asked.

"I guess he doesn't like fishing guides. He's known to hate Easterners. Especially Yankees. I didn't choose to be either; I was *born* in Connecticut. Davis told me I'm a blemish on the development of a great Western state."

"And so he goes after you and gets a lot of publicity and a conviction and then wins the election? And he doesn't care what happens to you?"

"That's about it," I replied.

"Davis called me from Cheyenne and made sure I knew he was our governor's cousin. He wants me to arrest you and send you to Cheyenne. You have to give him credit for his ambition."

"Do you know if I've been arrested in Wyoming?"

"Not that I know of."

"Has he given you a copy of a fugitive warrant and formally requested extradition?"

"No. He said I should respect the attorney general of a sister state and send you based only on his oral request. He offered to send a plane here to the Gardiner Airport and 'take Brooks off your hands.'"

"What did you tell him, Erin?"

"That there's a procedure for extradition that we take seriously here in Montana. I told him you'd have to have been arrested in Wyoming and given an opportunity here in a Park County court to object to extradition. Would you object?"

"Of course I would object to being sent to Cheyenne. You'd have to serve me with papers, and my house can be very hard to find. And we might just happen to have left for Florida."

"You *are* hard to find, now that I think of it. I doubt very much that I could find this cabin again."

"If you turn down Attorney General Davis, did he suggest he'd file papers in our courts for formal extradition?"

"He didn't expect to be turned down, and he quickly lost his composure. He said he'd call his cousin—our Governor Davis—and as a personal favor among family members, insist the governor 'make Brooks available.'"

"Have you met Governor Davis? You said you don't have any reason to dislike him."

"I've never tried to meet him. He's been very successful as a rancher but a failure at home. Broken marriage with charges of abuse and a court order not to approach his former wife. One kid in a Mexican jail for transporting drugs. And there's a thirteen- or fourteen-year-old daughter who just gave birth to an out-of-wedlock child. That's not a good record."

"Erin, I don't want a Montana State Highway Patrol car with a couple of burley troopers showing up here to take me away in handcuffs to a waiting plane at Gardiner."

"A kidnapping! I hadn't thought of it that way," Erin said.

"It is. More or less."

"Like the recent kidnapping of a U.S. citizen from the Bahamas. He was involuntarily dislodged from some Bahama island and taken to D.C. to be tried," Erin added.

"That sounds different," I replied. "Lucinda's been telling you stories. Don't believe her."

"We can talk about that another time, Macduffy."

"My suggestion," Lucinda said, "is that I call our governor's office, try to get through to talk to Davis, and ask if he's talked to his cousin about you."

"You probably won't get through, but if you did, let me know how I could help," offered Erin.

"It would give us some idea about where our governor stands on helping his cousin in this matter," said Lucinda. "He may not know about it, meaning he hasn't talked to his Wyoming cousin. Or he may *say* he knows about it and Montana is considering rendering some kind of assistance."

"Meaning I need to be ready to leave the state. . . . I can be in Idaho in a couple of hours."

"But you can't go to Wyoming or to Florida," Erin insisted.

"That leaves a lot of alternatives. I'd best not tell you where, Erin, but I will have a cell phone so we can talk, even if I'm in some place like Connecticut."

"Or the Bahamas?" she asked.

35

A WEEK LATER

ERIN STAYED ANOTHER HOUR, AND WE TALKED about everything other than Spence and the two Davis cousins and Lucinda's captivity by Ellsworth-Kent and Covington. We brought Erin up to date on Elsbeth's time at UF, our drive to Montana by way of Calgary, and the little fishing we had done except for Canada.

We didn't go into the details describing our few days at Hope Town. Telling her our visit was for rest and relaxation, I added a few facts she didn't know about the barbed wire deaths on the Gallatin, careful how I explained Grace Justice's role. I didn't mention Rachel Hart's death, and Erin didn't ask about it. And I said nothing about Juan Pablo Herzog in Guatemala and the skull on the mantle. All in all, there is much Erin doesn't know about us.

We agreed to keep in contact if either of us learned anything new about the Spence case. I viewed it as a case of where, as singer Waylon Jennings labeled it, "good ol' boy" politics could trump justice.

That I had not taken the Spence case seriously before Erin arrived bothered Lucinda. She had stuck pretty close to me since she arrived last Thanksgiving and I think was concerned I might be taken to jail. That would not help with her recovery. I tried to convince her Wyoming's Davis was another bumbling political hack who was not a threat.

Teton County has voted Democrat since 1992, except for the younger Bush. Jackson has proven to be one of the *least* conservative areas in Wyoming. Strangely, educated young people are often liberal and idealistic until they realize how hard it is to earn a living. Those few who achieve unexpected wealth and convert to conservatism along the way to retain that wealth often retire to places like Aspen, Bar Harbor, Nantucket, Taos, or Jackson, and convert *back* to liberal causes because they don't feel any financial pinches anymore. Tom Wolfe said it better in *Radical Chic & Mau-Mauing the Flak Catchers*. Jackson apparently has more than its share of Wolfe's "limousine liberals" and "upper class Leftists" and that worries AG Davis as he envisions himself moving up to be governor.

Wyoming papers have consistently predicted Davis could win the governorship *only* by not losing Teton County by a significant margin. That's where I came in, according to Davis' distorted view. I was the chance to shift the county to vote Republican. In Davis's view I'm a disposable asset.

When Erin went back to her office in Livingston, she decided to call the Montana governor. Erin was amazed when his secretary quickly put her through.

"Ms. Giffin, or should I say Undersheriff Giffin? What can I do for Ken Rangley's protégé and favorite deputy?" Davis said to Erin's surprise. How did he know her?

"Thank you. You seem to know me. Have we met? Have you talked recently to your cousin in Cheyenne?"

"I talk to him as infrequently as possible. We don't get along. He's power hungry. I ran here in Montana on a one-and-out basis. I said a second term was only possible if I received at least a two-thirds vote of support for a second term by the party officers and at least eighty percent of a primary vote. . . . How do you know my cousin, Undersheriff? May I call you Ms. Giffin?"

"Call me Erin, please."

"And I'm Carter. Even my grandchildren call me that."

Erin told the governor first about the Spence death, including the medical examiner's report that concluded that the death was accidental, and then about the call six months later from Attorney General Davis to Macduff Brooks. She said AG Davis was trying to convince Brooks to go to Cheyenne for questioning about the Spence death, for which Davis held Brooks responsible.

"I know who Macduff Brooks is, but I don't know him personally. Isn't he called the 'celebrity guide'?"

"For good reasons. He's a good guy, Governo . . . Carter. I've known him for over a decade. Sheriff Ken Rangley considers Macduff one of his best friends. They fish together when Ken can get away for a few hours."

"Brooks lives on Mill Creek," Davis said as a statement more than a question.

"He does. I had breakfast there today with Lucinda and Macduff. Do you know Mill Creek?"

"Very much. Do you know the house a little before the beginning of the national forest and the gravel road where there is a modest drop off to the north or left? It slopes down to the creek."

"I know that. You don't see the house from the Mill Creek Road. As a sheriff's deputy I've probably been on every road in the County."

"Go knock on the door there sometime. That's my parents' house. They moved there from Billings two decades ago when my dad retired. They're both in their early 80s."

"Do you know where Lucinda and Macduff live?"

"Yes. A little further upstream from my parents and on the south side of the road and the creek?"

"Do you know his wife Lucinda's ranch? The big place even further up the creek called Arrogate Ranch."

"It's beautiful. Which house do they live in?"

"The smaller cabin. They use the ranch house sometimes. It's where they met at a Thanksgiving dinner Lucinda had for some colleagues in her Manhattan investment firm. She also invited her new neighbor, Macduff, who she had not met. Macduff was the only guest to show up. That was fifteen years ago. They want to keep the house for now. But almost all the land has been given to the National Conservancy."

"My cousin wouldn't like that, giving up the land so it's out of the reach of miners, lumber companies, and developers. But I admire what Ms. Brooks did. . . . How can I help you, Erin?"

"You already have. I was worried that you and your cousin might do something together that's not according to the Montana extradition law and send Macduff to Cheyenne."

"Not a chance. And if my cousin does try extradition, I'll add my two cents to support any move to block Brooks's removal from Montana."

"May I tell Macduff that?"

"What? Did I say something? . . . Use your good judgment. Brooks probably *should* know. But the public needn't share that knowledge."

"Do you travel down this way very often, Carter?"

"To visit my parents, I do. It's about three hours by car. I sometimes fly from here in Helena to Gardiner. Mom or Dad pick me up there."

"When you come next time, let me introduce you to Lucinda and Macduff?"

"I'd like that. I know about Macduff's work in the state with Project Healing Waters. Anything that helps combat wounded disabled vets has my backing. . . . Next time I go to Mill Creek, I'll take my wife, and we'll all get together. When we finish talking, I'm going to call my parents and tell them to stop in and say hello to Lucinda and Macduff."

"I'll call Lucinda and tell her."

"Thanks. And I'd like to see you and Ken the next time I'm in Livingston."

"Consider it done. Thanks for your help."

Erin hung up, thrilled about her talk with Davis. She told Ken about the call and phoned Lucinda and Macduff.

36

A WEEK LATER

LUCINDA WAS WASHING WUFF ON THE BACK porch when Erin called. Wuff hates water, and when she saw Lucinda head toward her with the pail holding shampoo and an old towel, she bolted for the bedroom and hid back up against the wall under our king size bed. Lucinda finally coaxed her out with a third cookie, carried her to the porch, hosed her down, and applied the soapy shampoo. Then Lucinda's cell phone rang. She let Wuff loose from her grasp for the moment it took to pull the phone from her jeans pocket, and Wuff headed straight back into the house, leaving a trail of suds behind.

"What do you want?" Lucinda said curtly.

"That's not a very cordial way to greet a caller," said Erin.

"Would you like a dog? You need a pet."

"What did Wuff do? She's a sweet sheltie."

"Not when she's being washed."

"I'm going to make your day; I just talked to our governor. Can Macduff listen in while I tell you?"

"He's in Emigrant at the bank."

Erin related every word of her conversation with Carter Davis.

"I can't wait for Macduff to get back. He'll be ecstatic."

"Call me first thing when Macduff arrives, and we can talk about what to do."

Macduff drove in a few minutes later. Before he walked up the porch steps, Lucinda called Erin and told her Macduff was at home and the cellphone speaker was on."

"What's up?" asked Macduff. "You were here a couple of hours ago."

Erin repeated what she'd told Lucinda.

"What's next, if anything?" asked Erin. "You owe me a dinner, Macduffy."

"Give Attorney General Davis a few days to talk to and be rebuffed by his cousin in Helena. Then he'll have to decide what to do. He won't give up his intention to run for Wyoming's governorship next year, but he may think of a more certain way to get votes in Jackson."

"Bribing vote counters?" Lucinda asked.

"Not quite that. Maybe legitimately campaigning exclusively on issues important to Jackson folk."

"You mean taking a position whether he believes in it or not?"

"Sure," replied Erin. "And whether it's contrary to what he says to the voters in Laramie or Cheyenne or elsewhere. That's not unusual for politicians."

"I do owe you a dinner," I said.

"Forget it. You haven't paid off past favors yet. I gotta go. Duty calling." She hung up.

"Macduff, would it be safe to drive to Jackson and stay at Dornan's a few nights? We could float Deadman's Bar to Moose on the Snake, take John and Sarah to dinner, and maybe hike up Cascade Canyon to fish for brookies."

"I'll call John and ask what he thinks.

"Lucinda, what on earth is that wet mess on the floor from the front door to our bedroom?"

"Ask *your* dog, if you can coax her out from under our bed."

Just then Wuff appeared in the bedroom doorway. She was damp and most of the suds had dried on her back. She gave a slight bark. It was 5:05 p.m.

Her supper was five minutes late.

37

A WEEK LATER

GRAND TETON NATIONAL PARK IS HARD TO surpass for scenery and fly fishing. But I've had some bad moments driving U.S. 89 south from Moran Junction and passing the steep drive down to Deadman's Bar on the Snake River.

My first wife El died on an April day on that part of the river, when an incompetent guide floated us into a killer strainer, a twenty-foot high pile of tree limbs deposited in the middle of the river from the then recent ice melt. The melt had gushed down the creeks and streams and swarmed into the river, turning it chocolate with silt, increasing the flow rate, and randomly depositing debris carried downstream.

Our drift boat broke into pieces and left me hanging in the tree limbs, but swept El downstream to her death. Her body wasn't found. For seventeen years I believed our about-to-be-born child had perished in the womb of El. But a Maine couple named Carson pulled El from the water and the wife, a physician, saved the child by performing a Caesarian birth. She couldn't save El. The child was a girl who the couple named Elsbeth when they found that name on a bracelet on the mother. Childless, the couple kept and raised the girl as Elsbeth Carson at their home in Greenville, Maine.

Mr. Carson died when Elsbeth was sixteen. Just before Mrs. Carson passed away the following year, she told Elsbeth the true story. With some help Elsbeth learned I was her father, and she showed up at our door in Montana. She's been with us since, adores Lucinda and Wuff, and now is near receiving her B.A. at the University of Florida in Gainesville, my place of work and home for ten years on either side of El's death. For those twenty years I was Professor Maxwell Hunt at the UF law school. How I came to be a fly fishing guide in Montana is another story.

El is buried high in the Sierra Madre Mountains southwest of Saratoga in southeast Wyoming. A lone, small marker honors her. Elsbeth and I try to visit there every summer; it's a long day's drive for us from Mill Creek. I was concerned about making the trip this summer because of Davis. Cheyenne is only a two-hour drive east of where El's buried.

With Davis again on my mind—I had tried to forget him the past three days since talking to his cousin in Helena—I remembered I promised myself to call John Kirby and tell him about our conversation. It was a good time to call; I was sitting in our kitchen having a sandwich and looking at a map of the Smith River and thinking about doing the float between Camp Baker and Eden Bridge. It meant five days on the river and required a special permit to float through mostly privately owned land. It's the only limited-entry permit procedure for floating a Montana River. It's not easy to win a permit; the number of applications is approaching 10,000 for one of the nine launches allowed per day each summer. I made a note on the edge of the map to apply next year and at least give it a shot.

"Should I call John and tell him about my talk with Governor Davis?" I asked Lucinda, who was sitting across from me struggling to fill in a few words on a *N.Y. Times* crossword puzzle.

"Yes, because he should know what's going on. After all, John was supposed to guide Spence, but Spence never showed up. The next day, John guided Scott Bradford, and they found Spence's body. But since then increasingly it looks as though you're off the hook, as long as you stay in Montana."

"You mean if 'we' stay in Montana?"

"*No.* If it means staying here from December through March, you're on your own. I've decided warm blankets and a fireplace aren't enough."

"I thought marriage was sharing the good and the bad."

"There are limits when it's the bad."

I refilled my coffee and called John. Sarah answered and she didn't sound cordial.

"I didn't think you'd call, Macduff. You've left John dangling by staying in the safety of Montana while he's within reach of our attorney general in Cheyenne. Why don't you go to Cheyenne and talk to Davis. I think Davis knows you're in the clear. You'd already left when Spence went missing. The AG wants the matter pursued here, and if you're not willing to come and talk directly to Davis, John becomes the target."

"I can't imagine Davis would do that."

"Can't imagine! This minute John is in handcuffs in a state vehicle on his way to Cheyenne. Yesterday, he was arrested for the murder of Spence. I don't understand it all. The head of investigations at the Teton County Sheriff's Office, Huntly Byng, refused to go along with Davis and Davis is doing it through his Wyoming AG office."

"I'm mortified, Sarah. Did John say anything about Davis's brother, our governor here in Montana? The AG put pressure on our governor to send me to Cheyenne, without following the extradition procedures. The two Davises don't get along. They rarely communicate."

"What does that have to do with John?" Sarah asked.

"It may mean, since our governor will tell his cousin that Montana won't help, your AG is taking it out on John. In fact, I suspect Governor Davis talked to AG Davis in the last week and the AG was turned down. And he's probably furious."

"That's what must have happened. John told me before they left this morning that he'd heard through Byng that Davis was livid about not being able to deal with Montana. . . . John will be back soon. We think he'll be let out on bail but restricted to the Jackson area. So they'll bring him back in a couple of days."

"Does John have a lawyer?" I asked.

"He does. You know the guy here in Jackson who wears Western buckskin, tooled leather boots, and a Stetson hat. And a huge gaudy silver belt buckle. He's on what seems to be half the billboards in the county. But he's a terrific lawyer when you want a successful defense."

"Only one person fits that description—Harry Smart. Is it true he's never faced a guilty verdict?"

"How much do you believe is true in TV ads? Especially about personal injury and defense lawyers."

"I don't know. How much can you read of the dozen or more lines of fine print at the end of a PI lawyer's ad that's on your screen for four seconds?"

"We have to play the game," Sarah replied. "Smart plays it best here in Jackson."

"Sarah, I know you're upset. Let me tell you about the conversation Erin Giffin from the Park County Sheriff's Office had with Montana Governor Davis. Do you know he and the Wyoming AG are cousins?"

"I didn't even know the name of the Montana governor. And I don't know anything about Erin Giffin. Tell me."

Over the next half-hour I repeated what Erin told me about her conversation with Montana Governor Davis and afterwards with Lucinda and me.

"It's politics at work," said Sarah. "It sounds as though Governor Davis called his cousin, or vice versa, not long after the governor talked with Erin. I'm thinking that the conversation didn't go well for our AG. If he was mad at the outcome, he decided that he'd focus on John and immediately got an arrest warrant. Why a court would issue one is a sad reflection on our justice system. The Jackson ME said the death was an accident, and I've not seen or heard anything different."

"Sarah, I'm coming down. I'll leave this afternoon and be there for dinner. If Lucinda goes with me, we'll stay at Dornan's."

"Macduff. Don't come. If Davis learns you're here, and he may be thinking you'd come as soon as you heard John was arrested, it's not hard for Davis to check who's coming south from Yellowstone or over the Teton pass from Idaho."

"I'll take a chance. . . . Lucinda's nodding about going with me. We may borrow or rent a car."

"Promise me you won't drive one of yours in this state?"

"OK. We'll go to the Bozeman Airport and rent a car in Lucinda's name and go south through Victor, Idaho, and over Teton Pass into Jackson. I'll call when we get in."

When Sarah hung up, Lucinda and I packed quickly.
"Why are you taking fly rods?" Lucinda asked.

"We have to come back sometime. We'll come through the park and fish. And if things work out, John and I might float the Snake and talk as much as we fish."

We reached Dornan's a bit before 10:00 p.m. and settled in. I plugged in my cellphone that showed seven percent power remaining. And only one bar of reception. In the morning we would find a spot with cellphone power and be back in touch with the world.

I promised to call Sarah before breakfast.

38

LATER THAT NIGHT - MOOSE

AS WE CLIMBED INTO BED, I WAS TIRED FROM the stress of talking to Sarah, weighing the alternatives, conversing with Lucinda during the drive to Jackson, and being too weary and missing dinner. I tossed and turned, trying to decide the most certain way to get John released.

A little after midnight I was startled by someone knocking on our door. When we arrived the keys had been in an envelope taped to the office door. A note said to stop by the office in the morning.

Could that someone be the owner of the cabins? I assumed not; he closed down in the evening and used the office door to leave keys in envelopes for late arrivals.

The knock came again, this time a bit louder.

Lucinda went to the living room window, slightly opened the drapery, and said quietly, "There *is* someone at the door. Turn the outside door light on."

I nodded and turned the light switch. The front stoop was flooded with light. Lucinda saw a person at the door, bundled with coat, scarf, and hat, but she couldn't tell if it were male or female.

The knock came again, and I decided to open the door. When I cracked it slightly, a voice said, "Macduff! It's Sarah. I'm freezing. Let me in."

She stepped in, brushing past me rubbing her hands for warmth.

"I had to come," she added. "You obviously haven't heard the 11:00 news, and I couldn't get through by cell phone."

"It must be important if you've come here at this hour. Is it about John? Is he OK?"

"He's fine. Look at this YouTube."

She tapped on her phone and then set it on the table. It was a video of a man getting off an office conference table. And getting off a small female who was beneath him. They were both naked and trying to cover themselves. The man hid behind a Wyoming flag next to the table and then behind a larger window curtain. The female sat on the floor sobbing.

"This hit the news about when you apparently went to bed this evening," exclaimed Sarah. "Guess who the man is?"

"He must be important to get your attention."

"A friend called me and said watch it. It's gone viral on YouTube. Lucinda! Macduff! That's the Wyoming Attorney General's office. And that's our Attorney General Myron Davis."

"Who's the woman?"

"You mean the *girl!* She's an intern in the AG's office. She's sixteen, a minor!"

"How was this video taken?"

"The last meeting on the AG's schedule was with some twenty members of the Cheyenne League of Women's Voters. They were apparently late and being rushed to the AG's office before he left. He must have assumed they weren't coming. The group had pledged to support him for governor. One of the women had her cell phone ready to take a video of the group meeting with the AG. She certainly got an impressive video!"

"Have you come twenty miles on a cold night to show us a video?"

"Yes. There's more to tell you. Davis was arrested immediately because the intern was underage. She turned out to be the *daughter* of Davis's most generous financial supporter. Davis wasn't handcuffed; he was a miserable sobbing wreck and no threat to run. He told his private secretary something, and she issued a statement an hour later.

"Davis resigned effective immediately. His statement said he had been seduced by the girl! And that when the truth was told, he would be exonerated. He said he resigned only because he was thinking of the best interests of the state.

"One of the women asked him about his intention to run for the governor's position and he said that was off. But, he added, he knew the good people of Wyoming would understand the truth and he expected his supporters would forgive him and demand he run."

"How does this affect John?"

"I called Harry Smart. He was in his law office listening to the news about Davis. He knows the person in the AG office who will be acting AG. Smart had talked with him a few days ago about John's case and the assistant said it was crazy and some kind a vendetta Davis had against John, or more likely against the town of Jackson, which might cost him the election. But he said he couldn't convince Davis to drop the charges and accept the Jackson ME's conclusions."

"Will John be released?"

"He's out and should be home tonight. One of the attorney general's assistants is driving him. Come for dinner tonight. You *must*."

John arrived home in early afternoon. A dozen family and friends were at the house to meet him, plus a couple of reporters and a TV crew.

Lucinda and I arrived at six. To pass the time, we had borrowed John's drift boat and floated the Deadman's Bar to Moose section of the Snake. We both caught some nice cutthroats.

I estimated that my biggest one was an inch longer than Lucinda's!

39

THE NEXT DAY - JACKSON

LUCINDA AND I SLEPT IN THE NEXT DAY. IT WAS 10:00 when we finally sat and had coffee on the porch of our Dornan's cabin. The Grand Tetons stood out as grand as ever, and we knew they were live and growing. It looked like a good day to do something we hadn't done in a long time.

Grand Teton National Park had opened the prior weekend, and we would be among the year's first hikers to circle Jenny Lake. Sarah took a day off, and she and John joined us. Lucinda went to the grocery at Dornan's and bought us all lunch.

Two hours later, half-way along the west side of the lake, we stopped on a grassy slope overlooking the water. It was so smooth and reflective that the image of landscape above the lake was suspended upside down on the water below. Lucinda took dozens of photographs.

"Can you believe what has happened in the last few days?" Sarah asked.

"It was a scary adventure," I admitted.

"It was just one more day in the lives of a couple of popular fly fishing guides," John said.

"Couldn't you pick your friends more carefully, John?" Sarah asked, grinning at me.

"I didn't pick Macduff. The truth is, and this stays with us, Sarah," John added, avoiding looking at me, "in my first year of guiding more than two decades ago, I was scheduled to take a couple from Gainesville, Florida, fishing. He was a Professor of International Law at UF in Gainesville."

"Is this something you made up, John?" I asked, aghast at John's connection with the fatal float that took my wife El. Where was he going with this?

"I had to fly to Georgia," John continued, avoiding my stare, "because my dad had a sudden heart attack. The outfitter I guided for found a substitute. His name was Steve Brewster, and he was known as Brew, an obvious reference to his drinking habit.

"Brew took the couple down the Snake from Deadman's Bar to Moose. It was spring, and the melting ice streaked down the creeks and streams and the rivers. It had abated sufficiently to clear the river enough to fish. But the water had propelled tree parts downstream that formed numerous strainers on the river.

"The part close to Moose was the worst. Brew apparently panicked at a particularly large strainer and ran into its middle. The rest I've told you about before, Sarah. It was gruesome. The papers covered it extensively, including photographs of Professor Hunt.

The woman died, we believed taking her unborn child with her. The woman was named Elsbeth. She was called El.

"We can guess what happened next," John said, looking at me, "because *you* have an Elsbeth Brooks whose age fits perfectly with the age that child would have been today. We know Elsbeth Brooks as the daughter of you, Macduff, but her mother's name was not Brooks. It was *Hunt*. She was the wife of the law professor who survived the crash, but for nearly two decades lived a life believing his daughter had perished."

What I was hearing was causing me to sweat profusely. John had not looked at me since he began his story.

"I suspect Lucinda knows all this, but Sarah doesn't, and I have some gaps. But it's clear to me that Macduff Brooks was once Maxwell Hunt." John turned his head for a second to see my reaction.

"Why is he saying all this?" I wondered. "What good can come of it?"

"I met Macduff Brooks a little more than a dozen years ago, a decade after the accident on the Snake," John continued. "His appearance had changed from when he was Professor Hunt. Different hair length and style, moustache, and what had to be a little plastic surgery to his nose and ears. And eyeglasses. I've never seen you without those, Macduff. Let me have them for a minute." He was finally looking at me.

Reluctantly, I took mine off and handed them to him.

"Macduff," John said as he handed me his fishing license. "Read the finest print to me."

I did.

"Now, look down near the edge of the lake where there's a pile of brush. What do you see?"

"Is this a game?"

"Humor me. What do you see?"

"There are three trout about two feet deep, both facing the shore."

"Anything more?"

"A bird on one branch. It looks like a White-Crowned Sparrow. It has black and white streaks on the top of its head."

"Now look across the lake toward the boat dock. That must be a couple of miles away. How many boats are at the dock?"

"One, two, and now I see a third."

John handed my glasses to Sarah. Lucinda sat amazed at what was going on.

"Sarah, is this a pretty strong prescription?"

"No. I suspect its clear glass," she said holding the glasses to her eyes. "What's the point of this?"

"Macduff," John asked, still looking at me directly, "did Professor Maxwell Hunt wear glasses?"

"He had perfect vision," I murmured.

"You've never told me about your life before you arrived in Montana. We know that until a decade after El's death, you taught international law at UF in Gainesville. What we don't know, and would like to learn from you, is where were you between the time Professor Hunt was reported to have died of a stroke and the day you arrived in Montana?"

"Why do you need to know that?" I asked quietly.

"You've helped us beyond measure. Lucinda has told me about your unwillingness to stay out of Wyoming and leave me alone facing Davis. Davis is through, as is any further investigation of you as a suspect in Spence's death. . . . I'd like to fill in the gaps in the life of a best friend."

Lucinda was looking at me, nodding.

"Lucinda learned about my past bit by bit," I said, knowing I had to be honest with John and Sarah. "I avoided telling her for a long time after we met. There still may be a few short gaps. . . . The short response is that what you have said is true. What's missing are two things. One is what I did between El's death and my reported death and what I did between that latter time and when I moved to Montana.

"The first period lasted ten years. All I can tell you is that for the last decade that I taught, I was despondent over El's death and increasingly accepted work abroad for the State Department. Finally, in Guatemala, I was beaten nearly to death by the man who is currently President—Juan Pablo Herzog. Since that reported death, he has refused to accept that I died and has vengefully been seeking to learn who I became and where I lived. Fortunately, with the help of some government people, Herzog has been frustrated.

"The time between my reported death, which obviously ended my teaching and living in Gainesville and when I arrived in Montana was spent in . . . ."

"It was only a few months or so," John interrupted, "and I suspect was spent in D.C. It began with you being placed in a protection program from which you emerged as Macduff Brooks the fly fishing guide who soon moved to Montana. That's my guess."

"You're right."

"One question. In your time abroad before and after becoming Macduff, were you working with a government group known as the 'Agency'?"

"I don't know what you're talking about," I said, a slight smile breaking across my face and Lucinda showing her engaging Cheshire cat grin.

"What on earth has just happened?" inquired Sarah, who was staring at the lake as she listened.

"Nothing," Lucinda replied, "except that now you have knowledge that few possess. Elsbeth, of course, and Dan Wilson in D.C. There's an Agency person based in Montana who's assigned to Macduff, but knows only he is in a protection program and not why or who he was before."

"There must be others at the Agency who were involved in placing you in the program that know all about this," said Sarah.

"A few. Several have died. Three because they were threats to my protection and all related to Herzog's search for me."

"What good is there in telling *me* about this? " Sarah asked us both.

"I can answer that," I said. "I knew that John was aware of certain gaps in my life. Until today I thought what John didn't know included everything before my becoming Macduff. John and I have developed a friendship too close for keeping him wondering."

"When John wonders about you, I do, too," added Sarah. "I've lived with suspicions about you, Macduff. Aren't you worried I might accidentally disclose something useful to Herzog?"

"No. Knowing more will hopefully result in your saying less about me to other people. . . . Herzog doesn't know about me and doesn't know about either of you. That differs from the agents who were at the meeting placing Macduff in the protection program. One met with Herzog and was about to turn over the information for a very large sum when he was shot by a sniper from an adjacent building.

"Herzog is getting closer. He knows Hunt did not die of a stroke. He learned from another agent that Hunt was involved in something to do with fish. Fortunately, Herzog's off on a wild goose chase now, thinking whoever Hunt is lives in Alaska."

"Are you sure Elsbeth and Wilson are the only ones who know?" Sarah asked.

"No, others know part of what I've told you. That includes Elsbeth's college roommate and best friend, Sue. Possibly Erin

Giffin and Ken Rangley in Livingston. Maybe Huntly Byng here in Jackson. Our two housekeepers, here and in Florida, are assumed not to know. Luisa in Guatemala. Grace Justice, who died a year ago, knew probably as much as anyone other than Elsbeth and Wilson. That's about it. . . . Remember that there are two groups with some information. A few knew Professor Hunt but don't know about Macduff. The others, like you two, are those who know Macduff but not about Hunt."

"I'm exhausted, and not from the hike," said Sarah.

"I feel good about you two knowing," interjected Lucinda. "If anything happened to the two of us, we need you to help Elsbeth. We want you to know what she's dealing with."

"John," I said, "I've been looking at that bird. It's the male, not the female."

"You don't need these," John said holding my glasses in front of him. "But I assume you want them back."

"I do. It's one of the minor prices I pay to be alive, have a partner like Lucinda, a daughter like Elsbeth, and friends like you two."

John handed me the eyeglasses, and I put them on. I didn't need them to see but to *feel* more like Macduff Brooks than Professor Maxwell Hunt.

After our walking circumnavigation of Jenny Lake, we drove the few miles to Jackson. John's attorney Harry Smart was coming out of the Wort Hotel. We later learned he had arranged a press conference at the hotel and taken full and exclusive credit for convincing the Attorney General's office that John was innocent and his arrest had no basis.

He never mentioned that the reason for John's release was not the offer Smart had placed on the table, but the intern Davis had placed on the table.

40

A WEEK LATER – MILL CREEK

ATTORNEY GENERAL DAVIS WAS SULKING IN A Cheyenne jail, arrested for having sex with a minor and denied bail.

Erin Giffin called the other Davis, Montana's governor, and filled him in on what I had learned and passed on to Erin. His reply expressed embarrassment for his cousin's actions. He said he hoped his cousin had the sense to face his punishment and wished, like British convicts from 1788 to 1868, his cousin could be "transported" to live out his life if not in Australia perhaps in Greenland. At least he wanted him "to get the hell out of Dodge."

Sarah and John sent Lucinda and me a postcard from Hope Town, where they went to celebrate their fifteenth wedding anniversary and avoid us for a week. The card was an aerial view of the town, and Lucinda pointed out Reginald Covington's mansion. Sarah and John wrote a note on the postcard that they had a meal at the Conch Shell and sat at the table we described as using the evening we kidnapped Covington.

Lucinda and I returned to Mill Creek driving through Yellowstone Park. Nothing unexpected happened. We liked that.

41

TWO DAYS LATER – MONTANA

JOHN KIRBY CALLED FROM JACKSON. JOHN AND Sarah were home from the Bahamas. Sarah had fished for the first time in years and caught three mahi mahi. John caught one ladyfish and the flu. He told Sarah that was the end of her fishing career.

"We're delighted to be home, Macduff. We were gone eight days. I have twenty-three messages from people whose names I never heard who want me to guide them on my drift boat. Now I know what it's like to be a celebrity guide. Maybe not as well-known and in demand as you.

"There is one matter I can't get out of my head. It's the only thing about the whole Spence episode that bothers me. *Was he murdered?*"

"John, you and I know the Jackson ME concluded that it was an accidental drowning, that Spence was in the water presumably fishing and somehow became tangled in the bottom grasses. He fell and drowned. The Park Service accepted that."

"The guy I took guiding when we found Spence—Scott Bradford—says he saw nothing about Spence that suggested a murder. The local Jackson paper supports the ME's view. Former Attorney General Davis's chief assistant says Davis called it a murder only to get votes in Jackson. The public agrees it was an accident. I'm happy to live with that. But I have this overriding notion that no murder should go unsolved and unpunished and that Spence was probably murdered."

"Don't let it become something that affects you or Sarah," I suggested. "Or us. I know how you feel about seeing justice prevail. . . . What is it specifically about Spence's death that bothers you?"

"The black fly. I can't figure it out," John replied. "You and I know about the body found in Florida that also had a black fly. The second time makes me wonder. Not only what the black fly meant but why was it used another time? Was it a trademark by the same killer? A serial killer who may strike again? But two deaths a couple of thousand miles apart doesn't earn the 'serial' label. Maybe wearing a black fly is becoming popular with guides? *I've* never seen one on anyone else. Nor for sale in any fly fishing catalogs."

"Do you know if the police checked different fly shops in Jackson," I asked, "to see if any carried or knew anything about black flies like the one found on Spence?"

"I talked to two fly shop owners and they said 'no.' One looked through the shop's fly sources and found nothing similar. They had black Wooly Buggers that were slightly different. The truth is, Macduff, I've never tried to compare the two flies from photographs. I wonder if Byng or Abbott has. Of course, if they don't know about the other, they can't compare them."

"Couldn't a black fly be worn, for whatever reason, by fly fishermen in Maine or California or Oregon or Georgia?"

"Of course," said John. "But there's no reason for them to raise questions in any other places. There are only the two deaths associated with black flies.

"If we told Huntly Byng about the black fly and Rachel Hart's death in Florida, would he open a new investigation about Spence?" John asked.

"Probably. And that puts you back in the spotlight. And maybe me. I don't wish that on either of us. We don't know that Byng isn't aware of Hart's death. It was in many Florida papers. He has access to them online, but I don't know why he'd read one."

"Do you think Byng has checked *every* state for information about the black fly?" John asked.

"No. . . . Hart's death received scant attention in Florida. No one in St. Augustine asked *me* about it. Forget it. Let your notions about perfect justice moderate. Recognize we have imperfections throughout our system. Not just the justice system. Election fraud. Police brutality. Professional sports and the World Cup and Olympics. Oceans filled with plastics. You can name a dozen more."

"OK. But I'm still going to wake up at night wondering about the black fly."

"Don't do anything more than count sheep and go back to sleep."

"I'll try."

42

THE NEXT AFTERNOON - MILL CREEK

I WAS INSTALLING BETTER TIE-DOWN STRAPS ON *Osprey* in my drift boat storage shed, oblivious to sounds from outside. Lucinda was removing invasive weeds along the creek with a boisterous gas-powered trimmer. And my cellphone, sitting under the morning newspaper on the kitchen table, was ringing and playing a noisy Perez Prado 1940s Cuban piece called "Que Rico el Mambo." Lucinda and I didn't hear a single note.

A half-hour later we finished our projects and made two afternoon cups of coffee. She had a Colombian decaf; I had my favorite Guatemalan Antigua. Keurig had brought the world of coffees to the rural mountains of Montana.

Back in the cabin, we both dropped into chairs in the living room.

"That's hard work," complained Lucinda.

"It wasn't hard for you a decade ago," I said.

"Are you implying I'm getting old?"

"Maybe not old, but *older*."

"You're treading on thin ice."

"Does it make you feel better for me to say *I'm* worn out from an hour's work on *Osprey?*"

"That's because you're getting old," she answered.

"I can't figure out the difference. I seem to be aging faster than you. When we were allegedly married, I was a decade older than you. Now, according to your calculations, I'm two decades older. Please explain."

"Never ask a woman a question about age."

"That's not an explanation."

"I never *explain* to you. I only *inform* you. *No more* questions or comments!"

The only thing that saved me from further confusion was the phone ringing from beneath the newspaper. Lucinda beat me to it.

"Hello, this is Lucinda."

"It's your protector in D.C."

"I *need* protection from Macduff, Dan."

"My abilities don't extend that far," he said.

"Is this going to be a pleasant call?" I called out so Dan could hear.

"When have I called you with good news?"

"Maybe today?"

"No such chance. Ready for some bad news?"

"Depends on what it is," Lucinda answered.

"It's about Reginald Covington."

"He's dead. Tell us. Get it over with. But I assume you're going to inform us that regrettably he escaped and is a fugitive somewhere in the U.S."

"He didn't have to escape. He had clever lawyers and the benefits of having political power at home in Nassau."

"Do we want to hear this?" Lucinda asked. "It's a beautiful day here in Paradise Valley. I can hear birds singing and Mill Creek cascading down the mountain. There are trout just waiting for us to cast an Adams or Royal Wulff their way. Do you have to tell us about Covington?"

"I thought you'd like to know. Not that you'll be pleased."

"Give Lucinda another minute to pour out our coffee and replace it with a Montana Whiskey and a Gentleman Jack, and we'll be ready."

The minute passed, and Dan began.

"You know something had to be done with Covington. Either be charged or let go."

"Wasn't he wanted by you on federal charges as well as by Florida, Montana, Idaho, and Wyoming authorities?" I asked.

"In an ideal world, yes. We keep proving it's not ideal."

"What did you prove this time?"

"Montana, Idaho, and Wyoming didn't want him. It's Ellsworth-Kent who was wanted for the wicker man and mistletoe murders. We don't know how much Covington knew about how Lucinda came to be with Ellsworth-Kent."

"And Florida?"

"We went through all that when Covington was implicated in one of the airboat murders—the killing of Grant Borders. It probably took place in the Bahamas, not in Florida. Covington likely killed Borders and took the body to the U.S.

The only person who might have testified against Covington was Grace Justice, who said Covington admitted to her in Florida that he had killed Borders. He was taunting her. Her office dropped the matter. Now Grace is dead. . . . That means any state trial in the U.S. is out."

"You didn't bring Covington here against his will to let him go. He was responsible for keeping Lucinda for eighteen months, hypnotized and deteriorating physically. It wasn't only Ellsworth-Kent. What about conspiracy by Covington? Or a deprivation of her civil rights?"

"Not provable according to Justice Department lawyers. As to Covington's allowing Lucinda to be kept hostage at his house, that occurred in Hope Town. Proof would be difficult. Especially without Bahamian cooperation."

"What about the hypnotherapist, Mira Cerna? She can testify."

"We've talked to her. She says 'no.' It might damage her reputation in Europe. We can't make her say anything to help us. We can't force her to appear as a witness in the U.S. The most we could do would be to take her deposition in Budapest, but even that has problems."

"There's more to this you haven't told us, Dan. What is it?"

"Politics. Which too often trumps justice and fairness."

"What's happened?"

"The Prime Minister of the Bahamas apparently has made a fortune from his business associations with Covington. Last week the Prime Minister was here in D.C. complaining about our holding Covington without charges being made. He talked with our Secretary of State, the Vice President, the top three at the Justice Department, the head of my Agency here in Langley, and the head of the DEA. The Bahamas help our DEA deal with the islands being used for drug trafficking. The trouble is that the PM's cards were better than ours. He has the aces."

"Where is Covington right now?"

"We know he flew to Miami to stay with friends as soon as we released him yesterday. When he arrives home in Hope Town, it won't be long before he learns that his lady friend, Candi, found his cash in the house and took it. That should quickly lead to his discovering she also took his Cayman account number and has all his money. Undoubtedly, the proceeds from his Cayman account are in a new numbered account in Switzerland or Liechtenstein. And Candi is nowhere to be found."

"He won't like that, Dan."

"Understandable."

"And he may blame *us*. Meaning Lucinda and me. And you. And John Smith, whoever he really was."

"Understandable."

"All meaning that he might want to take it out on us."

"Also understandable."

"That's your only comment?"

"I was thinking that, unlike the case with Juan Pablo Herzog, Covington knows where we all live."

"Yes."

"Just maybe," added Lucinda, "Covington doesn't know exactly where our place is here in Montana. But it wouldn't be hard to find this cabin. . . . I'll bet he knows your address in D.C."

"Thanks," said Dan. "Let's hope he spends his time tracking down what Candi's done. He knows she's now worth a lot more than he could ever get out of us."

"That's comforting. . . . Isn't it?"

43

A WEEK LATER – MILL CREEK

"WE TALKED THE FIRST WEEK OF APRIL, MR. Brooks, at the State Attorney's office in St. Augustine. Your lawyer, Muirhead, was there, but he didn't help keep the discussion on a very cordial level," Rosalie Abbott related to me on the phone very early one morning. She called when she arrived at her office at 8:00. I pointed out to her that it was 6:00 a.m. in Montana and that she woke me. She didn't apologize, and I expected it would be a brief phone conversation. Lucinda was still asleep. I had heard the phone and taken it into the kitchen.

"Ms. Abbott, you're a prosecutor. You're trying to win cases that you've concluded are worth prosecuting. What you don't seem to realize is that you have to do your own investigative work. You can't expect to identify someone you believe committed a crime and then have that person confess. Or answer questions that, if answered the way you hope, will be the main evidence to be used in the case at trial.

"Bill Muirhead is my lawyer. You can't blame him for being skeptical about your profession. Many, if not most, prosecutors aspire to build a reputation for success in gaining convictions that will lead to promotion. Maybe first at the county or state level, then perhaps to an appointment as a federal prosecutor, and even being appointed or elected to a judgeship, a state or federal attorney general position, or more. Would you like to be Florida's governor?"

"That's demeaning; I'm very pleased with my job."

"A lawyer from your county, who I assume prefers not to be named, told me soon after we last talked that you had been chair of a state committee on the future of the prosecutorial role in Florida and that you responded to a question about your future saying you hoped to be appointed head of the Florida State Attorney's office in your county because you had by far the highest conviction rate in the county."

"I think you're misstating the facts. What I said was that if I were asked to serve in such position, I would consider it my civic duty to accept."

"Same meaning, different words. . . . Why are you calling? You know my wife and I are in Montana. Today's only the eighth of July. We won't be back in Florida until after Thanksgiving. If you don't have something new about Rachel Hart's death, I suggest you find something to do other than revisit her death. Go read your ME's report again."

"That's why I called you. I did read it again. The report was lengthy. The District ME here was careful. He has a fine reputation. Like all MEs in Florida, he's a practicing physician in pathology. We don't have a state ME or county MEs. They are district based. Our ME is a licensed medical doctor, not like a lot of coroners across this country, who may be or have been funeral parlor directors or law enforcement officials. Ours also had a year of law school and then switched to medicine.

"The ME read medical records and investigator reports. That included toxicology reports searching for possible drug use by Hart. He had meetings with law enforcement officers from Crystal River and with Hart's family members. That included three of her four husbands.

"Since she was thought possibly to have drowned, water samples of the canal where her body was found were taken and examined.

"The ME's report on Rachel Hart was very detailed. With appendices it ran several dozen pages. It *was* thorough," she concluded.

"If it was so thorough, why haven't you accepted its conclusion that Hart died accidentally from falling in the canal and drowning?"

"Because I have *other* evidence."

"That contradicts the ME's conclusions?"

"I believe so. A matter he didn't want to cover."

"What is it?"

"Please understand that our ME is a very religious man. He's a Catholic extremely opposed to adultery or divorce. He sometimes turns his head the other way so he doesn't have to address those issues. He passes those cases on to an assistant ME. . . . But not in this case. His assistant was in the hospital.

"We know Rachel Hart was married four times and divorced three. She was apparently on her way to another divorce. Her fourth husband had moved out of their Sanibel condo. He was in California when Hart died."

"What does all that have to do with Hart's death?" I asked.

"When the ME was investigating the case, he expressed to his assistant when he visited him in the hospital that he was concerned about Hart having been married four times. He thought that was immoral and contrary to the commandments. He said he would not make any reference about that in his report."

"OK. But that doesn't answer my question."

"It will. Remember that Hart was still married when she was in Crystal River although it was apparently about to end.

The ME found semen in her vagina. That established she had sex with several people. It *didn't* include her husband. I believe you were one of the several people. I've learned you had adjoining rooms."

"Semen has DNA. I assure you the semen was not mine. Check my DNA. . . . Why are you pressing this? Who she had sex with was her business."

"I don't like Rachel Hart."

"Did you know her?"

"Not personally. I don't like the way she lived."

"Like the ME, you object to her multiple marriages and extra-marital sex?"

"I don't like divorce or infidelity."

"Are you married?"

"Divorced."

"Grounds?"

"Adultery. He was sleeping with my sister!"

"You're not displeased with Hart's death."

"No."

"Then why keep the matter alive by harassing me?"

"I don't like her and I don't like the people she knew."

"That includes me?"

"Yes."

"Knowing her did not mean having sex with her."

"You could have had sex with her using a condom. That would mean no DNA in the semen but there was your DNA in her room."

"On the fly rod she was using to give me instructions."

"Yes. That's enough to believe you killed her."

"Did you find a used condom in her room?"

"I can't discuss that."

"I assume your next step is to ask for a new report by the assistant ME."

"No, that would discredit the ME. He's very well-liked and respected."

"And thus you decided to blame somebody at the IFFF program and that happens to be me."

"*No*. It means I'm not dropping you as a suspect. There are a couple of other suspects as well."

"I'll bet you have no evidence against any of them that would stand up in court."

"I don't agree with that."

"If you don't drop this harassment, I'll call Bill Muirhead. He will certainly disclose to the press what the ME did."

"You can't do that. I told you about the ME in confidence."

"I don't remember agreeing not to use any information you gave me while you questioned me, but *you* can use anything *I* talked about?"

"That's what the Miranda warning says."

"I think Muirhead will explain the Miranda warning to you if this gets to court. . . . I've had enough of you for the day. Call me when you decide to be reasonable."

I hung up. . . . Lucinda staggered into the kitchen.

"Macduff. It's only 6:45, and you were on the phone?"

"It was nothing. A crank call."

"Go back to sleep."

I would tell her about the call later.

44

THAT AFTERNOON – MILL CREEK

"MACDUFF, WHO WERE YOU TALKING TO AT 6:00 a.m.?" Lucinda asked the next morning.

"Ms. Abbott in Crystal River."

"Did she tell you you're finally free of her incessant accusations?"

"No. But she did tell me some things about Rachel Hart that likely mean the case is going nowhere if Abbott insists on keeping after me. One thing makes me laugh, but I try not to show it. Whenever I say 'Muirhead,' her voice changes, and she stutters."

Over morning coffee on the porch, I told Lucinda everything Abbott had said.

"Abbott's one of those physically attractive people who impress you until you talk to them awhile and understand how socially unattractive they are and you break off any further conversation."

"You didn't break it off with Hart," Lucinda said cryptically. "You went to bed having had a pleasant evening with her."

"I broke it off when I separated and headed for the men's room after our dinner. I think that was why I left so early the next morning; I didn't want to run into her and have her ask me to join her for breakfast. . . . By the time we finished dinner the previous evening, I had begun to understand why four husbands had left her."

"You *could* have left her earlier," Lucinda said, hinting doubt about my decisions.

"She was entertaining, although listening to her talk about her husbands was disturbing, like Henry VIII talking about his wives. At least beheading was not an option Hart chose. But she had two more marriages to tie King Henry, and they could both have ended in beheadings."

The cabin was quiet the remainder of the morning. Although Lucinda hadn't returned at the time of Hart's death in late September—she didn't join Elsbeth and me until Thanksgiving—she wasn't pleased with my dining alone with Hart.

"I'd like to go on a picnic, Macduff," Lucinda suggested quietly in the early afternoon. It was a clear, cool day in the mountains.

"For two years I haven't been up Mill Creek to the campsite where we like to fish," she added. "It's the middle of the week, and the site is unlikely to be taken. Did you fish there while I was gone?"

"No. I didn't fish much when you were gone. Mostly a few times with Elsbeth."

"I'll take a camera along with my bamboo rod. Blackened, burned pines above beds of wildflowers make an attractive subject of contrasts—dead trees and new flowers. . . . Do we take Wuff?" she asked.

"It's grizzly country. With *big* cats. And moose. We don't want Wuff to scare them. Let's leave her here. I'll feed her early and get the fishing gear. You find your cameras, and we can make some sandwiches together."

"We should take marshmallows. Graham crackers. Chocolate bars. And matches. I *must* have some S'mores!" Lucinda pleaded.

It hadn't rained in weeks, and our SUV left clouds of dust as we drove up Mill Creek Road, passing Lucinda's ranch, some church camps, parking for the popular trail to Passage Creek Falls, and further on where we slowed and watched some young people climbing a sheer rock cliff face that rose abruptly from the edge of the road.

The picnic and camping site we've preferred is the last of a group, just before a small bridge beyond which the road turns and begins a much steeper climb.

"Darn, Macduff. Someone's at *our* spot," Lucinda said as the site came into view.

A small place for cooking fires was forty feet off the road, and a much smaller Mill Creek than what passes behind our cabin was twenty feet further. Lucinda and I have caught trout at the campsite in water that seemed too shallow for any fish to live. A small dry fly dropped in four to five inches of the moving water often brought a strike and sometimes a seven- or eight-inch cutthroat.

A fisherman was sitting on a rock by the fire pit, facing away from us toward the creek. He was engaged in serious concentration, presumably looking for rises. We hoped he had caught some trout and drove on, crossing the small bridge and winding up the steep slope. Over the top we found a place to pull off we'd never seen. It was perfect, but fires were not allowed. We unfolded two chairs and sat to enjoy a view new for us.

"There go your S'mores," I said. "No fires up here."

"That's OK. We can have our sandwiches and water and then on the way down, if the fisherman's gone, stop and have a fire. And our S'mores. It's so quiet here, Macduff. All I hear is the wind passing through the few trees that survive at this altitude. And an occasional bird I don't know how to communicate with. But I don't recognize many bird calls; I can't answer any but a few. The only thing missing is the sound of water; Mill Creek split off from us soon after the campsite and bridges."

We stayed an hour, not talking much because we welcomed some time to absorb our surroundings. The sun was a crescent flame wrapping the edge of the western outline of the Absarokas; it would set earlier than when we're in the grand expanse of Paradise Valley down to the west.

"Time to go?' Lucinda asked.

"Sure. We'll come back."

"Often," she said quietly.

"I hope the fisherman's gone," I said as our SUV maneuvered back down the steep road toward the campsite.

"His car *isn't* gone," Lucinda said glumly. "I don't see him; he must be behind some of the brush along the river. . . . Do you want to stop and say hello and see how he's doing?"

"Why not," I said, pulling over. I parked and reached behind for my rod.

"Macduff, should we invade his fishing space?"

"Absolutely not! You're right. That was an impulsive reaction caused by being in range of trout and not thinking. We'll come back and show those trout, maybe tomorrow morning."

"Macduff, that's looks like an expensive Winston rod the guy left near the fire pit. But I guess he can hear anyone coming."

"Let's walk to the stream and see if he's there. He might have hiked up or downstream."

"And left his rod here?" she asked.

We had been at the campsite many times over the years and headed exactly toward where we had caught the most fish. Half-way to the creek I noticed something on the ground along what served as a path.

"Look at this, Lucinda. It's a nearly new chest pack for small gear." I picked it up. "This one has leaders and tippet material, forceps, a small tube of sun screen, and some insect repellant. And a dozen flies stuck on a piece of foam pinned on the front."

Lucinda walked on a few steps while I went through the chest pack. I was looking at a poorly tied Royal Coachman when she screamed.

"Macduff! Look! The guy's *in the creek*. Face down in less than a foot of water. Help me pull him out. Maybe he's breathing."

We managed to pull the body to the bank, realizing how heavy he was from being in the water, especially because his hip boots were filled.

"He may have had a heart attack. He's too overweight to be wandering around at this altitude especially wearing heavy clothes and boots."

"Roll him over, Macduff. Is there any life left in him?"

"None," I said, checking for a pulse as we got him on his back."

"Go get your phone and call 911," I said. "Tell them we have a dead body."

"There's no cellphone service here," Lucinda declared. "Should I take the car down to where I can make a call?"

"I guess that's best. I don't want to leave the body. There's not much light left, so be quick. There's a new moon tonight, and that means it will be very dark here."

I went back to the fire pit and started a fire. The temperature was dropping. There could be near freezing temperatures tonight this high up Mill Creek.

It seemed forever before Lucinda came back.

"I had to go nearly to our ranch where I got through on 911, then called the Park County Sheriff's Office. Ken Rangley was there, about to go home for the day, but changed his plans and is headed our way. At best it's a forty-minute trip."

Only twenty minutes later a county sheriff's car arrived with it blue lights flashing. A deputy we didn't know got out and came over to the creek.

"I'm Forrest Starke. Ken called me; I was near Emigrant. I'm new to the force. *Very* new. This is the first time I've been called where there's a dead body. He *is* dead, isn't he?" Starke asked timidly walking with me toward the stream.

"No question," I said. "We pulled him from the water, but there was no sign of life."

Starke turned ashen looking at the body. He suddenly ran around to the other side of the brush. I could hear him gagging. He'll get used to it, I thought.

"Damn, Mr. Brooks, I'm not doing very well at this," he said apologetically when he returned.

"It takes time," I responded. "Don't worry. It won't go any further than my wife and me."

45

AN HOUR LATER

"WHY IS THIS CAMPSITE SO ATTRACTIVE?" asked Erin, who arrived soon after Ken who was, in turn, followed by the coroner. The two or three sites I passed coming up the gravel road here were so stark, but this site is charming, filled with firewood and free of trash."

"The answer is 'Pine Tree Pete,'" said Lucinda, smiling and knowing the next question.

"Who is Pine Tree Pete?" asked Erin.

"This place was pretty much the same as those downstream until about four years ago. One day, when people arrived here, they found a nice stack of wood all cut and ready to be used for a campfire. When they used some of the wood the next day, by nightfall the stack was full again. No one knew who did this."

"Most people assumed it was the National Forest people. But it wasn't."

"Forest elves?" asked Deputy Starke, looking better than an hour ago.

"Not unless Pine Tree Pete was an elf," Erin commented. "He wasn't. He's a retired Forest Service Ranger who lives in a modest one-room cabin further down Mill Creek. He was working here one day before he retired and a woman drove in with her disabled husband. They wanted to picnic and hoped there was a grill. There wasn't. Neither of them was physically able to cut wood and after explaining their disappointment to the ranger, they left. The ranger was Pete Sanchez.

"The next week on his day off he came here with a chainsaw and began to walk through the areas where there were dead trees burned by a month-long fire a couple of years ago. Taking only fallen and rotting trees, he cut the limbs into logs and carried them here and stacked them up. And he built a grill.

"The next week the wood was gone. So he did it again. And again and again. He's still doing it."

"So we can thank Pine Tree Pete for the fire we're sitting around?"

"Yes, and more. The next thing Pete did was bring some round river rocks to surround and protect the fire pit. They're the ones in front of you."

"And the six boulders we're sitting on?"

"Same guy. Using a borrowed front loader, he found some larger boulders that had a flat side and could serve as seats. We're each sitting on one."

"I'll think of him every time we're here fishing," said Lucinda, as I nodded.

"Shouldn't we be talking about the body that was just carried off by the coroner?" I asked her.

"I thought the coroner was a little strange," said Lucinda. "He only talked to Erin."

"There's a reason for that," said Ken. "His name is Victor Persey. He's called 'Cutter.' Bright but no training to be a physician. We have county coroners in Montana. There are also two to three medical examiners or MEs. The MEs have to be a physician with a Ph.D. and board certification in forensic pathology. Since Erin has a Ph.D. in Forensic Sciences, Cutter prefers to talk to her. He majored in biology in college and started medical school. But he left and took a couple of courses for coroners. He's been in Livingston for two decades. "

"What did Cutter say to you, Erin?" Lucinda asked as Erin rejoined us. "I don't think any of us overheard you two."

"He has an autopsy to do when he's back in Livingston with the body. He did a very quick examination and said probably drowning that might have been the result of heart failure.

"Cutter was not happy that the body was border-line obese and mumbled 'How in God's name will I turn him over on the examining slab?'" Cutter's small and can't weigh more than 150. The dead man may have been 275 or more.

"Cutter said he hasn't done an autopsy for months."

"When will he have his report ready?" I asked.

"Maybe a day or two. But he said he saw no sign of a struggle or any foul play and was reasonably certain the cause of death was either accidental drowning or suicide."

"Suicide? What does he base that on?" Lucinda asked.

"Didn't he explain?" I inquired.

"I know Cutter's record," said Erin. "He's prone to assume suicide if it's at all feasible. Then he sends the body to the ME in either Billings or Missoula. He prefers the ME in Billings because that guy rarely questions a coroner. Claims he's overworked. Truth is he has a thriving private practice he says is necessary to earn a decent living because Montana pays so little."

"Suicide!" I said, mirroring Lucinda's uncertainty. "I don't think so. Why would he come to a part of the creek that's so shallow? He'd have to lie down in the deepest part of the creek and start drinking. If he wanted to drown, he could have jumped off one of the bridges over the Yellowstone River, like the one not far from here at Emigrant."

"Let's wait for his report," Ken said. "He may change his mind. I have some authority over Cutter. I can talk to him."

"I don't know what the fisherman's name was. Do you, Ken?" I asked.

"Yes. I copied down his license info and have it here on my IPad," said Ken. "His name was Ben Norton. I don't know him. Do you, Macduff?"

"I don't think so, but it sounds familiar. Maybe someone I've heard about but have never met. I'm curious about something. Can you go on the Federation of Fly Fishers website and look him up."

"I know what you're thinking, and I'm looking," Ken nodded. . . . "Here he is. Ben Norton, Bozeman, Montana. . . . Guess what?"

"He's a Master Casting Instructor." Lucinda guessed.

Ken nodded, looking questioningly at Lucinda.

"Like Spence and Hart," Lucinda said.

"The next question you're going to ask, Lucinda, is was he wearing a black fly around his neck?"

"Was he?" she asked. "Macduff and I didn't notice one."

"No. He wasn't."

"Then maybe this wasn't related to Spence or Hart," I said.

"Wishful thinking at this stage. Let's wait for the coroner's or ME's official report," Erin suggested.

"Suicide?" I mumbled. "I don't believe it. No way."

46

TWO WEEKS LATER

THE AUTOPSY REPORT WAS ISSUED TWO WEEKS later. Signed by the state assistant ME in Billings, it approved Cutter's report that concluded Norton died from suicide by drowning. Ken Rangley called the Billings ME and asked how Norton committed suicide. The ME said he hasn't the resources to personally view the area where Norton died, and he accepted Cutter's conclusion. Unless the Montana attorney general rejected the report, it stood firm. Ken contacted the AG's office in Missoula but was directed to a young staff lawyer who did nothing other than look at the report online and say he saw no red flags. But he added that he appreciated Sheriff Rangley's interest.

Ken called me and asked me to come to Livingston and meet with him. He invited Erin to join us and asked me to bring Lucinda. He proposed lunch and said his office would pay.

Lucinda and I locked Wuff in and drove the twenty-four miles in a half hour. We went the speed limit, and not one car passed us heading north to Livingston, and no more than six passed us later heading south going home. That couldn't be said of traffic around St. Augustine. If only Montana didn't have winters!

Erin insisted we have lunch at the Northern Pacific Beanery near the railroad tracks. It was crowded, but the owner knew Ken and found us a table.

"What's up?" asked Lucinda, peeking over her mound of roasted pork loin on a small mountain of noodles.

"Each of us has read the coroner's report and the MEs approval," Ken began. "I've been abruptly turned down by the AG in Missoula regarding the possibility of any further investigation."

"Do we have any choices?" I asked.

"In theory, yes. Practically, no," Erin replied. "It would require a legal challenge, and we don't have county funds to do that."

"What's our interest in this?" I inquired, taking a bite of my Nathan's All Beef Natural Hot Dog. Natural? It came so loaded with toppings the beef was both invisible and without taste. I sent it back, reminding the waiter I asked for it plain. Or *natural* as advertised. No onion, relish, tomato, sauerkraut, or cheese.

"Do we really care about Norton, other than a life was tragically lost?" Lucinda asked. "Norton is dead. The papers say that he had no spouse. His one daughter lives in Dijon, France, where she teaches English to French adults. She was notified but didn't respond."

"Norton must have left some assets which she would likely inherit," I added.

"Yes," said Erin. "But that's a matter for probate to sort out. No will has been found, and that means an administrator will be appointed to deal with his estate."

"I have a problem with one thing," commented Lucinda, frowning. "The Billings, Bozeman, and Livingston papers all described the death as 'involving' Macduff and me. They said we found the body and 'claimed' that it was in the creek. And they went through and repeated every past instance where Macduff alone or the two of us had been linked to deaths, including some murders. They started with the sniper killing in Wyoming of former ambassador Ander Eckstrum on Macduff's drift boat. That was a decade and a half ago. . . . I want our names cleared of any responsibility for Norton's death."

"You mean you want it further investigated?" Ken asked. "We *don't* have the resources. Journalistic hints of foul play and blame aren't enough for us to act."

"I know, Ken. Macduff and I have placed enough burdens on your time and the county's budget. But I'm going to do whatever I can to keep newspapers and people from thinking we were involved in another death."

"What do you plan, Lucinda?" asked Erin.

"The autopsy report was only *two* pages. I'm going to ask to see every document the coroner and ME used to reach their conclusions. There isn't even a good description of the body by Cutter when he first saw it at the picnic site."

"Cutter and the ME in Billings won't be happy. Be prepared for some rejections," Ken promised.

"Then we'll be in court. And not at the county's expense. Mine."

"Let's get started," Lucinda said, taking the last bite of her noodle pile.

47

THAT AFTERNOON - MILL CREEK

THE DRIVE HOME TO MILL CREEK PASSED BY fields with scattered white tailed deer, prong-horn antelope, one wandering red fox, and a young bison that must have escaped Yellowstone Park or a bison ranch around Gardiner and slowly progressed north in the valley.

"More game than we see between St. Augustine and our cottage on the salt marshes," I commented.

"Maybe not," Lucinda noted. "We've occasionally seen a wandering red fox like here, plus gopher turtles, an alligator, and a nearly six-foot Eastern diamondback rattler. In a few years, as they migrate north, add a twelve-foot African python eating 100 pounds of young calf or a loved pet. One python ate a 30-pound porcupine that punctured the snake's insides and killed it."

"You have such broad knowledge of the animal kingdom," I added. "Did the porcupine escape?"

"No, it suffocated. Maybe it was suicide, like Norton! . . . We're almost home. I'd like to do something," she suggested as we turned into Mill Creek Road. "Macduff, please drive past our cabin and on up to the camp site where Norton died. Maybe we'll find something."

"It's been two weeks."

"But it was wrapped with a yellow 'Crime Scene' tape. People have likely avoided using Pine Tree Pete's campsite."

Lucinda was right. The tape had not been removed.

"Should we go under the tape?" I asked.

"Of course, in the name of justice and curiosity."

We walked to the fire pit and sat on the rocks, as we had the evening we discovered Norton's body. Lucinda searched carefully around the fire pit, but found nothing.

"Do you want to toss a fly into the creek?" she asked. "One of our small bamboo rods is in the SUV."

"Why not? Between the front seats is a small square of foam with some flies. You choose. You did better than me in Canada."

"I think a #20 Blue Wing Olive is what you need," Lucinda decided as she pulled the rod and flies from the SUV. "Here, go to it. I'll watch from my boulder seat."

I walked the twenty feet to where the creek had a bend that left a quiet spot on the inside of the curve. I could have walked to the edge and dappled the fly into the water, but no bushes were behind me, so I stayed ten to twelve feet off the creek, false cast once, and dropped the fly on the upstream side of the quiet water. It moved slowly through the calmness of the bend and just before it was pulled away into faster water, what proved to be a 7" cutthroat—a red slash maturing on the throat of the young trout—rose and engulfed the fly.

After I carefully set the fish back in the creek and started back to Lucinda, I thought maybe there was another trout in the same calmness. Turning back again, I did a couple of false casts while I walked the bank and this time dropped the fly in fast running water above the bend. It was immediately taken, not by a fish but a rock or a twig. I pulled gently because I wanted my successful Blue Wing Olive back. I had hooked what first looked like a twig, but then became a piece of string. Someone had tossed something into the creek. I pulled more and it suddenly came free and flipped my way, landing at my feet. Reaching down, I picked it up. It was a piece of string. But there was more. The string formed a loop. But it wasn't the string that held my attention; it was what was tied at the end—a black fly.

"You won't believe what I hooked," I called to Lucinda, scurrying back to the fire pit and handing her the black fly.

"My God! It must have come off Norton and became caught on the bottom. It was exactly where we had found his body. Now we have *two* common parts of all three deaths. They were all Master Casting Instructors. And they all had a black fly on a string!"

"What do you suggest? Let's first put the black fly in anything that will protect it."

"And call Erin or Ken," she suggested.

"What if we didn't? It's only going to link us to the Spence and Hart deaths, which now seem more like homicides. . . . The Norton case is closed but the local papers might start to do an online search and investigate Hart's death and link me to that."

"But if Norton's death *was* a homicide, it should be reopened."

"Let's drive down to our cabin and talk. Come sundown, I'd like a drink."

"Or two," she added.

48

THAT EVENING – MILL CREEK

ERIN AND KEN HAD BOTH GONE HOME WHEN we tried contacting the sheriff's offices.

"It's after hours. Who should I try first on their cell phones?" Lucinda asked.

"Call Erin. She spent more time than Ken did talking to Cutter."

Erin answered the call. "Where are you two? That was a great lunch. Has something happened since you left for home?"

"We didn't go straight home, but we're there now. . . . We went to the campsite next to where Norton's body was found."

"Not *another* body?" Erin asked, not laughing.

"No," I said, sitting next to Lucinda. "I went fishing in the creek *exactly* where Norton fished."

"You've called me to tell me you caught more fish than Norton did?"

"No, to tell you that I hooked something caught on the bottom and that something was a black fly tied to a string!"

"Tell me you're joking and that you two were drinking at the fire pit."

"Not a drop until we got here. We're on our porch. . . . We want your advice, Erin. What happens now?"

"I'll call Ken," Erin stated. "We have some choices. One would be to call Cutter and show him the black fly and tell him about the same black flies found with Spence and Hart. He may not know about either of those cases."

"He might say forget it," responded Lucinda. "It doesn't affect Norton's suicide. Even if we claim it was not a suicide but was either an accident or a homicide, he might do nothing more than take the black fly and add it to the file, and not even pass that information on to the ME in Billings."

"What if he thinks it's important?" Erin considered.

"In that case, he will probably want to tell the ME and suggest he review his report," replied Lucinda. But you know Cutter and the ME are busy. If neither believes it would cause any changes to the report, they might say add it to the file, but do nothing more. You know the ME's decision is not subject to appeal unless it goes to a court."

"Or one of the two might say the fly makes a big difference and agree the deaths may not have been suicide," Erin surmised.

"Probably only if they don't know about Spence and Hart," I affirmed.

"Do we tell them?" Lucinda asked.

"Let me think about. And discuss it with Ken."

"Erin, does finding this make *you* think I might have killed Norton by drowning him?" I asked.

"Don't be silly. You weren't arrested for the Spence or the Hart death. I don't know whether Cutter looked for DNA on Norton, but I assume, if he did, it wasn't yours. . . . If you were guilty, you wouldn't be calling and telling me about the black fly. You would have destroyed it. . . . But then again, maybe you just went to the campsite to search for the black fly and get rid of it."

"And then call you and tell you?"

"Maybe you even tied a black fly earlier this afternoon at your cabin, tossed it in the creek, and then retrieved it."

"You have some imagination, Erin."

"What I really think," she interrupted, "is that Lucinda was delighted with finding the black fly so she can pursue her own investigation."

"Erin, Lucinda's nodding her head and smiling. Do you want to come and arrest her?"

"I'll ask Ken about that, too. If Lucinda went to prison, Ken would be able to fish with you more."

49

THE FOLLOWING DAY

KEN RANGLEY CALLED US THE NEXT DAY. IT was difficult to gain an understanding about what he was thinking from his quick and unemotional hello-and-how-are-you greeting. But it didn't take long for him to change after Lucinda interrupted and asked, "What are you planning to do about the black fly we discovered?"

"I was up most of last night because of you two, considering choices."

"You can sleep other nights. What are you going to do?"

"Options? The buck seems to have stopped in front of *me*. The easiest option is to do nothing and assume with time all will be forgotten. Maybe the choice of accident versus suicide will continue to be debated, but by who?

"Among some coroners? So what? The black fly is meaningless without two additions. First, they would have to link the black fly to Norton. Remember that it was found days later in the stream, *not* on the body around Norton's neck."

"What if there's a trace of Norton's DNA on the black fly?" asked Lucinda.

"Obviously, the black fly hasn't been tested yet for DNA. I do remember reading Cutter's report that stated there was someone else's DNA on Norton that can't be linked with anyone because whoever the DNA belongs to never had it registered. Dead end."

"If the third black fly is tested for DNA, it should have mine and Macduff's because we both handled it when we discovered it in the creek."

"I might have Erin talk to Cutter about testing it. But I don't know where we're going. Without more, the black fly has little meaning as part of a possible homicide. That more is for the three black flies to be linked. If it were added to all three persons being Master Casting Instructors, I grant the question is raised: Do these two common facts mean enough to re-open the investigations?"

"There is another common factor," added Lucinda. "Each was found in *water*. Each was fishing. Each *possibly* drowned, regardless of the suicide conclusion here in Wyoming."

"We know Spence and Norton appeared to be fishing for trout," agreed Ken. "Hart, however, was casting on *salt* water. Maybe for sea trout or maybe for anything, such as redfish or snook."

"That makes me wonder if Hart was casting a fly with part of a hook or the kind of practice fly used in giving lessons," Lucinda noted. "She might have been practicing some complex form of roll cast because she couldn't sleep. Maybe a Spey roll cast. But I don't recall that the rod found near Hart on the bank was a double-handed Spey rod."

"Lucinda, those are questions I agree might appropriately have been raised during the original investigation. Investigations aren't perfect."

"Do you think any newspapers would undertake investigations on their own if they were told what we're discussing?"

"Newspapers? They never challenged the suicide conclusion. I don't think the Bozeman or Livingston papers would pursue any further investigation based solely on knowing about the black fly. Remember that it wasn't found on Norton's body."

"It's a mess," Lucinda said, frustrated. "I guess I have better things to do than second guess your office or the coroner and ME."

"But you're not going to quit, are you?"

"There are a couple of things I want to try on my own. Will you or Erin help?"

"I have an office to run. But, of course, I'll listen to you. And Erin would be thrilled to help you, if she agrees it makes sense to go further."

"I have one idea," Lucinda whispered, half to herself. "I'll call Erin tomorrow."

50

THE FOLLOWING WEEK

"ERIN," LUCINDA ASKED THE NEXT MORNING when Erin returned to her office from a boring traffic case in a Livingston court, "may I have a copy of Cutter's autopsy report and any follow-up on DNA found on Norton?"

"Looking for anything specific?"

"I'd like to know for certain if any DNA other than Norton's was found on Norton."

"I'll humor you, Lucinda, at least this time. I'll send you what I can get. Cutter owes me a few favors."

Cutter's file on Norton, including the final report, came the following week. Erin called while Lucinda was reading it.

"Lucinda, you see that the autopsy report stated that DNA *was* found on Norton but said nothing further about it. It was not much DNA, but possibly enough for identification."

"My understanding is that it doesn't take much," Lucinda said. "It helps to find some in different locations on a body, but some from under a fingernail could be all that is needed. Norton may have struggled with someone and scratched him. Or her. Why didn't Cutter try harder to find a match after they had a DNA profile?"

"Cutter was a little evasive," Erin replied. "He told me he was overloaded with work when Norton died. He admitted he didn't search for a match outside a Montana state DNA bank.

"Erin, can we try to find a match? Will you help me?"

"Of course. It may be the only way the two of us can spend some time together. We haven't seen each other for a long time. Years, not months."

"You won't get in trouble, will you? . . . Will you tell Ken what we're doing?"

"I'll tell Ken. I'm not sure how he'll react. He's concerned with our budget. If he thought we wanted the case re-opened, I think he'd say 'no.' I've never dealt with DNA and the possibility of a suicide being a homicide."

"Erin, don't use that 'h' word. Call it a chance to use an already concluded case—where there was DNA—to help you learn about DNA in general in the event that knowledge is needed sometime in the future. It shouldn't be hard for you to do with your Ph.D. in Forensic Sciences."

"Aren't we deceitful?"

"Absolutely."

"Where shall we start?" Erin asked.

"You have the black fly, don't you?"

"Yes."

"Did you give it to Cutter?"

"No," Erin responded. "Ken finally decided to leave it in a sealed bag with the Norton file here. It wasn't used in the autopsy. Remember that the coroner and ME issued the report before the black fly was found."

"Then a start would be to have that black fly separately examined for DNA," I suggested.

"Why wasn't the black fly found around Norton's neck?" Lucinda asked.

"Maybe there wasn't time to get the loop around Norton's neck," said Erin, "if a second person *was* involved and drowned Norton and wanted to get away quickly."

"All Macduff and I did was pull the body out of the creek. We assumed we shouldn't touch it further. We were certain he was dead and knew you and the coroner would carefully search the body and scene, which would have included where we found the black fly."

"Why don't we look at the black fly together. I haven't seen it since Macduff and I gave it to you."

"Come here a week from today in the morning, and we'll start re-examining the file. . . . I should know more about the black fly and DNA. I'll urge Cutter to help."

"I'll be there at 7:00 a.m."

"Try 8:30. I want my wake-up coffee."

51

A WEEK LATER – LIVINGSTON

E RIN HAD JUST POURED HER FIRST COFFEE AS Lucinda arrived at 8:50. She would have showed up earlier, but when she walked out of the Mill Creek cabin, a black bear was nosing around the yard. It looked at her for ten minutes, walked into the woods, and disappeared.

"I was held up by a bear," she told Erin, taking off her jacket.

"Bare what?" Erin asked. "Macduff chasing you around in the cabin without his clothes on?"

"Much less exciting. A black bear in our yard."

"My thought was more fun."

"Let's talk about black flies. Did you find it?" Lucinda asked.

"Of course. It's on the conference table with the rest of the info."

They both took coffee to the conference room. On the table was less than Lucinda expected."

"This isn't much of a file for an unsolved death," commented Lucinda.

"Oh! But it was solved. It was a suicide."

"Look me straight in the face and say you agree with it being a suicide."

"Am I here to be interrogated?" Erin asked.

"Answer the question!"

"It was . . . *not* a suicide," Erin admitted.

"OK. So it was a drowning that was accidental or induced by another party."

"Agreed. And you'll see the info confirms that there was DNA on Norton's body *and* on the black fly."

"Was it the same DNA on the body and black fly?" Lucinda asked.

"I wasn't very clear," Erin apologized. "Norton obviously has his own DNA. The black fly does not. Norton had DNA on him other than his own. And there *was* DNA on the black fly."

"How did DNA get on the black fly? The person might have been rushing to attach the black fly around Norton's neck and pricked himself, leaving DNA on the fly," Lucinda offered.

"Or the person who tied the black fly might have been stuck by the barb while tying the fly, and bled on the fly."

"The flies were barbless," reminded Lucinda. "But there was part of the hook left when the barb was cut off, and the remaining bit of metal should have been rough enough to scratch. . . . Would the DNA wash off when the black fly was in the water?"

"Hard to answer. It would degrade but there could be enough left."

"What's next, Erin? The newspapers have never been told that Macduff and I found the black fly. What would they do if *you* told them?"

"I'm not going to tell them because I don't think there are enough new facts to re-open the case. And you'd best not tell them because they will immediately link you and Macduff to whatever foul play they can think of that would make a good article."

"Erin, we haven't achieved much other than adding the black fly to our discussion. What will make a difference?"

"Finding a match that identifies a second party."

"We want to learn if the DNA on Spence and Norton is the same. If it is, we want to know the identity of that party. Sounds simple but it isn't."

"Who can help us?"

"That's where Cutter comes in. I talked to him yesterday. He's frankly excited about checking and matching. He'll call me."

"Let's assume Cutter *doesn't* find a match. I'm pretty certain that in the Spence death in Jackson a search was made but nothing was found. That doesn't mean there wasn't anyone with that DNA. It's just that they couldn't identify who it was."

"I have an idea, Erin, but I don't want to discuss it until we hear from Cutter and Byng."

"I can't wait, Lucinda. But I need to get back to the work I'm paid to do."

"Erin, isn't this more fun than vehicle violations and domestic disputes?"

52

THREE DAYS LATER – MILL CREEK

"MY TURN TO COME TO YOUR PLACE," ERIN suggested in a message left on Lucinda's phone a few days later. "Is it worth my coming?"

Lucinda reached her an hour later.

"I've mostly confirmed what we agreed on about Spence," Lucinda said. "But you have to come. I have something you must see. ASAP. It's laid out on a table."

Anxious to meet, Erin arrived in record time. She and Lucinda had not been together much and enjoyed working with each other.

"I drove 80," she admitted. "And I turned on my flashing lights. Don't ask me if I passed many cars. I passed *all* of them. I'm exhausted. . . . I don't see anything on your tables. You said it was all laid out, whatever it is."

"Sit on the couch with me for a minute. It's chilly, and I started a fire. We can enjoy it before I show you what I promised."

Erin sat and looked quizzically at Lucinda. "Do you have a secret you're reluctant to share?"

"Yes. Something you've never known about. Only two others besides Macduff and me know about it—Elsbeth and Dan Wilson. The same people who, along with Sarah and John

Kirby, know something about Macduff's past before he moved here.

"You learned more than we wanted you to know when you saved Macduff's life while I was in a coma after being shot on the Snake River. Macduff was so worried about me he wouldn't eat. . . . This secret is about where Macduff and I spend private time and where I'm going to show you my ideas about the cases."

"Sitting *here* I can see most of your cabin. What are you talking about?"

Lucinda stood and walked to the side of a bookcase and reached behind the books. The bookcase swung out into the room, exposing a steep staircase.

"You have a *basement?*"

"We call it our music room," Lucinda said, taking Erin's hand and leading her down the steep steps.

"That's about the last thing you need a room for! You two don't play any instruments."

"That's true about me, but as you can see, there's a music stand, and on the table next to the chair are an oboe and an English Horn."

"That sheet music is for a Cimarosa concerto! That's serious music. Since when did Macduff start playing?"

"When he lost El."

"Is he any good?"

"Better than I ever tell him he is. I don't want him to get too serious."

"He might leave you and join the New York Philharmonic? You could go back to work at your old investment firm, and you two could date or live together in your 57th Street apartment."

"That's not going to happen. Wuff doesn't want to live in NYC and have to learn to pee on cement sidewalks."

"Lucinda," Erin exclaimed, "there's more to this room than music. What is all this stuff? . . . I know the face on that life size paper target on the far wall, with the half-dozen bullet holes. It's Abdul Khaliq Isfahani, the Islamic terrorist from the Sudan who Macduff assassinated in Khartoum."

"You know about that?"

"Some things are obvious about Macduff. In addition to what I learned when he was delirious, he tells us too much. You both have let a few things slip over the years. . . . And *all* the fancy equipment here isn't your normal household word processing gear."

Erin walked around the room carefully looking at some of Macduff's communications equipment. Then she went to the large table in the middle.

"What have we here?" she asked. "Is this what you wanted to show me?"

"Yes. They're close up photos of the three black flies, each hanging from a string loop."

"Are these the real black flies?" Erin asked.

"They are *exact* photos of the real flies. Don't ask me how I got the photos, but I did. Each shows one of the black flies close-up. You can see where the barbed point was clipped off, what the fly was made from, and the string and how it was knotted. And you can see the length of the strings."

"What do you want me to do?" asked Erin. "We know the real flies may carry DNA from the person they were attached to and from the person who apparently made the specific black fly necklace."

"We know which body was found with which necklace. But look at them and tell me where they differ. No one else has seen these photos or the real flies together. This is the first time they have been compared. Maybe comparing them will tell us more than merely confirming that the three bodies had black fly necklaces. Of course, *I* know which is associated with which body. Humor me."

"Aren't they all the same?" said Erin, still wondering what Lucinda was trying to prove. "We all knew that the black flies looked like standard Black Marabous."

"Erin! Look at them *carefully* and tell me if you see *any* differences."

"Well, the strings are different. Two are the same, but one has more prominent strands, not as smooth as the other two."

"OK," Lucinda said. "I'm laying the two that seem similar together. The two with smooth strands are on the left; the one with coarser strands is on the right. What else?"

"Something else becomes apparent. One of the two similar strings is shorter."

"Long enough to get over someone's head?"

"Not a chance," Erin said. "Lucinda, we know who is associated with each fly. The real flies are in the three case files in the three locations, Florida, Montana, and Wyoming. The short one has to be from Norton. So what does this display mean?

"First, my guess is that the murderer tried to put the fly on Norton, but couldn't because the loop was too short. Trying to get it on, he pricked Norton's neck with the end of the hook where the barb was cut off. When it didn't fit around Norton's neck, it was tossed next to the body. Someone was in a hurry. Maybe they had seen us go by the campsite earlier.

"Second, we know the other longer smooth strand necklace, which you placed next to Norton's, is Spence's," Lucinda continued. "The Spence black fly photos were taken and sent to me by Huntly Byng. It shouldn't surprise you to figure out that the resemblances in the flies suggest the two in Montana and Wyoming were the same. After all, Spence and Norton were each killed not far apart—maybe 150 miles—one in Montana and one in Wyoming."

"Is that all? I'm not sure the different string of the third fly means that much. But go ahead."

"You do agree that the two smooth strand necklaces are from Spence and Norton?"

"Yes," Erin agreed. "Of course. They were sent to you from the place they were found. That adds nothing."

"I want to be very sure we can establish a *difference* between the necklaces. I accept the DNA findings so far. But some judges are uncomfortable with placing too much reliance on DNA tests."

"As I look more closely," Erin said, "the necklaces are different. Each was tied to be at the rear of the neck. But the way they were tied differed."

"How?"

"Look at the knots, Lucinda. On the Spence and Norton strings, there is a small square knot, like you tie your shoe but without the bow."

"I know my knots; you don't need to give me a lesson."

"The third string isn't tied with a knot; it was whipped with black thread."

"Now look at the flies and not the string," Lucinda said. "Anything more to mention?"

"At first glance," Erin said, "they are all the same Black Marabou, tied on a #4 hook."

"And?"

"Easy. Two are very different."

"Which ones?" Lucinda asked.

"The two associated with Spence and Norton are the same and differ from the one associated with Hart."

"How are they different?"

"First, the tails are longer, maybe a quarter inch."

"Does that mean the persons who tied them were different?"

"No," answered Erin. "It's easy to change the tail length when you do a final trim. But, look at the black fly wings. There are half-dozen strands of green pearl flash mixed into the wings on the two flies that are on the left—the Spence and Norton flies."

"Anything more?"

"Yes, but a little hard to see. The body of the same two with the green flash looks like black chenille wrapped with a copper wire. On the fly from the Florida death, the body is the same black chenille but has a black rather than a copper wrap."

"Do you have any doubts now?" asked Lucinda.

"The same person made the necklaces found on Spence and near Norton. It could have been the same person also made the Hart case fly and necklace, but I doubt that because there are so many differences."

"Does this mean Hart wasn't murdered?"

"Not at all," said Erin. "But by someone else if it was murder. Remember that the DNA on Hart, other than her own, was *not* the same as the DNA samples in either the Spence or the Norton case."

"Should Rosalie Abbott in Florida be told about our observations?" Lucinda asked.

"Only if she asks. All she's done so far is look like a cranky horse's ass. She wants to use Macduff for the same kind of political gain Davis tried in Cheyenne."

"I have one more thing to raise," said Erin. "Probably not too important with what we already talked about."

"I see you made a chart and wrote Spence at the top of the left side and Norton at the top of the right."

"Yes. And below I noted that there is DNA of Spence on one fly and of Norton on a similar fly."

"The same DNA?" Erin asked.

"Yes," replied Lucinda. "I believe we've got ourselves at least one murderer who killed both Spence and Norton."

"And Hart in Florida?"

"Hart is a separate case, maybe murder, maybe accidental. Let's leave that to another day."

53

A WEEK LATER

"YES, YES, YES" ERIN WAS yelling when Lucinda picked up her cellphone. Only one thing could have excited Erin far beyond her normal exuberance: she must have received the results of Cutter's examination. Was the DNA on the two similar black flies found with Spence and Norton the same?

"They match! They're the same, Lucinda. Whoever was around Spence when he died was also around Norton when he died."

"So we have a murderer?" Lucinda inquired calmly despite her excitement because she wanted Erin to calm down.

"If we have a murder, there must have been a murderer. Spence's death was ruled an accidental drowning and Norton's a suicide. But this match challenges both rulings."

"Can your Norton case be re-opened?"

"For a murder, absolutely. I asked Cutter what should be done. He said he would contact the ME in Billings. The ME previously insisted on confirming the suicide conclusion Cutter had reached. He didn't go into the reasons. Cutter has a task to convince the ME they were both wrong."

"And if he can't, I assume the ME's conclusion stands."

"Technically, but I imagine the papers, at least in Livingston, Bozeman, and Jackson, will be very interested."

"I'll bet they will label it a 'serial killing.'"

"And we're back to personally being harassed by the media and possibly some authorities."

"Maybe. But *this* office is not going to investigate you and Macduff. None of the DNA we're talking about is from you or Macduff. Huntly Byng in Jackson will not re-open the Norton case and include you. Harassment seems most likely to come from Abbott in Florida, when or if word gets out there about any revived investigations of the Wyoming or Montana cases."

"Erin, we have a match to the two black flies. Now find a match that provides the *name* that fits that DNA profile."

"Cutter tried that without any success thus far. I have to go slowly with him; he's excited but can only do so much."

"When did he say he'd know the extent of the available match info?"

"He asked me to give him a week."

"Assume that he *finds* a matching name. What then?"

"See whether Wyoming or Montana will try to extradite the person, if he or she is out of state. My guess is that the person's from one of those two states or possibly Idaho or Utah."

"Will your office pay for this?"

"I think Ken will want Cutter to do, it but Ken will be concerned with the costs involved. He might be able to get some extra funds from the state because homicides are unbecoming to tourism. . . . The same goes for Huntly Byng in Jackson."

"And if Cutter *doesn't* find a match? A lot of cases end with knowing the DNA found at two different sources is the same, but not being able to match it with a specific person on any data bank. When a match does happen, it's like having all the bells line up on a slot machine, except the DNA match doesn't set off bells."

"I guess we wait for Cutter," Lucinda commented.

"We have no choice. I'll be one anxious gal," exclaimed Erin.

"Me, too. . . . Erin, I'm so glad to be back here working with you."

"Macduff and John Kirby in Jackson are called 'celebrity guides.' What if people begin calling us 'celebrity sleuths'?"

"I'll deny ever having met you," Lucinda responded.

54

A WEEK LATER

ERIN WAS LOADING BAGS OF GROCERIES INTO her car when her phone rang. She thought she wouldn't answer. It had been a long and frustrating day, and it was already 9:30 p.m. She had missed the only sit-com she watched each week and wanted to go home, eat whatever didn't take long to prepare, and flop in front of the TV, whether or not it was turned on.

She looked at the phone, ready to turn it off, but saw the call was from Cutter and quickly answered.

"Cutter, what have you got?"

"No match. Dead end. Zilch. Goose egg. I tried every DNA date bank I could find and came up stymied. You can't imagine how frustrating it was. You think you're on to something and it will only take a quick computer search for a DNA match to link a name, and, when the last source you can try flashes a big nothing on your screen, you're ready to head to the nearest bar. In fact, that's where I am, at the bar in the old Murray Hotel in Livingston. I'm on my third drink, and I'm not even sure now what I'm drinking. I can still mumble 'another' and probably will a couple more times. . . . What was it you wanted to talk to me about?"

"Cutter! *You* called *me*."

"Did I? I guess I did."

"And you've already told me why we're at a dead end; there's no DNA match with a person who might have murdered Spence and Norton. Not because there isn't such a person, but that person's DNA isn't listed."

"What use is knowing there is *one* person who killed *both* Spence and Norton," asked Cutter, stumbling on his words, "without knowing who that person is? Are we supposed to hang the DNA findings on post office walls next to photos of the most wanted? You know that DNA results appear as a group of dark-colored parallel stripes. It would be like hanging pictures of fingerprints and asking 'Do you know this person?' Are people supposed to look at the fingerprints and say, 'Oh! I know who has that fingerprint.' Or, in our case, 'I know who has that DNA.'"

"Are we out of choices?"

"Yes, other than having another drink."

"Are you driving?"

"I think so. I got here somehow. I don't own a bicycle. Do you know what kind of car I drive?"

"Don't even *think* of getting into your car. Stay where you are. I'm coming to take you home."

Erin hung up, got her car keys, and drove off headed to the bar at the charming hotel that has hosted the likes of Sam Peckinpah, Will Rogers, Buffalo Bill, Calamity Jane, and even the Queen of Denmark.

She wondered if the matter of the Spence and Norton deaths was over.

55

THE FOLLOWING DAY

MORNING ARRIVES LATE AT OUR MILL CREEK cabin tucked against the base of the Absaroka Mountains on the east side of Paradise Valley. Our first glimpse of the sun has to wait until it rises above the ridges surrounding our cabin. Folks living in the valley close to the Yellowstone River see the sun earlier, even though they're west of here.

If we walk to our mailbox before sunrise, we see the sun's impact first lighting the top of the Gallatin Mountains across the valley to the west. The light moves slowly down the Gallatin slopes and heads our way across the valley and river, and by the time we return to the cabin, it is chasing or has caught us. Watching this light show repeated never tires us.

Lucinda has been busy with Erin—phone conversations and visits to her office in Livingston or our cabin at Mill Creek. She hasn't told me much of what has happened; she didn't want to bother me in the middle of my week of guiding for Project Healing Waters, commenting that a vet, however disabled from combat, was far more important and rewarding to work with than re-opening the Spence, Hart, and Norton deaths.

But this morning at breakfast Lucinda said it was time to talk.

"I've pretty much put Hart aside for good," she stated. "It's pleasant to answer the phone and have it not be Rosalie Abbott. I don't want to think about her until we're back in Florida after Thanksgiving, if then. . . . Erin and I have made some progress on Norton. It's time you knew, Macduff. It could affect us."

"That worries me," I said. "I was hoping that when you and Erin finished you'd tell me you two knew nothing more about any of the deaths, especially Norton's. . . . You'd let it go. Out of sight, out of mind. No way, Jose. Sayonara."

"I don't think Erin's told Ken *anything*. But she may be talking to him right now. We agreed last night to bring you both up-to-date today."

"Before we talk," I interrupted, "I want to ask you something that has nothing to do with the cases. Why did you take Erin to the music room?"

"How do you know? I closed the bookcase entrance carefully when we came up."

"I'd been practicing a Cimarosa concerto. The music page has been turned over to an Albinoni piece. I know you never even dust around my oboe and the music stand."

"Wow! I didn't know you'd been in the music room in the past week or two," Lucinda exclaimed.

"Getting ready for Carnegie Hall?"

"If you'd heard me practicing you wouldn't ask that."

"Back to my first question and then a second one—is it wise for anyone to know about that room other than you, Elsbeth, Dan, and me?"

"I'll answer that first. No, it probably isn't. I was using the room to lay out some things on the table there that I wanted to explain to Erin and later tell you about. I thought it was easier to leave them there and take Erin down.

"I thought about your question before I took her to the room. Few know about the room. Dan's only been there once. Elsbeth's not in Montana from the time UF begins in mid-August until she's out in mid-May. She rarely goes downstairs and only with one of us. We're here from her late summer departure to a few days after Thanksgiving when we leave for Florida. We come back in early April before she arrives here in late May to work at Chico Hot Springs. At most she's been in the music room two or three times.

"When I was contemplating taking Erin downstairs, I decided maybe it was good for her to know about it. What if you and I went down and closed the bookcase door behind us, which we often do. And then something happened to both of us, and we couldn't or weren't able to get out. Erin would be the first person to come to the cabin, probably after being called by Elsbeth when she couldn't get in touch with us."

"There is a phone in the music room," I said. "We could call for help. And wouldn't it be more likely that only one of us was hurt, perhaps falling on the stairs, and not both?"

"Both true, but I don't want our need for secrecy to govern our lives," she said.

"It already does. But maybe not for long."

"What do you mean?"

"We have only one certain worry—Herzog. And one less certain—Covington," I responded. "Isfahani is gone, as I'm reminded every time I go downstairs and his face on the target is staring at me."

"Do you remember *shooting* at that paper target?" she asked.

"I do. . . . I scared you."

"You terrified me. But that's over. And so, maybe, is Herzog. After all, he looks at his mantle in Guatemala City and sees your skull on display. As long as he believes it's you, we're safe."

"Another 'if.' Let's talk about Herzog another time. I understand your concern. I'm glad Erin knows some facts about Herzog. We've kept his attempts on our lives separate from our life here. . . . Back to Spence and Norton. What do you have to tell me?"

"Please don't interrupt while I tell you. I'll lose my chain of thought. No words. No hands raised. Just be quiet. OK?"

"This must be important."

"The conclusion Erin and I have reached is that Spence and Norton were murdered, probably surprised from behind and pushed over in the water and then held under. Someone strong."

"That's impo . . ."

"No interruptions!"

"Go ahead."

"The same person killed the two here in the West. Forget about Hart in Florida. We didn't pursue her case beyond the black flies. . . . We accept that she accidentally drowned."

"But Hart isn't ver . . ."

"Stop it, Macduff. When I'm done and *not* before."

"OK. Sorry."

"The black flies found on and near Spence and Norton were *identical,* quite probably tied by the same person. . . . There was DNA on the two black flies that wasn't from either Spence or Norton, but on each fly it was from the *same* person. We're assuming that person was the killer of both. Cutter helped us with Norton, and Huntly Byng helped with Spence.

"So we reached the point where we concluded that the same person murdered Spence and Norton. But who was that same person?

"I have an idea I want to run by you. I want you to read this article on forensics from a recent *National Geographic*. I know that's not a science magazine, but it speaks intelligently in clear, lay language. Erin read the article and explained a lot to me. After all, she has a Ph.D. in Forensic Sciences.

"Erin and I intend to get Cutter to help again. He has become so excited about these two deaths that he's reversed his conclusion about suicide and gone from thinking it was accidental to currently agreeing it was a homicide. He's the one who found the match that told us the same person killed Spence and Norton.

"We intend to have Cutter do the DNA *phenotyping profile* discussed in the magazine article. The profile won't give us a name, but it may tell us the killer's skin, eye, and hair color, extent of freckles, and ancestry, such as Asian, Middle Eastern, Native American, African, or European. It acts as an *exclusion* test, not an identification of a *specific* person. But it can very much narrow the search. . . . That's it. What do you think?"

"I'm overwhelmed!" I said. "I assumed you were out taking photographs for a magazine article, like you did in Cuba."

"I did some of that, too; I'm tracing the origins of the Snake and Yellowstone rivers. Next year I want us to get a guide to take us up both rivers to their sources."

"A guide with a gun."

"I think so," she agreed. "Grizzlies are protected and rapidly increasing in numbers in Yellowstone and Grand Teton parks, and now outside their borders. Meaning for us, more here at Mill Creek. For John and Sarah Kirby, more in Jackson Hole. We can take a gun into Yellowstone, but we aren't permitted to fire it. You figure that out. I didn't know grizzlies would turn and run away when a gun was merely pointed at them."

"The evening while you were gone, having a dinner with Erin, I took Wuff outside our cabin at dusk. We were standing at the edge on our side of the creek. I saw movement across the creek, and as my eyes focused in the dim light, I watched a female grizzly rise up on her hind feet and stare at us. She made what I understood to be threatening noises. She could have easily crossed the creek, but apparently she didn't want to leave two cubs that were beside her."

"Did you have bear mace or a gun in your hands?"

"No, I had a glass of Gentleman Jack. Next time I'll have a gun. This cabin is not in the park. Montana says I can shoot."

"*May* shoot. . . . You haven't asked much about what Erin and I did. No questions?

"I admit I need to read more about DNA phenotyping," Lucinda admitted. "I understand that if we take the DNA for the person who presumably killed both Spence and Norton and have Cutter undertake DNA phenotyping, we may discover that the person is European, has fair skin, brown hair, blue eyes, and a few freckles. I know that must apply to a huge percent of the people in the U.S.

"Let's assume we find that the person has light olive skin, that's 25% of the people, has black hair, 27%, brown eyes, a little less than 1%, and some freckles, 60%. We've *eliminated* a lot of people. Add that the person is Middle Eastern, and we've eliminated Europeans, the most prevalent group."

"Agreed," I said. "But we haven't come close to identifying any *specific* person."

"Macduff, do you have light olive skin?"

"No."

"That alone tells us something."

"Meaning in your hypo the killer had skin different than you and me?"

"Exactly, light olive, and thus the killer *can't* be you. Or me. Are your eyes brown, Macduff?"

"You know they're blue. At least I hope you do."

"Is your hair black?" she asked.

"No, but it could be dyed black."

"Good point. If you had dyed your hair black, you might want to return it to its natural light brown. . . . Finally, are you Middle Eastern? Meaning all you've said about your Scottish ancestry was a fairy tale."

"My response, Lucinda, is that we send the phenotyping profile—if it *excludes* me—to prosecutors who think I 'did it.' The first copy goes to Abbott in Crystal River."

"So I'm exonerated. But wait a minute. The DNA phenotyping hasn't taken place yet. What if the profile comes out European, brown hair, blue eyes, and fair skin embellished with a few freckles? Haven't we in that case narrowed the pool to a group that *includes* me?"

"We have," she agreed. "The pool has been reduced, but to a very large group. What we accomplished is to narrow the search, but not very much. Maybe enough to make those excluded happy."

"But I'm not excluded yet," I pointed out.

"At least any racist authorities in Florida may not try to hang it on a Black or in Wyoming or Montana on a Hispanic or Native American. But Abbott might use it to harass you a little more if you're not excluded. . . . What do we do now?"

"Go to bed. You've exhausted me."

"OK. Put a sign on the front door that says only 'DNA.'"

"Meaning?" she asked.

"Do Not Arouse!"

"Can I count your freckles?"

56

TWO DAYS LATER - GUATEMALA CITY

JUAN PABLO HERZOG ARRIVED AT HIS OFFICIAL office before any of his staff members. He made coffee, ironically the identical Antigua coffee Lucinda and Macduff were sipping in their kitchen at Mill Creek at the very same time.

President Herzog took his cup and looked out the windows as the first light gave a glow to the Parque Central that was the attractive hub of the nation's poverty. Nothing Herzog had undertaken during his time in office gave any hope to the people, a majority of whom were Maya speaking twenty-some different native languages. To his credit Herzog had worked hard and tried to make a few changes for the better, but he was always thwarted by the ineffective Guatemalan Congress, which had recently refused to enact recommendations of the United Nations International Commission Against Impunity, which had addressed the nation's crime and corruption.

Herzog wondered if he should have remained in the United States years ago after he attended a University of Florida graduate program. The U.S. was a far safer place to live and continually the choice of Guatemalans who entered illegally by way of Mexico. But when he thought of Gainesville and UF, immediately he thought about his former professor, Maxwell Hunt, who Herzog had tried to locate and kill over the past fifteen years. Was he foolish to have spent so much time and money pursuing Professor Hunt? It had cost him the lives of a niece, María-Martina, and a nephew, Martín Paz, who were shot and killed on the UF campus in Gainesville, and recently the refusal of another niece, Luisa Solares, to return from studying at UF to become Herzog's legal assistant. She was still in Gainesville, currently enrolled in the law college's JD program. Luisa had a job offer to practice in Miami, and she vowed not to return to Guatemala as long as her Tío Juan lived.

Turning from the window and admiring the skull on his mantle, Herzog mused about how he told people who visited his office and asked about the skull that it was a relative and Guatemalan hero who led the nation to independence from Spain in 1821. He related how the skull had been passed down in his family and added that he had promised to bequeath it to the National Museum on his death. But Herzog knew it was not the skull of his ancestor, but of UF law professor Hunt.

He did not know that the skull actually was from an obscure Alaskan ex-con. Herzog had sent trusted General Hector Ramirez to Alaska to locate and bring back Professor Hunt, who allegedly was living there as Walter Windsor and working in the fishing industry. The Windsor who Ramirez found was not Hunt, but rather the unfortunate victim of mistaken identity whose skull now graced the mantle of President Herzog's office.

Herzog had wanted Ramirez to bring Professor Hunt—Walter Windsor in Alaska—to Guatemala alive. Ramirez thought that would be difficult; the man likely would not go willingly. Ramirez believed that it was better to kill the man, and when he found the boat where Windsor worked, he locked him in his cabin and incinerated the boat and Windsor. The charred skull was all that was left.

Herzog stared at the skull, remembering for the first time since he was in Gainesville as a student that Professor Hunt had told him during his naval service he suffered an injury and had a small metal plate inserted at the back of his head. Herzog was curious and slowly turned the skull around. There was no metal plate nor any sign of an injury to the head! He thought for a moment and suddenly realized it could *not* be the skull of Professor Hunt. Admittedly, according to General Ramirez, there were a number of Walter Windsors in Alaska. Did Ramirez kill the wrong one?

Herzog now accepted that the skull could not be Professor Hunt, and he took the skull and threw it against the bricks in the fireplace, where it shattered. There would be no nineteenth century skull of a Guatemalan hero to leave to the museum.

How would he solve his dilemma? Was there another Walter Windsor in Alaska who was really Professor Hunt? Or was the information totally false that he obtained about the deaths of both his security advisor Alejandro Olviedo and former CIA agent Ralph Johnson in the small Italian hilltop town of Barberino val d'Elsa in Italy? Did Professor Hunt remain free?

Herzog was furious and all the more determined to find and kill Professor Hunt and every member of his family.

He called his personal secretary, ordered her to have General Ramirez arrested and executed for treason, and decided to send another nephew to Gainesville to start the search once again.

57

THE FOLLOWING DAY – MILL CREEK

"MACDUFF, YOU KNOW I DON'T VERY OFTEN dream at night. But I did last night."

"A dream or a nightmare?" I asked.

"A mixture of both. It was about Herzog so it had to be part nightmare."

"Did Herzog finally catch us?"

"It wasn't about that. We received word that Herzog was killed in an accident on the road to Antigua."

"That's good," I said.

"You'd think so. . . . But what would it mean for us?"

"Dan Wilson might be through with us, although we've developed a friendship over the years I wouldn't want to lose."

"I meant you and me. What would *we* do?" Lucinda asked.

"If you like what we're doing now—be here in the summer and Florida in the winter—it's been quite a life."

"Why did *you* come here to Mill Creek in the first place, Macduff? And why are *we* still here?"

"The protection program got me here. It was my choice and proved to be one of the best decisions of my life."

"Why? You could have settled in Durango or Missoula or any one of a number of places in the West where you could fish and be a guide."

"I wouldn't have met you."

"So you don't regret coming to my ranch that Thanksgiving dinner years ago, even though you were the only invited guest who showed up?"

"Meeting you for the first time and being alone with you were what made it so nice."

"Then why were you so slow to agree to become engaged and then married?"

"I couldn't believe how lucky I was; I wanted to give you time to be sure and maybe back out," I said.

"Sometimes a fish is so good you have to keep it and not throw it back in. I used a barbed hook on you. Can I still throw you back?"

"Only if I begin to smell," I responded.

"I guess my analogy with fishing wasn't so good."

"You asked about Herzog and us. What did you mean?" I asked.

"If he dies, today or any time in the future, we no longer have to hide."

"Truthfully, it means we don't have to *worry*. We can stop worrying and still not leave here. And we can go to Florida every November for the winter, as we do now."

"Do you like being a fly fishing guide?"

"On most days, yes. But there are occasional clients who make me think of doing something else."

"Such as teaching international law?"

"That's a shock! I haven't been in the classroom for years. Even if I wanted to teach or write or consult or lecture about law, I've lost my edge. The world has changed, and so have I."

"Would you like to walk into the law school at UF and say hello to the few teachers you knew who have remained there? They would be shocked to know you're alive. And pleased."

"I think I'd go in to ask for all my years of retirement pay. I was there twenty years and earned it."

"Dean Perry would be happy to see you," Lucinda said. "He's the only one who knows that you didn't die in D.C."

"He's gone. Apparently he had enough with being a dean and moved back to the mid-West to take a chair and teach. . . . UF hired its first woman dean a couple of years ago. . . . Why do you ask all this? It's very hypothetical."

"It does affect me," she added. "We would live in Gainesville most of the year. I don't know what I would do."

"What do *you* want to do?" I asked.

"Live in this cabin in the summer and in the Florida cottage in the winter. No changes. Maybe do more photography, like the Cuban photos for the Canadian magazine. . . . I know you like being in Florida for the time Elsbeth is at UF. What about when she graduates and leaves?"

"I think she's going to law school at UF and that gives us a few years to think about possible significant changes in our time in Florida each year."

"I can't leave Mill Creek," Lucinda pleaded.

"We won't leave Mill Creek. . . . If Herzog died, would we tell our friends here the whole story? How would we explain the music room to them?"

"And tell friends about Khartoum, when you assassinated Isfahani? Or what you were doing in Italy. Why the airplane escape from Cuba? How you rescued me in the Bahamas? Macduff, you have connections to D.C. that may not go away."

"I hadn't thought of that."

"Connections that might call on you for some task in some exotic unstable place in the future."

"I hope that's over," I mumbled.

"But once you work for the Agency in Langley, you can't get out. It's a federal mafia. They have too much on you. Dan would feel you still have an obligation to his group?"

"That worries me. But maybe he does feel that way."

"Can I tell you my suggestion?"

"Yes," I responded.

"If Herzog dies, we do essentially everything we are now doing. What we don't do is worry about Herzog showing up."

"Then we might still be asked to travel to places like Cuba or Spain or Portugal or Italy or Guatemala," I said. "All paid for by our government and traveling first-class carrying diplomatic passports."

"That sounds good, especially first class using diplomatic passports."

"One more thing. I'm not giving up my CheyTac rifle."

"The one with the two notches?"

"There's room for more."

58

A WEEK LATER – LIVINGSTON

CORONER VICTOR PERSEY, BETTER KNOWN AS Cutter, received a report from the lab that contracted to undertake the DNA phenotyping. When completed, he immediately called Erin at the Park County Sheriff's Office.

"I have the report, Erin. I wish it were more helpful."

"Why? Something missing?"

"Remember that with phenotyping we're talking *exclusion* of groups of people. The report profiles a person who at first glance might be Macduff. It suggests the person is of European ancestry, has fair skin color, blue eyes, and a few freckles."

"But that *all* describes Macduff."

"But not the remaining characteristic," he said, smiling. "The report says the person's hair is *red*."

"That's wonderful. It lets Macduff off the hook. What number of people have red hair?"

"Five percent. Nevertheless, that means thousands of people fit the profile."

"Is there any way to narrow the group?"

"I'm afraid not."

"I guess I was excited about *identifying* the person who has the DNA. Anyway, what this should accomplish is remove Macduff from any blame for Spencer's or Norton's deaths."

"It should, without question."

"But," Erin added, "the work you did confirmed that the deaths were murders—forced drownings—and each of them in Montana and Wyoming was done by the same person. . . . Before you helped me, Cutter, we had no proof of accidents or homicides, and accusations were made against Macduff. Now we have homicides, and the investigations should be reopened, but Macduff won't be a part of those investigations."

"What we know," responded Cutter, "is there is a murderer out there, and he's European ancestry, has fair skin, blue eyes, and freckles, and—most important to Macduff—he has red hair."

"Now we have to start thinking about what red haired person had a motive to kill both Spence and Norton. That's not your problem, Cutter. It's ours here at the sheriff's office, and the same for Huntly Byng in Jackson. I'll let Byng know as soon as we're through. But first I'll call Macduff and Lucinda.

"Say hello for me," said Cutter, "and tell them if they ever need my services, give me a call."

"I'll tell Macduff if he doesn't reach you at your lab to try the bar at the Murray Hotel."

59

SIX HOURS LATER – MILL CREEK

LUCINDA AND I WERE PULLING *OSPREY* OUT OF the Yellowstone River at Carter Bridge after a day's drift when my cellphone began its new ring, Eddie Fisher's 1952 song, "Wish You Were Here." For some callers I disconnected after the first line: "They're not making the skies as blue this year. Wish . . ."

Lucinda and I were struggling with the trailer winch and the cellphone finished its ring and shifted to our recorded answer, which opened with the Big Bopper singing "Chantilly Lace," starting with the deep and drawn out greeting: "Hellooo, Baby!"

"And 'hellooo, baby' to you, Macduff. It's the Little Bopper—Erin. I've tried to get you for several hours. Call me. I have news from Cutter. Good for both you and Lucinda, but not so good for my office or Huntly Byng's. Bye."

As soon as *Osprey* was loaded, Lucinda and I sat in the front seat of our SUV, and I called Erin. She answered quickly.

"Where were you two all afternoon?"

"Exercising," Lucinda said. "Tough, but good for the heart. And builds muscle. Glad you asked."

"I'm not sure if I should believe you," she said. "Is Red there with you?"

"Red?"

"Yeah. The guy you married. Didn't you tell me once that Macduff had red hair he didn't like and dyed it brown?"

"Erin, what are you drinking? Are you and Cutter at the Murray Hotel bar again?"

"No. I'm about to leave the office and go directly home. I wanted to reach you first. The DNA phenotyping profile arrived. The guy we're looking for is European, with blue eyes, a fair complexion, and some freckles. And *red* hair."

"I do *not* have red hair," I replied forcefully. "I am *not* among the group phenotyped."

"*If* you can prove your hair isn't red, you're no longer a suspect—assuming you accept the finding."

"We accept it! How lucky! The killers's profile was so close to matching Macduff," added Lucinda. "What does this mean?"

Erin explained everything Cutter had told her.

"To make it easy, Cutter and I have been calling the killer 'Red,'"

"I hope you find Red," I said. "Unless there's something else, tonight Lucinda and I can celebrate our release from the clutches of the law."

"Sure, while I spend the evening wondering how we'll find Red. There's been a murder on my turf we have to solve."

"You don't have much to go on," I said. "Spence and Norton were both Master Casting Instructors. Who wants to single out MCIs and kill them?"

"People they've flunked taking the CCI or MCI exam. I'm going to check the IFFF records and see if there's any test taker for CCI or MCI who both Spence and Norton failed and who fits the profile. If Spence and Norton both failed the same person, we may have a suspect. If so, I'm not sure what we do. Try to get some DNA from that person. Then see if there's a match. If so, arrest him. If not, keep searching. . . . Put the word out to all the IFFF casting instructor test sites to let us know immediately if a red haired guy shows up to take the CCI or MCI test."

"Does what we know about the black fly help?" Lucinda asked.

"No. There were two different black flies, although the two found on Spence and near Norton were identical. We're trying to track down the fly tier who made those two flies."

"That could be some 15-year-old-girl in China or Nigeria who does nothing but tie flies. And supports her family being paid two dollars a day. A lot of outfitters and online stores probably have no idea where the fishing flies they sell come from. I suspect that idea has a dead end."

"Macduff, do you have to fill out anything before you go to fish in Cascade Canyon?"

"No, unless you're camping overnight. On a busy summer day, hundreds of people hike up the Canyon to get a closer view of the Grand Teton and maybe see a moose. Cross the permit idea off your list. Anything else?"

"Not right now, but I'll be thinking about it all evening while you two relax on your porch with drinks."

"We've earned the right to do that after being harassed by so many prosecutors," I said.

"Including me?"

"No, Erin, you harass us *all* the time, not just when there's some serial killer on the loose."

"Who says Red's a *serial* killer?" Erin asked.

"Two victims killed the same way," Lucinda commented.

"Some argue more than two," Erin added. "And there must be commonalities, which the black flies and the MCI certificates provide. Maybe there are some psychological reasons like the choice of victims, both being MCIs. Or maybe just being fly fishers. And the same way the bodies apparently were pushed under. . . . What I worry about is I don't want to hear 'and then there were *three*.'"

"Would that make the killer a *mass* murderer?"

"No, the rules of the game are strict. A *mass* murderer kills all at once. Indiscriminately. Like the Colorado school shootings."

"What about a *spree* killer? Do we have one here?"

"No again. A *spree* murderer doesn't have specific targets. It's like a shooting from a rooftop at a bunch of unidentified people below on the street."

"Erin, you're good. You know your murderers."

"I learned them at police school. It's unprofessional to call a homicide by its wrong name."

"I don't think there will be a third killing in the Mountain West or a fourth or even more, Erin," I added. "If there is a third, it probably won't be in this jurisdiction. I have a hunch Red will choose a different creek; that way it will scare people—at least MCIs—on every creek in the West."

"I hope you're right."

"One last question for you, Erin. What if the murderer of Spence tried to kill everyone fishing along the creek, ten people in all. But he was a terrible shot and although he aimed at and tried to kill all ten, he missed all but one. Was he a *spree* killer?"

"That would be like taking the exam to be a Master Casting Instructor. There are about fourteen parts to the test. If you only pass one, you're not an MCI. You have to do better, just like a *spree* killer. Any more dumb questions?"

"Could we call the killer of Spence and Norton a *terrorist?*"

60

TWO DAYS LATER - LIVINGSTON

ERIN WAS TALKING TO A BOZEMAN DEFENSE lawyer who wanted her to drop charges against a ninety-two-year-old Livingston woman for going through a red light and slamming into an emergency van that had its lights flashing and siren blaring. The woman said she was crying while listening to Sirius radio replay an old radio soap opera—the *Romance of Helen Trent*—and didn't see or hear the emergency vehicle. It turned out she was also smoking and trying to text.

When Cutter walked in, Erin was relieved. She told the lawyer an emergency had come up, and they would have to continue their conversation another time.

"Cutter, you look happy about something. Find a gold coin in someone's stomach when you were doing an autopsy?"

"No, but I'll keep searching. Would you like to hear my news or make nasty comments about my profession?"

"Speak!" Erin said, impatiently.

"I was unhappy when we discovered that both Spence and Norton were almost certainly killed by the same person, but I couldn't find a DNA match to a specific person. Now I have! I learned about a big DNA databank coming on line in London and again tried to find a match. Guess what?"

"You found who Red is?"

"YES!" Cutter exclaimed. "His name is Lance Appleton. He's a New York City lawyer, a partner in a two-hundred lawyer firm. Two years ago he was asked by his partners to manage the firm's London office for five years. He applied for a UK work visa and part of the process was a medical exam to check for any communicable diseases he might bring into England. That exam included taking a DNA sample. When I checked the new data base, it showed Appleton as the match."

"Does he fit the DNA phenotyping profile as well?" Erin asked.

"He's European ancestry, fair skin, blue eyes, and has a few freckles. And, he has *red* hair!"

"How could he have killed Spence and Norton if he's in London?"

"He may not have been at the time. I think we need to talk to him."

"Will you go to London with me and see him? *If* he agrees to talk to us?"

"Do we have the funds?"

"Yes, the state has given us a special supplement."

"How did you get that?"

"I talked to the governor. He's interested in our case, and also the Spence part in Wyoming, where his cousin was the attorney general. He believes Macduff is innocent and wants to help. He also said he would like to float a section of the Yellowstone with our celebrity guide!"

"When do we go to London?"

"I'll call Appleton."

61

A WEEK LATER – LONDON

APPLETON AGREED TO SEE ERIN AND CUTTER. He said he was curious about what a Montana deputy sheriff and coroner could possibly want from a London-based attorney.

Neither Erin nor Cutter is large. Erin is *very* small and Cutter is *more or less* small. That was fortunate because they chose to fly Delta to London by way of Minneapolis, and their size allowed them to fit into Delta's vanishing seats. But it didn't keep them from experiencing the abominable air quality, the dirty restrooms, or the stink from the food brought on the plane by the couple behind them. All in all, it was a routine flight.

They had reserved two rooms at a small hotel on Holborn near Chancery Lane, which placed them a ten-minute walk to the law offices where Appleton worked.

The firm's reception area and the small conference room to which Erin and Cutter were escorted the day after they arrived had a subtle luxury appearance, like the firm's two Bentleys parked at the front door. The décor was a mixture of Burberry, Laura Ashley, and English oak.

"I'm glad we're not paying Appleton by the hour," Erin said quietly to Cutter. "I don't know his hourly rate, and I prefer not to know it."

"He'll probably see us for fifteen minutes and excuse himself to do something more profitable."

"Doesn't that make you wonder why he so quickly agreed to see us?" Erin asked.

"He can't be hiding anything. I'm sure he has documents to show us he was nowhere near the United States on the two different days Spence and Norton were murdered. But we need to check."

"It should be interestin. . . ." The door opened and in walked what had to be Appleton. Fair skin, blue eyes, a few freckles, and—most notably—red hair."

"I'm Lance Appleton. Please use Lance. Sorry about being a few minutes tardy."

Erin and Cutter introduced themselves as Appleton seated himself at the head of the small conference table.

"I took the liberty, after we arranged this meeting, to have my secretary search newspapers and other sources for whatever information was available about Spence and Norton. I know you believe them to have been murdered, even though the two county sheriff's offices and medical examiners ruled them an accidental drowning and a suicide. He set his pencil down, looked up, and waited for Erin or Cutter to respond. Where do we go from there?"

"What's your hobby," Erin asked.

"A strange question. If you mean do I fly fish, the answer is 'no.' I'm a golfer. I have never held a fly rod in my hand."

"We have some additional information about the deaths, info which I don't believe was in the papers. It has to do with both the usual DNA sample matching and something called DNA phenotyping."

"I don't know anything about that. This firm never accepts criminal cases," he said condescendingly.

"Mr. Appleton," Cutter said, ignoring his request to use Lance, "I'm the coroner in the Norton case. I wrote the report that wrongly concluded that Norton committed suicide.

"Later I discovered the DNA found on the two black flies matched—the same DNA was on the black fly on Spence and the one found near Norton. That suggested that the same person killed both Spence and Norton. It meant the conclusions in both coroners' reports—including mine, embarrassingly—were wrong, and the cases should have proceeded as homicides. We re-opened the Norton case and confronted an insurmountable obstacle—we could not match the killer's DNA with *any* DNA profiles in dozens of DNA databanks in the U.S. and Europe.

"We next had the DNA phenotyped, a relatively new process that doesn't *identify* a specific person, but *eliminates* many. Our phenotyping determined that the person was of European ancestry, had pale skin, blue eyes, and some freckles. It also told us that the person had red hair."

Appleton squirmed in his chair, swiveled around, and stared out the large window. Without turning back, he said, "That narrowed group must include thousands of persons," he said, "perhaps hundreds of thousands. . . . I fit it, but why have you come all this way to see me?"

"I can explain that," said Cutter. "We knew we were at a standstill. Then I learned about a new DNA databank of profiles established here in the U.K. by the government. You know that everyone who wishes to work in England must apply for a special visa, which includes adding the person to the DNA databank. You applied for such a visa and, I assume, as is required, you carry it with you."

"I do," he said, producing his visa and handing it to Erin. It was dated well before the first death.

"Let me finish, please," asked Cutter. "The DNA which we tested against the DNA profiles here in England provided us an exact match with *your* DNA. The likelihood of an error is perhaps one in ten million. Or even one in a billion or even trillion."

Appleton's complexion altered from fair to white.

"You may be losing me," he said. "The DNA from the test here in England can't possibly connect me with two murders in two states I have never visited. Furthermore, I have my work records here for the days the deaths occurred and the time in between. On each of the days the two died, I had several meetings with clients here in London that began with breakfast at 7:00 a.m. I believe that would be about 11:00 p.m. the previous night in Montana. I did not return to my lodging until nearly midnight on each day. That would have been about 5:00 p.m. for you. Look at my records." He passed a number of sheets across the table.

"I hope you don't mind if we check with some of the people you stated you were with," Erin said.

"Please go ahead. These are copies are for you."

"Assuming they are correct, and I have no reason to believe otherwise," Erin interjected, "we have unfairly taken your time. You have been thoughtful. Please excuse us."

"One moment," Appleton responded. "If DNA is as reliable as it is alleged to be, how can this have happened?"

"Frankly, I don't know," Cutter admitted hunching his shoulders. "I'm going to have to learn more about DNA. This case is my first experience with it. . . . I think we are back at square one. We're sorry to have bothered you."

Visually embarrassed, Erin and Cutter walked out of the firm.

"I don't know what we expected," Cutter uttered glumly, "other than to find Appleton was missing from his firm when the two deaths occurred. But the deaths were ten months apart, and he was unlikely to have been away in the U.S. for so long. His records seemed to confirm that he wasn't away from London on either date or in between."

"Drink?" Erin asked Cutter as they walked the crowded street.

"You're bloody right," answered Cutter.

They looked for a pub and soon came to one called the Cittie of Yorke, which boasted the longest bar in England. They each had two bottles of Samuel Smith's and then walked toward their hotel, detouring to join the activity at Leicester Square and Piccadilly. They reached the hotel at 3:00 a.m.

Twenty-four hours later the two walked out of the Bozeman airport, ready to confess their failure to Ken Rangley in the morning.

And then face Lucinda and me in the afternoon.

62

THE FOLLOWING DAY - MILL CREEK

CUTTER AND ERIN MET WITH KEN RANGLEY IN the morning and described their meeting with Appleton without mentioning the Citte of Yorke Pub or what they did at Piccadilly until 3:00 a.m.

"What did you expect to discover in London?" asked Ken. "That Appleton had flown to the U.S. twice to murder Spence and Norton? You haven't discovered any flight records which support that. Even if he had been in the U.S. at those times, what possible motive existed?"

"I don't know what we expected," Cutter answered. "Maybe to meet someone with *other* than red hair, telling us Appleton was not within the profile that suggested red hair. But when he walked into the conference room and we saw his red hair. That lent credibility to the phenotyping and helped exclude other suspects including Macduff. But our focus was on the DNA match I had discovered in the London DNA bank.

"I was confident I had done a good job, but I quickly realized his records affirmed that he wasn't in Wyoming or Montana when the two were killed."

"What do you recommend we do?" Ken asked. "You tried and came up against one of the anomalies of DNA accuracy. Don't blame yourself, Cutter."

"We wait," said Erin, with Cutter nodding. "Patiently. There's no statute of limitations for murder. Maybe we'll find the killer in some other DNA profiles. We were never able to get them from several states because of different attitudes about privacy."

"If you found another DNA match in some New England state DNA databank, for example—which you won't—and the matched person lives in Bozeman," stated Ken, "no Montana court is going to accept DNA that pointed to both one person in London and another in Montana."

"Do we close the cases," asked Erin, "but update the file for each case to show the same person killed both Spence and Norton?"

"Yes, and call Huntly Byng in Jackson and tell him about your trip and our intentions. I assume he'll do the same with the Spence case."

"And I'll call Lucinda and Macduff and tell them we struck out in London—or better we lost a wicket. But we're still at bat."

63

THAT EVENING – MILL CREEK

THE CREEK'S FLOW HAD DIMINISHED DAILY. Roaring high water rushing down from melting snow was only a memory. The dryness and heat of summer had reduced the creek's flow to barely sufficient to sustain trout. Irrigation dams on Mill Creek diverted so much of nature's flow that it endangered fish life in the creek.

Lucinda had called Erin, Ken, and Cutter at the last minute inviting them to come for an informal dinner on the cabin's rear porch overlooking the creek.

Erin had responded, "I'm so tired of all this. I was going to have Albertson's make me a sandwich and eat it in the car on the drive home. . . . But I'll come!"

Ken had replied, "I haven't talked to Macduff about fishing for months. And I haven't fished in months. I'll come."

Cutter was excited and stumbled over his words. "I probably would have ended up at the Murray Hotel bar—again. I'll be at your cabin on time."

Lucinda bought Chilean farmed trout, scallops, white asparagus, corn-on-the-cob, baby potatoes for roasting, and, adding a touch of Florida, a frozen Key Lime pie.

My role was cleaning the grill, setting up the bar, and arranging five chairs so all could see the mountains.

The three invited guests arrived within fifteen minutes of one another. After they fixed their own drinks, we all stood quietly watching the sun setting beyond the mountains.

For the first hour we talked about everything *except* Spence, Norton, and Hart. Cutter told us about dissecting his first cadaver, Erin about her recent Kendo match against an opponent a foot and a half taller, and Ken about his daughter Liz's first month on the Yellowstone as a fly fishing guide. I outlined plans for developing some side streams that flow into Mill Creek along Lucinda's ranch to form a Spring Creek and, hopefully, create a breeding area for native cutthroats, and Lucinda caused uncontrollable laughter by her rendition of our first meeting at her ranch for Thanksgiving dinner. I didn't say one word in my defense.

Our Montana and Wyoming friends draw us back to Mill Creek every year. We do less socializing in Florida, where a similar number of guests might discuss calling in favors to get their kids into expensive private schools, so-and-so's brand new *very* expensive Porsche Carrera GT, and the *outrageously* expensive gown one had just bought to wear only once to a forthcoming charity ball.

After dinner, which left nothing for another day's meal or even a snack, our conversation turned to the black fly cases.

"Ken," Lucinda asked, "is the Norton case finally closed?"

"Essentially, yes. We'd open it only if we determined we made a mistake about how Norton died. Huntly Byng in Jackson feels the same way about Spence; I talked to him just before I left for this much appreciated and relaxing meal.

"Even if the case were re-opened, you two are out of it," he said nodding at Lucinda and me. "Period! You never should have been suspects. If I ever showed doubt in either of you, I apologize."

"Thanks," Lucinda and I replied simultaneously and barely above a whisper. Lucinda was sitting next to me and without looking reached and squeezed my hand.

"I've seen enough of Norton's cadaver," exclaimed Cutter. "His cadaver has been cut open and reopened. Next time I'm putting in a zipper."

"Is that why you're called 'Cutter'?" Lucinda asked.

"No. It's because of the skill and delicacy I exhibit doing autopsies."

"I don't believe that," Ken said laughing. "I had a turkey dinner with you a year ago. You made such a mess of that unfortunate bird I thought, 'And this guy may someday do that to me!'. . . Lucinda and Macduff, you must be relieved about Spence and Norton. Update us on the Hart case in Florida."

"Our last conversation with the prosecutor in Crystal River ended poorly," I commented. "In fact, every time Abbott and I talked, we've ended a step further from any cooperation. . . . I hope it's a cold case. Dead. Buried away in the records boxes. Forgotten. I hope I never hear from *her* again."

"Don't count on not hearing from Abbott," said Erin. "It depends on when a prosecutor *wants* to prosecute. Not when he or she *should* prosecute."

Together, the group broke up at 10:30. It must have been successful—all stayed five hours.

64

AN HOUR LATER – MILL CREEK

THERE WAS LITTLE TO CLEAN UP. EVERYONE had brought dishes into the kitchen, and a half-hour after they left, no remnants of the dinner were present except memories and two full trash bags.

Five minutes after we retired to our bedroom and turned out the lights, only thirty minutes into the new day we heard a car coming up the gravel drive. Someone must have forgotten something. I turned on lights again. They flooded the yard, and I watched a vehicle approach. It was a small, late model with Utah plates. I lifted the Winchester 30-30 from over the front door and walked out into the headlights of the mysterious vehicle.

"Are you going to shoot your own daughter?" the invisible voice called out. The car lights went out, and heading toward me was Elsbeth.

"What on earth are you doing in Montana?"

"Visiting. Am I not welcome?"

"I thought you were flying to London from D.C. at the end of your summer job. Your coming year abroad will be exciting. When are you leaving?"

"In a few days. I'll leave from here. I thought I'd surprise you."

"Surprise!" exclaimed Lucinda. "We haven't seen you since April in Florida. We missed you not being here and working at Chico Hot Springs. And we missed Sue. Where is she headed?"

"St. Andrews in Scotland. Too far north and much too frigid and gloomy in the winter for me. But we'll visit each other every couple of months and on the holidays."

"Come in. I'll get you a Moose Drool."

"A beer would be good. I haven't had a Moose Drool since last summer. I doubt I'll find it in London."

On the porch, wrapped in blankets, Elsbeth asked, "What's with the murders? At least you're not in jail."

"We're out of it," I answered. "At least the two deaths here on our Mill Creek and on Cascade Creek in Grand Teton Park. The Florida death also remains ruled an accidental drowning, but a prosecutor wants to change that to homicide and has warned me I'll be a suspect. Let's talk about nicer things first."

For the next hour we heard about Elsbeth's summer in D.C. The memory of the experience seemed better than the experience itself. Like the DNA phenotyping, it *excluded* rather than added. She vowed never to live and work in D.C., especially for the federal government.

After we told her about our return to Montana by way of Calgary and the few days of fishing we had managed to fit in since arriving, she asked about Erin, Ken, and his daughter Liz. And John Kirby in Jackson.

"So you haven't been to Jackson to see John and Sarah and do some fishing."

"I was advised not to because of Wyoming Attorney General Davis's vendetta against me. But we did anyway, just in time to see Davis disgraced. We'll go again the week after the One Fly tournament. That's when the hopper fishing gets really good. And we'll stop on the way back and fish the Firehole *if* its temperature has dropped and the trout are moving back into the main part of the river."

"Do you know anything about DNA and phenotyping?" I asked Elsbeth, offhandedly.

"Of course I do. You don't remember what I've studied at UF? Last year I aced a course in criminology. DNA was a big deal. Profiling to find out the matching person was a major topic. But what's DNA phenotyping?"

I outlined the basics of phenotyping and told her how we used it in the Spence and Norton cases, and added how Cutter had discovered that DNA found on Spence and Norton matched. I admitted we ran into a dead end trying to match that DNA with a specific person after Cutter used the new UK DNA databank that identified London Attorney Lance Appleton. I described how we came to an abrupt halt when it was clear Appleton was nowhere near Spence or Norton when they were murdered. He hadn't in his life ever been west of the Mississippi.

"Dad, the chances that the DNA profile identifying Appleton was wrong are *indescribable*, at least according to the current science. What are the error odds? One in a hundred million?"

"Something like that. Too big to challenge."

"Where was Appleton born and where did he grow up? Do you know?" she asked as she pulled out her iPad. There's a directory that includes personal information about lawyers. I have it! You said his first name is Lance?"

"Yes."

"Ok, here he is. Lance Appleton. Born in 1960 in Albany, New York, to Roger and Eva Appleton. One brother named Henry. Educated at. . . . I have all we need."

"What do you mean?"

"I will bet you *anything* that Lance's brother is an identical twin."

"Meaning what?"

"Dad! You're so uncool. The one time when one person's DNA is *exactly* the same as another is when they are twins. Not just twins, *identical* twins."

"I don't believe you," I said, with no reason to doubt her.

"Why didn't Lance Appleton tell Erin and Cutter he had a twin brother?" Elsbeth asked.

"I guess family blood is thicker than trout water."

"Elsbeth, I'm surprised Erin didn't know about twins having identical DNA. Are you?"

"No. Remember, she did her Ph.D. nearly three decades ago. DNA has been known for several decades, but accepted and applied not much more than twenty-five years. I missed out on hearing about phenotyping in my forensics course, Erin missed out on hearing about DNA in her Ph.D. studies. And also remember Montana has few murders.

"If I'm right, Dad, you owe me a new car. A four door Jeep Wrangler. My used Jeep is on its last legs from driving back and forth between here and Florida and checking in on you every week in Florida. Deal?"

"Deal? What do I get if you're wrong."

"My continuing undying love."

"You'll be out working for a living in two years. You'll be able to afford your own vehicle."

"I won't be out in two years. Sue and I have decided on law school. With next year in London, one more to get my B.A.

and three years of law school, it'll be five years before I start a steady job. And I might go somewhere for a graduate law degree."

"Why is it that whenever you walk in here my heart rate goes up?"

"Because you love me and are excited to see me."

"Or because you cause me so much anxiety?"

"I'm going to cause you more. In the morning you and I will call Erin and Ken, and then Huntly Byng in Jackson."

"What for?"

"To tell them how fortunate you are to have me and to start searching for Lance Appleton's twin brother. I'll bet he lives in a Western mountain state."

"Another bet?"

"Of course. And I've just upgraded my new car when I come back to a Range Rover!"

Elsbeth left me thinking I had lost another expensive bet with her. Sleep came slowly. But it didn't last; the phone started playing Chopin's "Funeral March." I was sure Elsbeth had put it on my phone after our bets.

"Macduff, are you awake?"

It was Dan Wilson. "Awake? Its 1:40 here, 3:40 where you are in D.C. Have you taken up Gentleman Jack?"

"First, I'm not in D.C. I'm in Guatemala City. I arrived an hour ago. Five Guatemalan Army generals have ousted Juan Pablo Herzog from the presidency."

"Is he dead? In jail?"

"Missing. He had friends who helped him flee the country. We don't know where he is. I thought you'd like to know."

"Right now I'd like to know how the hell I'm going to go back to sleep."

EPILOGUE

Elsbeth's Diary

Dad and I settled on a Tahoe. He agreed the Range Rover was a great looking car, but it had to be serviced every few hundred miles.

The day after we made that bet, Dad drove to the Park County Sheriff's office in Livingston, asked Erin if she'd ask Ken to join us in their conference room and get Huntly Byng on the line. When they were all listening, Dad said Lance Appleton's identical twin brother was named Henry Appleton and he lived in West Yellowstone.

Further inquiry told them that Henry was a problem ever since grammar school in Albany. From 13 to 16 he was confined in a New York 'House of Refuge for Juvenile Delinquents' where he met experts in all manners of deceit, fraud, and mayhem and came out a very capable criminal. For the next few years he was in and out of one or another ascendingly secure institutions for ascendingly severe crimes. His parents disowned him.

Ken in Livingston and Huntly in Jackson decided not to pursue why Lance Appleton withheld information about his brother. Truthfully, Lance hadn't talked to his brother in years and had no idea he lived in the West.

Henry made no attempt to escape arrest. He was tried in Jackson and sentenced to life. He spent much of his time in prison tying hundreds of flies. All were black. Two years later he was found dead in a corner of the prison exercise yard. He was wearing a black fly tied on a string around his neck. I have always wondered if Henry put it on himself.

Dad never heard another word about Rachel Hart from Rosalie Abbott, except an announcement a decade later that Abbott had been appointed the Florida State Attorney.

M.W. GORDON – The author of more than sixty law books that won awards and were translated into a dozen languages, he wrote one book on sovereign immunity in the U.S. and U.K. as a Scholar-in-Residence at the Bellagio Institute at Lake Como, Italy. He has also written for *Yachting Magazine* and *Yachting World* (U.K.) and won the Bruce Morang Award for Writing from the Friendship Sloop Society in Maine. Gordon holds a B.S. and J.D. from the University of Connecticut, an M.A. from Trinity College, a Diplôme de Droit Comparé from Strasbourg, and a Maestria en Derecho from Iberoamericana in Mexico City. He is a pretty competent fly caster, an average small plane pilot, and a terrible oboist. He lives in St. Augustine with his author wife Buff and their sheltie, Macduff.

AUTHOR'S NOTE

You may reach me at: macbrooks.mwgordon@gmail.com
Please visit my website: www.mwgordonnovels.com

I answer email within the week received, unless I am on a book signing tour or towing *Osprey* somewhere to fish. Because of viruses, I do not download attachments received with emails. And please do not add my email address to any lists suggesting for whom I should vote, to whom I should give money, what I should buy, what I should read, or especially what I should write next about Macduff Brooks.

My website lists appearances for readings, talk programs, and signings.

Made in the USA
Columbia, SC
22 August 2023